EPIC

BESTSELLING AUTHOR
TRUDY STILES

LOVE

EPIC FAIL SERIES

Cover Design by Sarah Hansen of Okay Creations
Interior Design and Formatting by Elaine Hudson York of
Allusion Graphics www.allusiongraphics.com
Editing by Erin Noelle
Proofreading by Julie Deaton of Author Services by Julie Deaton
Poetry by J.R. Rogue

HEATH STRICKLAND, the son of a prominent district attorney, lived his life surrounded by violence and crime. He was an unwilling witness to the corrupt lives his father swore to prosecute and keep behind bars. His escape was his music, which eventually led him to replace the iconic singer of the world famous band, Epic Fail.

NOELLE DURAND lived in luxury, growing up on a sprawling estate, with everything she could ever want or need. Her life, to everyone else, seemed perfect. Perfect house. Perfect things. Perfect family. But nothing at all was perfect. She lived in hell. A hell that nobody on the outside could see.

As a neighbor and childhood friend, Heath would have done anything for Noelle. He would have given up the world to protect her and keep her safe. Their friendship grew into something that neither of them expected. But then she suddenly disappeared, vanishing from his life as if she never existed. He never stopped hoping that one day she would resurface, alive and well. But as time went by, and her family gave up hope, he surrendered his heart to his lost love.

Twelve years later, one phone call changes everything.

EPIC LOVE is the third book in the EPIC FAIL series and can be read as a standalone novel.

This series is a spinoff from the FOREVER FAMILY series.

Content Warning:
This book is not suitable for young readers. It is intended for mature adults only (18+). It contains strong language, adult/sexual situations and potential trigger subject matter.

DEDICATION

For my children.
I hope you always believe in the
magic of fireflies and fairies.

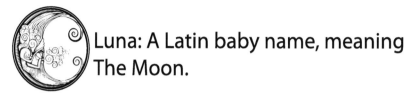 # Luna: A Latin baby name, meaning The Moon.

In Mythology, Luna is one of the names of Artemis the moon goddess. She was known to be the goddess of hunt, wild animals, wildness, childbirth and virginity. She was also known as the protector of young children. Her hunting companion, Orion, won her heart, who she eventually placed in the sky, forming one of the most recognizable constellations seen today.

TAKE ME BACK

Take me back to two weeks ago.
My blue oil lamp painting
the fireflies dancing in the ink night sky
of your backyard in amber rose mosaics.
When the moon is asleep I will
find a way to rescue you.

Take me back to two nights ago.
Your eyes afire again with the tales
your father told.
I know his promises taste like a lie
or a line or paper stack of let downs.
When he has forgotten I will
find a way to rescue you.

Take me back to two moments ago.
Setting fairies free to twirl
under the watchful moon, back with her
unwavering glow, moving the tides of
unruly seas and your smile pulled at the
corners of your mouth like a forgotten
treasure.
When all is forgotten you find
new ways to rescue me.

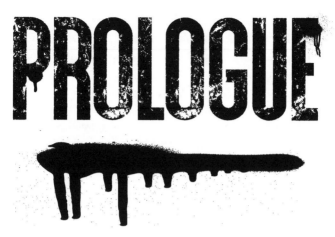

PROLOGUE

Melanie Durand
Past

SOFT COOING DRIFTS from the bassinet next to our bed, stirring me from my light slumber. It's been just about three hours since I last fed her and she's awake again, like clockwork. Tom delicately places his hand on my arm. "Mel, I've got this. You need your rest." His words are a subtle reminder of the news we received this morning, and I'm not about to pass on the chance to hold my daughter.

"No, Tom. I'll feed her. I *want* to." *I need to feel her heart beat against mine.*

"Are you sure?"

"I've never been more sure in my life."

His eyes soften and he nods.

"I'll warm up her bottle while you get her ready. Is that okay?"

I sigh and situate myself so I can get Noelle ready for her bottle. "Perfect," I respond. Tom is doing everything he can to make things easier for me, and for that I'm so incredibly grateful. But I don't want it to be easy. I want to experience as much as I can with my daughter before–

He presses his lips against mine then slips out of bed, making his way around to her bassinet. I see her hands waving in the air as her feet kick in place. Soft grunts and coos continue as Tom picks her up, carefully cradling her in his arms until he can place her into mine. He looks at his daughter with so much love in his eyes. Every time I witness his intense affection for her, my heart hurts. He's going to be an incredible father–he already is. She's going to be showered with so much love, she'll never want for anything.

He softly kisses Noelle's forehead and places her into my arms, his hand resting over the crown of her head. "The both of you are so beautiful and perfect." His words hurt me so much more than he can imagine. Knowing what we now know. I suck in a breath, trying to hold back the sobs that are fighting to escape. "I'll be right back," he assures. His eyes are full of love but pained. *And we both know why.*

The moonlight shines through our large windows and Noelle's eyes are open wide, her mouth searching for the nipple that's just a few minutes away. She's just three weeks old and the warm, summer moon is still in full force. It's so much brighter than the small night light plugged into the wall next to her bassinet. "Hey, you," I whisper, stroking her forehead. Her eyes look toward my face, attempting to focus on where the sound is coming from. "Daddy is getting your bottle warmed up. He'll be back soon." She makes a small 'o' with her lips, another coo escaping. "And Daddy's right. You're perfect, Noelle. Our perfect little Christmas in July present. We're so blessed." Tears sting my eyes as she begins to calm down at the sound of my voice, anticipating the warm formula that's about to fill her tiny belly. This moment is so simple, but so vital. She'll never remember the bond that we're forming right now, but I know I will. Forever.

Tom emerges from the hallway and quickly places the warm bottle in my hands. "I tested it, just like you showed me. On the inside of my wrist. It's perfect." He's been so intent on learning every nuance in preparing her bottles and feeding routines.

I touch the nipple to her lips and she quickly begins sucking the warm formula down. She's an incredibly good eater, rarely fussing. A twinge of sadness emerges as I wish I could be breastfeeding her instead of bottle feeding. But, it's not something I'm able to do.

Tom places his head on my shoulder, softly stroking Noelle's legs as she drinks. "I love watching the two of you like this. It's so amazing to see how trusting she is of both of us. She needs us so much, and she doesn't even realize how much we need her."

I nod silently as I look into her wide-open eyes. She's staring up at me as her mouth pulls the formula into her belly, alternating sucking and breathing through her nose. It's astonishing to watch. Instinctive and beautiful.

She takes an ounce and I pull the nipple from her mouth, adjusting her into a sitting position as I cradle her neck and head. I slowly rub and pat her back, a loud burp quickly erupting from her body. Tom chuckles, "That never gets old."

Her lips are already moving as I rest her back into feeding position. She's ready for more. She sucks down another ounce as quickly as she did the first one, and she's once again ready to be burped. This time, though, her eyes are heavy, struggling to stay open. I rest her cheek on my shoulder and slowly rub and pat her back. This burp takes a little longer to come, but when it does, she completely relaxes in my arms, fast asleep.

"Do you want me to hold her for a little while so you can go back to sleep?" Tom knows we try to keep her upright for at least twenty minutes after each feeding, so she doesn't burp or spit up in her sleep.

"No, that's okay," I answer, pressing my head back into the pillow and placing my free hand firmly on her back, holding her against me.

He sits silently, looking pensive. He huffs and turns to face me. "Are we going to talk about today?"

I hold my breath, knowing this conversation was inevitable, but not wanting to have it.

"I can't talk about it now." Tears fill my eyes and I tense. Noelle can feel it, and she immediately twitches in my arms. "Shh, shh, shh," I whisper against her ear, my lips kissing her softly.

"When are we going to talk about it? We need to make some serious decisions."

I've already made my decision. "I'm going to fight as hard as I can."

He chokes on a sob. Something I've been dreading since we left the oncologist's office twelve hours ago. He was stoic and supportive, but now he's about to fall apart, and I'm not ready for this.

"Tom–"

His hands cover his face as he leans over his lap. "How can this be happening? Why is this happening to you?"

Our daughter rests peacefully on my chest, and I wish I could wrap my arms around my husband to comfort him. To tell him everything's going to be fine. But I know it's not.

Dr. Lehman's voice is still fresh in my head, his prognosis hanging in the air throughout this room.

Tom squeezes my hand as he rocks Noelle's carriage with his free one. She ate just before we got here so she should be asleep for at least a couple more hours. She's resting peacefully and looks so content with her fluffy pink blanket tucked around her.

"I'm afraid the news I have isn't good," Dr. Lehman says somberly as he pulls his chair around the desk so he's sitting next to Tom and me.

I wait silently, grasping onto Tom's hand tighter.

"Tell us," Tom urges and stops pushing Noelle's carriage.

"The cancer has spread to your liver, lungs, and pancreas. And the tumor in your stomach is completely inoperable."

I look away as Tom stands up and starts pacing the office.

"How can it be inoperable? You just found out about it. It couldn't have been growing for more than a few months." His voice waivers and I hold my breath, trying to fight back my own tears.

"Your pregnancy sped things along, unfortunately. Pregnancy hormones have been feeding the cancer cells planted throughout your body. Had we known about this before you got pregnant, we could have fought this aggressively. But it's already metastasized to stage four. I'm sorry, but we have to talk about time, and how much we can realistically give you."

"What? Time?" Tom shouts angrily. Noelle stirs in her carriage, and he quickly mutes his tone. "I don't understand."

I can't speak. I'm frozen.

Dr. Lehman turns to me and asks, "Melanie, do you have any questions?"

My eyes widen and I shake my head, holding my breath.

"Help us understand how nothing can be done?" Tom begs. He places his hand on my shoulder, softly squeezing to let me know he's there.

"We just don't know how long she's had this cancer in her body. Like I mentioned before, it's metastasized so far beyond what would happen during a normal progression of the disease. We think you've had this much longer than we originally thought. It's possible that the cancer has been in your body for many months prior to your pregnancy." He addresses me directly, his eyes are sad, almost apologetic.

We found out about the tumor in my stomach during my second trimester, when severe pains sent me to the hospital. We thought I was going into premature labor, but they told me the progression of my pregnancy, and the displacement of my abdominal organs, exacerbated the pain the tumor was causing me. They gave me the option to terminate the pregnancy so we could focus on fighting the cancer that, at the time, was limited only to my stomach. Or so they thought.

"I wouldn't have done anything differently," I admit, stunned. And I wouldn't. I refused to abort my child. Our child. I had hope that I would be able to deliver her and we'd fight this with everything that we had. But now that it's spread so much, our hopes are dashed. The end of my life within reach.

"Of course not," Dr. Lehman says apologetically. He knows that option was never on the table, and he fully supported us.

"What does this mean?" Tom interrupts.

"We need to start treating this aggressively to give you a few more months to spend with your daughter."

"Months?" I gasp. Not years? Panic sets in, and my heart begins to race. I feel faint. And I think I'm about to vomit.

"I'm so sorry. I wish I could give you a better outlook." His eyes are heavy, and he looks as if he's about to cry.

"How many months?" Tom presses.

"Without treatment, I would say you would have up to three months. With aggressive treatment, I would like to give you six to twelve."

Oh my God. Oh my God. Oh my God.

The room begins to swirl and Tom kneels down next to me, holding my hands tightly.

I look at our daughter sleeping peacefully in her carriage. She's so dependent on me. She needs me. How can I say goodbye to this precious life that I brought into this world? How can I have so much stolen from me? From us? Time is gone, evaporating as we sit here.

I need to get out of here.

"I wish there was something more we could do. You have no idea." Dr. Lehman stands up and walks toward us. "I never do this. I never recommend anything unconventional, but maybe you can reach out to a holistic healer. Someone who can help supplement what we're going to do with drugs and chemotherapy. Maybe that will help extend your time." Everything he's saying sounds like nonsense. He's even grasping at straws, and I'm losing hope every second we sit in this office.

"We need to digest this. We have a lot to think about," Tom states.

"Please take a day or two, but no more. We need to get your drug cocktail started as soon as possible if we're going to have the best chance we can to keep you with us as long as possible."

His words are so foreign to me, as if this conversation isn't even happening. His voice echoes throughout the room and all I can do is stare at my beautiful daughter.

"Mel?" Tom's voice brings me out of my trance as I shake my head. I can't believe the news we received today, and I don't want to continue to think about it.

"What do you want me to do?" I ask him. Beg him. Tears flow down my cheeks and his hands cradle my face, thumbs wiping them before they can land on Noelle's back.

"I want you to do what will make you most comfortable," he sobs, his own tears running.

Dr. Lehman explained to us that the chemotherapy is going to be aggressive and strong. My days would be filled with nausea and vomiting. Rapid hair and weight loss would follow along with a lot of pain and sores. I'm scared of what the coming weeks and months are going to be like. Terrified of the unknown, but also terrified that if I don't follow the medical protocol, I'm going to be gone that much quicker, and I'm not willing to take that chance.

"I'll do everything I can," I announce.

"And what's that?" his voice falters.

"I'll start chemo right away, but I need some assurances from Dr. Lehman. I want to be coherent before it kills me. I want to be able to hold Noelle, feed her, bond with her. If the chemo is too strong and I feel myself fading too quickly, I want to be able to stop it. I need it to be this way, Tom. I can't do all of the drugs and medicine if it's going to cannibalize the time I have left with you and Noelle. I just can't. I need to be able to control my fate."

"But–" he interrupts.

"I'm still going to fight. But please, let me have the option to stop all medication if it jeopardizes my time with you."

He drops his head again as his shoulders shake. "I can't lose you."

My own sobs join his as he curls against my side, his hand on Noelle's back.

"I don't know what else to do," I cry.

Despite the amount of crying coming from the two of us, Noelle remains peacefully unaware of the dire situation that has unfolded.

We don't say another word to each other, our silence speaking volumes. Our lives withering away each second we sit curled on our bed.

Nothing will be the same for us from this moment forward. My life will be over soon.

I pray that Noelle gets to know the person that I am, and maybe remembers me, even just a little.

The moon shines brightly through our windows, blanketing the three of us with its protective warmth. Watching over us.

A moment of clarity overtakes me as I hold my family close. I'm going to fight as hard as I can so I can give my daughter everything of myself during the time I have left with her.

I hope she knows how much I love her in this world. And beyond.

CHAPTER 1

Heath

Past

Age 10

I WATCH THE MOVING TRUCKS pull away and the newly constructed house next door is quiet. For the last six hours, big men have been hauling furniture and boxes inside. Now, there's nobody.

"Heath, will you stop stalking the new neighbors?" my mother scolds me. I didn't hear her walk into my room, and my cheeks flush with embarrassment.

"I was just watching the trucks pull away. Geez." I hop down off my bed and drop back onto the floor where the one-thousand-piece puzzle of guitars is partially assembled.

"I don't want them to think you're spying on them. You've been staring out that window all day. The last thing we need are complaints from the new neighbors about a nosey kid next door," she jokes as she ruffles my dark brown hair.

"Do you think they have a son my age?" I ask hopefully. We live on a very private street and most of the families here have grown children. I'm the only kid that gets picked up by the bus on our block. My only friends are in school.

"I don't know anything about them," she comments, looking out the window to spy for herself.

"Maybe you can make cookies and welcome them to the neighborhood?"

"Honey, I don't think people even do that anymore." She smiles and walks toward the hallway. "Our neighbors enjoy their privacy. I think we should give them some, okay?"

I nod and slide a puzzle piece into place. "Yes!" I exclaim, pumping my fist in the air as I admire the guitar I just completed. Only nine hundred more pieces to go.

"Why don't you get some fresh air? Your father will be home later, and we're going out to dinner with the McCarthys tonight."

"Can I stay home?" I huff. Dinner with the McCarthys is always boring. They have five-year-old twin girls that are annoying. Most of the time, I wind up with some kind of food thrown at me for being a 'stupid boy.'

"Absolutely not. I don't even know why you bother asking. You're not old enough, Heath."

I jump to my feet and walk past her. "I'm going outside."

On my way out, I pass the television in the kitchen that's tuned into the local news channel and see my father, unfortunately a familiar sight. "Did Dad win?" I ask my mother.

"I don't think we'd be going out to dinner tonight to celebrate if he didn't," she admits, and I smile. *Good.* He's been on this case for too long. My mother hasn't given me many of the details because it's violent and lots of people got killed, but he's been in court prosecuting this case for almost a year.

"I hope that bad guy stays behind bars for the rest of his life," I state.

"Me, too," she responds quietly, lips pursed together. "Stay in the yard," she calls after me. Like where else am I even going to go? I also know that my father has a full-time security detail around us. Even if I can't see them, I know they're watching me and my mom. The people he puts in jail must be very dangerous.

After I slip on my sneakers, I grab a Wiffle ball bat and a bucket of balls. The game I was playing last night had a rain delay and it's the bottom of the ninth inning. I'm down four to two; there's runners on second and third, with two outs. It's all up to me to win this game. *Let's do this.*

My field is already set as I take a few practice swings, pointing my bat Babe Ruth style, to left field. "Strickland is warming up, getting ready to take this game back," I state in my best announcer voice. I take a deep breath and toss the first ball into the air, smacking it toward the trees that line the back of our property. I drop the bat from my hands and yell, "Home Run!" I throw my arms into the air, imagining all of the ghost runners clearing the bases. It's now my turn, and I begin my winning jog. "He does it again, folks. Heath Strickland drives in another three runs, enough to come from behind and win." I hear the yells from the stands as the fictional crowd cheers me on.

"What are you doing?" Startled, I open my eyes, mid stride as I round third base, hands still in the air.

A girl with long brown braids emerges from the trees with my winning home run ball in her hand. She looks to be about the same age as me, and I've never seen her around here before. She tosses the ball toward home plate as if she's throwing back an opposing team's home run.

"What does it look like I'm doing?" I reply, reaching down to pick up the ball.

"It looks like you're crazy and talking to yourself as you run around in circles."

"I'm playing a game, and I just won."

"Against who?" she asks looking at my empty backyard. "We're the only two people here."

Girls. They don't understand the idea of ghost runners and Wiffle ball.

"Forget it. I was just having fun." I shake my head and begin to pick up the bases.

"Explain it to me. Seriously." She looks at me curiously and walks toward home plate, picking up the bat.

"I was playing Wiffle ball, ever heard of it?" I ask as she swings the bat, a whoosh of air breezing by my face. "Hey! Watch out!"

"Oops. Sorry." She drops the bat as if it burns her hands. "I didn't realize how long it was."

I swipe it from the ground, tucking it underneath my arm. "You should know never to swing any kind of bat this close to someone."

"I said I was sorry." Her eyes glisten, and I suddenly feel bad. I don't want her to start crying.

"It's okay. Really."

She nods and backs away.

"Where did you come from?" I ask her, gesturing toward the woods behind us.

"I was walking through the paths back there," she answers. "I thought I was lost, but then I heard you playing."

"Do you live through there?" I didn't think there were any homes past the tree line behind my house. I've explored enough to know that there's a creek and a large retention basin and then a whole lot more woods. She must have come very far. "Are you lost?" I ask, changing my question.

"No. I live over there." She points to the house right next door. The house I'd been staring at all day.

"Oh."

"The movers were here all day and I wanted to get out of their way, so I went for a walk in the woods."

My mother often scolds me about disappearing back there by myself. She says that I shouldn't wander through there all alone, but my father usually jumps in to tell her that I'm a boy and that's what boys do. Besides, we own most of the land behind us, over fourteen acres. And I'm sure it's monitored by his security team. I was surprised when the house next door was built since I thought we owned everything on this side of the cul-de-sac. My father explained to me that the land was subdivided, and he only owned up to their property line and back.

"You shouldn't play back there all by yourself," I scold, sounding like my mother.

"I didn't go very far."

"Still. There are bears everywhere." I attempt to scare her a little and it works. Her eyes widen, and she steps away from the tree line.

"What?"

"Kidding!" I laugh, but she isn't amused.

"That's not very nice," she says, and her eyes once again get glassy.

"I'm sorry." I take a step toward her but she backs away.

She kicks the grass in front of her. "I guess we're neighbors?"

"Yeah," I reply. "I'm Heath."

"Noelle," she answers.

"It's good to have you in the neighborhood."

She nods, a faint smile spreading across her face.

"Where did you used to live?" I ask, wanting to know more about her.

"Connecticut."

"Why did you move to Pennsylvania?"

"My father's company moved to Philadelphia from Stamford. So now we're here."

"Oh, relocation."

"Something like that." She nods and picks up one of the spare white balls. "Maybe you can show me how to play, so you know, you don't have to play by yourself."

"Okay," I respond, wondering if that's even a good idea. She is a girl, after all.

"Noelle!" a woman's voice calls from the back of the new house, causing her to flinch, worry spreading over her face.

"I gotta go."

"Is that your mom?" I ask an obvious question.

"No! I mean, she's my–"

I raise my eyebrows, she's visibly uncomfortable.

"She, she, she's my father's wife," she stammers and starts jogging toward her house.

"I'll be out here tomorrow, same time, if you want a lesson!" I call after her.

She waves behind her back and picks up her speed. She reaches the door, and the woman glares past her in my direction. I suddenly get nervous, wondering if I did something wrong. She grabs Noelle by her hand, yanking her inside.

I feel terrible that I just got her into trouble, but I have no idea why. The door slams, and the woman is still glaring out the window. "Man, what's your problem?" I mumble. She disappears from the door and I see movement in a nearby, first-floor window. Noelle moves her curtains aside and waves to me. I raise my hand slowly in the air to wave back.

Her stepmother, or whoever she is, gives me the creeps. Noelle's face is drawn and she looks sad as she backs away from the window, my hand still in the air. A clap of thunder booms overhead, and I scoop up my bat and toss the remaining balls into the bucket. As I make a beeline toward my own house, I look back and catch a glimpse of Noelle watching me.

And I can't help but think that she looks like a prisoner in her own home.

CHAPTER 2

Heath
Present

"INCREDIBLE SHOW TONIGHT, gentlemen!" our manager, Stuart, yells. The pop of a champagne cork sounds in the dressing room and it flies through the air, barely missing Garrett's face.

"Dude! What the fuck?" Garrett yells as he ducks.

Tristan and Dax burst out laughing, and I follow suit.

Tonight was the last night of the European leg of our tour that started fourteen weeks ago, Germany being our final stop. We've been on the road for a total of almost twenty-six weeks, and we're all ready to go home. Dax, Garrett, and Tristan have each taken quick trips back to the states to be with their families or significant others. But I've stayed with the crew, exploring the cities we've visited, taking advantage of the time away. This is what I love about traveling the world with Epic Fail–and it never gets old.

Small juice glasses filled with champagne are passed to each of us, and we raise them in the air. "Cheers!" I say and quickly drink, the bubbles tickling my throat.

"You couldn't splurge for actual champagne glasses?" Garrett sneers.

"Next time, I'll put it in the rider," Stuart jokes. "Along with the special vanilla-scented moisturizing liquid soap you require everywhere we go."

Tristan's laugh reverberates throughout the room. "Seriously? You ask for girly soap, Garrett?"

Garrett's ears turn red as he swallows his mouthful of the bubbly, and glares at Stuart for spilling something that was clearly a secret.

Our riders are usually straight forward, and none of us are high maintenance at all, but hearing that Garrett requires a specific soap is hysterically funny to me and apparently to all of us.

"Shut the fuck up," Garrett grunts, jutting his arm out toward Stuart, "and fill this up."

Dax cups his free hand underneath his chin as he almost spews the liquid from his mouth all over the place.

"I like the way it smells," Garrett continues to defend himself as the rest of us erupt in laughter once again.

"I bet it makes your skin so soft and supple," Tristan teases. He attempts to reach out and touch Garrett's arm, but misses.

"It does," Garrett replies, a smile breaking through his serious face.

I'm glad to see he's not taking all of our digs to heart.

"Are manicures going to be next?" Dax asks, practically doubled over in hysterics.

"Guys," I interrupt, all of their eyes now on me. "If G wants soft, vanilla-scented skin, his wish should be granted."

"Whatever happened to just plain soap?" Tristan cackles.

"He likes to exfoliate!" Dax yells.

"No! *Moisturize!*" Tristan corrects him.

"Okay, enough. You've all had your fun. So fucking what if I like a certain body wash–"

"Now you're calling it body wash?" I interrupt him. "Do you have one of those pink poofy things to wash yourself with packed away somewhere?"

Garrett swipes one of Dax's drumsticks and it suddenly whizzes by my ear. I raise my hands in the air, laughing, "Hey, no need to get defensive. It was just a simple question."

Everyone's chuckles begin to die down as Garrett shakes his head. "Are you all happy now that you know what kind of *soap* I like?"

"Dude, best revelation ever," Tristan chuckles as Garrett sinks into the couch.

The room gets quiet, and a single voice pipes up.

"Let's go home," Dax says, walking around the room, bumping fists with us all.

We finish the rest of our champagne and walk out the back entrance. Our large, rented bus is waiting to take us from Hamburg to Munich so we can fly home tomorrow. Our crew has already broken down most of the stage, our gear packed in a large semi. They'll be shipping that home for us, where most of it will go into storage until our next tour, with the exception of some of our personal instruments.

Tristan gets the large room in the back of the bus tonight. The room that I had last night. We all take turns being able to stretch out in the queen-sized bed. I've already taken what I need from the back room as Tristan swipes his pillow and blanket from the bunk I'm inheriting tonight. "Good night. I'm wiped," he declares, closing the door partially.

Dax yawns, stretching his arms above his head. "Holy shit, I think I'm going to sleep for two weeks straight." He unzips his jeans and starts to drop them down to his ankles as he walks toward his bunk.

"Dude. Really?" Garrett yells at him as he slides into the booth in the front lounge area.

"It's not like you haven't seen my ass before," Dax laughs as he starts shaking it, doing his best twerking impression.

"C'mon, nobody needs to see that shit." I cover my eyes, falling onto the small couch across the aisle from Garrett.

"Hey, at least I'm wearing my boxers. I could have been commando. And you know you would have liked it."

I cringe, laughing uncomfortably as Dax finishes undressing in the hallway in front of our bunks. "Goodnight, punks."

He pulls the curtain in front of him and turns the lights off in the bunk area. His cell phone immediately shines light behind the curtains, and I know he's already texting Giselle.

"Tell G that G says goodnight!" Garrett yells as he twists a bottle off the top of a cold beer.

"She says fuck off," Dax yells back, "and save her some vanilla body wash." Cackles come from the back room, indicating Tristan is still awake listening to our chatter.

"Fuck all of you," Garrett growls, raising a middle finger high in the air as he swigs from his beer.

I reach into the small fridge at the foot of the couch and grab my own beer. "Right back at ya," I respond to Garrett. "And cheers." I take a long drink of the ice cold beer and lean back into the couch.

"Are we over the soap thing yet?" he chuckles and shakes his head. "I'm never going to live this down, am I?"

"No fucking way," I respond. "Not a chance, bro."

"Great."

"Seriously, I've got to know. Why that soap?"

He hesitates for a moment, taking another sip while contemplating his response carefully. He then lowers his voice, "You really want to know?"

"Uh, yeah."

"It reminds me of Sam. It's the body wash she uses." His eyes light up, and he relaxes into his seat. "Happy now?"

"Oh my God, yes!" Dax yells from the bunk. Tristan's cackles come from the back room.

"Thank you," I croak, choking on the last mouthful of beer I took. "You're all a bunch of douchebags."

"That's why you love us," Dax laughs, and I nod in agreement.

Garrett picks up one of my Wiffle balls from the bench next to him and tosses it across the aisle to me. I catch it and quickly toss it back. We play this game of catch for a few minutes, when he fumbles the ball and it rolls toward our driver, Mick. "Sorry," he says. Mick just raises a hand in acknowledgment, tipping his head slightly.

"Another beer?" I ask him as I reach for my second.

"Yeah."

I toss the bottle to Garrett, and he easily swipes it out of the air, using the opener on the table in front of him.

The interior cabin is dim, but oncoming car headlights shine through the front windshield. Suddenly, something from above the dashboard shimmers, catching my eye. I've never noticed it before, but there's a light catcher hanging from a hook above Mick's head. "Mick, where did you get that?" I call out.

"You're gonna have to be more specific, man. I'm driving, and I have no idea what 'that' is."

"The light catcher."

"Oh, that. Tammy insists I take it with me everywhere. She says it's good luck."

It's a glass shamrock, filled with all shades of green sea glass.

"How do you even know what a light catcher is?" Garrett asks, stretching his legs out in the booth. He has a smug look on his face, and he knows he just stumbled across a gem.

"My mother collects them." I admit and hesitate before I continue. A smirk spreads on Garrett's face. "And they remind me of someone I used to know."

I brace myself for Garrett's onslaught.

"Oh?" he asks, genuinely curious. "Who?"

I tip back the beer bottle, taking a long swig. And then another.

"Just someone I was close to when I was younger. Bad stuff happened to her, and in the end, I couldn't save her." *She didn't want to be saved.* It's been a long time since I thought about Noelle. My chest tightens as I think about the last few days she and I spent together. Some of the most amazing and most devastating times of my life.

"I'm sorry, dude," Garrett replies. "What was her name?"

"Noelle."

"Why haven't you ever told us about her?"

"There hasn't been a reason to."

"We've got seven hours until we reach Munich and I've had a ton of caffeine today, so I'm all ears."

I close my eyes briefly, her silhouette in the moonlight is the only thing I see. She was beautiful, but doomed.

"I wish I could go back in time, man. Do you ever feel that way?" I deflect Garrett's line of questioning back to him. I can't bring myself to tell him about Noelle, some of the wounds still feel too fresh in my mind, even though it's been almost twelve years.

Garrett nods without answering. "Who is she to you?"

I'm afraid to admit it out loud. Afraid of the feelings that are going to come swarming back, tearing out my heart once again.

I exhale deeply as the words slowly escape my lips. Words I can never take back.

"She was the first girl I ever loved."

CHAPTER 3

Noelle
Past
Age 12

I GRAB MY BASEBALL hat and jog toward the back door when I hear my father's voice, "Noelle?"

"Yeah, Dad?" I call back, my hand on the doorknob. Heath is outside waiting; I saw him through my window waving to me from the field we built together. He's my best friend. *My only friend.*

"Aren't you going to say goodbye? I'm leaving." My heart sinks in my chest, and I exhale harshly. I absolutely hate it when he leaves.

"Coming!" I call out, rushing to meet him in the large library near the foyer.

He's waiting with his arms outstretched and I run into them. He sweeps me off the floor, nuzzling his nose into my hair. "I'm going to miss you, Buddy," he says, calling me the nickname he gave to me when I was a little girl.

"You, too, Dad." I hug him tightly as he eases me onto the floor in front of him.

"You behave yourself with Tonya, okay? I don't want to hear that you gave her any problems."

He's always worried about how I treat Tonya. She's nothing but mean to me, and I dread being alone with her when my father's not around. He travels quite a bit, so that's a lot. I didn't tell him about the last time he left, when she slapped me across the face for questioning her when I found her in my father's office, rifling through the drawers of his desk.

"I'll behave," I huff.

"I'm serious." His eyes scrunch together, causing that crease to grow between his eyebrows. It's become a permanent fixture on his forehead, making him seem much older than he really is.

"I promise, Dad."

He pulls me into a huge hug and kisses the top of my head. "I'll see you in ten days."

"Why so long?" I whine. He's never gone for more than a week at a time. Ten days seems like an eternity.

"I'm visiting half a dozen European countries during this trip, trying to secure financing for the next year. You know that I need to have face-time with my investors to keep our relationships solid." He winks and messes up my hair.

"But that's a long time, Dad."

"I know. I know. I promise I'll call every few days to check in."

"Okay," I pout, dreading his absence. When he's here, Tonya leaves me alone. But when he's gone, I walk on eggshells. I don't ever want to feel the cold slap of her hand on my face again.

"I'll bring you back something, I promise."

"You don't have to."

He walks around to his desk, opening the top drawer. "Here." He reaches his hand out toward me, and I see a wad of money. "Take this in case you need anything."

I open my hand and see a couple hundred-dollar bills. "What do I need this for?" I ask. He's never given me money when he's left before. Tonya's always bought me anything I needed.

"It's fun money. Just in case you want to go shopping or need anything at all."

I shove the bills into the pocket of my shorts. "I doubt I'll need it, though." It's the middle of the summer, and I've hardly left the house since the last day of school. I can't imagine what I'd need to buy.

"Don't ask Tonya for anything. If you need to shop, just call my driver and he'll take you to the mall. Got it?" His voice is stern, and I wonder why things have suddenly changed. As much of a jerk Tonya has been to me, she always enjoys shopping and never hesitates spending my father's money on herself or me.

"Got it."

He kisses me again quickly and grabs his briefcase, "Gotta run, Buddy."

"Bye." I raise my hand as I watch him leave the office and out the front door. His car backs out of the driveway, and the house is eerily silent. Tonya went out a few hours ago, and I don't expect her home for a while. I shrug my shoulders and jog toward the back door.

Heath is taking warm-up swings in his backyard, and he looks up at me with a huge smile. "What took you so long?" He drops the bat and kicks the Wiffle balls toward the pitcher's mound.

"My dad needed to say goodbye. He just left for Europe. *Again.*" I pick up the bat and the grip feels warm from Heath's hands.

"Oh. Where's Tonya?" He looks toward the house, worried that our playtime is going to be cut short.

"Who knows. Out somewhere," I shrug.

"You're home alone?" he asks, concern on his face.

"Yeah, so?"

"My parents would never leave me alone. You're lucky. You can do anything you want."

"Not really," I respond, swinging the bat to stretch out my arms and shoulders.

"Simmer down, slugger," he smirks. "No need to take my head off! You always do that, remember what I told you about swinging that close to anyone."

"Sorry." I smile, and he backs up toward the mound.

"Are we picking up where we left off last night?" Our game went into extra innings; we were tied at twelve runs each.

"Why don't we just call it a tie and start over?" I suggest.

He takes a small notepad from the pocket in his cargo shorts and digs around for a tiny pencil that he got from the miniature golf course we played at last week. I watch as he writes down the score from the game.

"How many is it?" I ask, wondering what our records are.

"The same as yesterday, since the last game ended in a tie."

"Oh," I say.

"I lead our series still. I'm up by six games. You need to have a long stretch of wins to catch me." His grin widens as he shoves the notepad and pencil back into his pocket.

"Whatever." I roll my eyes, only causing him to smile bigger.

"Are you ready?" he asks, windmilling his pitching arm and causing me to chuckle. He takes Wiffle ball very seriously.

I swing the bat a few more times, the whoosh of it hanging in the air. "I'm ready. Give me what you got." I get into my batting stance and lift my chin.

He brings his knee into the air and covers the ball with his free hand, trying to hide the pitch he's about to throw. But I know what's coming and I back away from the plate a little bit. The ball leaves his hand with the familiar *swish* and the ball practically flutters in the air in front of me, confusing me. It's coming toward me slower than usual but it's *dancing*? I swing hard, missing by a mile, and his laughter fills the air.

"What the hell was that?" My cheeks burn, flushing from embarrassment and anger. I've never seen a pitch like that.

"You like it? I perfected my knuckleball," he declares. "And do you kiss your mother with that mouth?" His smile disappears when he realizes what he just said.

We don't talk about my mother very much, but he knows she died when I was an infant. He also knows that I don't consider Tonya my mother.

"Sorry–" he apologizes before I can react. "I didn't mean–"

I kick home plate and shrug my shoulders. "No big deal." But it is a big deal. Huge. I hate not having a real mother. I hate that my father is never here. I hate not having a family. Tears sting my eyes, and I close them, trying to calm down.

"Noelle?" Heath walks toward me, and my eyes pop open.

"Just pitch the ball, please?" I inhale deeply through my nose, sniffling a little. *Get a grip.*

He backs up and pulls his hand into his chest, once again hiding the ball. If he throws that wonky pitch again, I'll be ready for it this time. I'm surprised when the ball leaves his hand and it is thrown in the perfect spot. I swing and it flies over his head, into home run territory. A smile spreads across his lips as he concedes that he just gave me a gift–I've never seen him pitch that slowly and easily to me before. I drop the bat at my feet and run ceremoniously around the bases, watching him turn on the pitcher's mound to follow my strides.

"Good hit, slugger."

"You gave that one to me–and you know it." My accusation hangs in the air between us, and he shakes his head.

"That was all you. But you won't ever see a pitch like that again." His grin widens, and he kicks the ground in front of him.

"Heath!" his mother calls from their large deck. "Time for lunch. Noelle, join us?" Mrs. Strickland is one of the nicest women I've ever met. Her love for her son is so obvious, and he doesn't seem embarrassed by it at all.

"Sure! I was just about to wipe the field with your son," I joke as he and I jog toward the house.

He sprints ahead, reminding me that I could never beat him in a foot race, but stops at the bottom of the stairs to let me go first. "Such a gentleman," I say, and he tips his hat.

"Dorks before dudes," he smirks, then ducks before I can take a swing at him.

"Heath," his mother scolds. "apologize to Noelle."

"She knows I'm only joking."

I smile and nod. "It's fine, Mrs. Strickland. He knows who the real dork is here, and it's not me."

He ignores my comment as we walk into their kitchen. "What's for lunch, Mom?"

"Turkey sandwiches. Plus, I have some fresh fruit and chips. Help yourselves." She gestures toward the table, and the lunch spread is impressive. We both fill our plates with as much food as we can fit and slide into the benches in the sizable nook off the kitchen. Large windows surround us and it feels like we're in a greenhouse. His mother has plants hanging in the windows alongside beautiful light catchers. I almost expect to see a butterfly perched on the windowsill.

"I love these light catchers, Mrs. Strickland. Where did you get them?"

"Palmer finds them in the most unique places. This one is from a little shop down the shore." She points to the large seashell shaped light catcher that looks like it's pieced together with different color sea glass.

"It's beautiful."

They sway in the windows, a kaleidoscope of colors reflecting off the glass.

Heath is chomping on handfuls of potato chips, trying to ignore the conversation I'm having with his mother.

"Don't you think they're beautiful?" I ask him, overly enthusiastic.

"Boring," he says, pretending to be disinterested.

"I saw you looking at the dolphin-shaped one."

"Heath gave that to me for my birthday two years ago," his mother interrupts. "He even named it. That's Dusty the Dolphin."

I almost spit out my mouthful of food as Heath's ears turn bright red, his embarrassment spreading to his cheeks.

"Dusty the Dolphin! I love it!" I exclaim as he closes his eyes.

"You're lucky you're a girl," he mutters.

"Or what?"

"Heath," his mother says sternly.

"Nothing." He goes back to eating his sandwich, taking the biggest bite I've ever seen.

Our eyes lock onto each other, and I feel bad for embarrassing him. He obviously shared a tender moment with his mother over Dusty the Dolphin and he's afraid to admit it. It's so sweet.

We eat the rest of our lunch in silence as his mother straightens up the kitchen. "The McCarthys are coming for dinner tonight." His shoulders fall and he drops his head, shaking it slowly.

"Again?" he moans.

"Yes. Your father and Mr. McCarthy are working on a case together, so he's bringing the girls, and we're going to have a movie night." She turns to me. "You're more than welcome to stay, Noelle."

Heath's attitude suddenly changes. "Please stay. Please. Don't make me hang out with their twin daughters by myself." I remember him talking about those girls. They're in second or third grade, and they drive him crazy.

"I think I can stay," I respond, knowing I really don't have anyone I can officially ask.

"Thank God." A long exhale escapes Heath's lips causing me to smile.

"Glad I could help."

The doorbell rings, chimes reverberating throughout their huge two-story foyer. Mrs. Strickland walks through the house to answer it as Heath looks back at me. "Seriously, you're a life-saver. I don't think I could sit through a movie with those two kids. It's like I'm their babysitter or something."

"It'll be fun!" I proclaim. I'm secretly happy to spend some time with other people since I don't get out much at all, other than to play ball and go on hikes with Heath.

Voices get closer to the kitchen, and I look up to see Tonya standing with Mrs. Strickland. The look on her face alarms me, her lips are tight, and she looks angry.

"Thank goodness you're here!" There's no worry on her face at all.

"I–I'm having lunch," I stammer as she walks toward me, one arm outstretched.

"Come home with me this instant. I've been looking frantically for you! I almost had your father's plane turned around because I thought you'd disappeared!"

I swallow hard, a huge lump in my throat. *What is she talking about?*

"I've been here all day. Playing out back."

"I invited her in for lunch." Mrs. Strickland tries to intervene, but Tonya yanks me from the chair. Heath grabs the table when my left hip smashes into the corner, pain shooting up my side.

"You can't just vanish like that and not tell me where you are." Her fingers burn into my skin as her nails dig in.

"I'm sorry," I say as I'm dragged to the front door.

"Mrs. Durand, she didn't do anything wrong!" Heath is following close behind, but his mother stops him. Our eyes meet, there's confusion in his eyes.

It's okay. I mouth the words to him, and he shakes his head. He looks as terrified as I feel. Besides the slap a while back, she's never been this forceful with me.

Tonya tugs me out the door and across their vast front yard. When we reach our front door, her hand leaves my arm and grasps my ponytail, causing my scalp to throb. "You little bitch!" she hisses, slamming the side of my face into the door jamb. I see stars, pain radiating across my cheek. "How dare you talk back to me in front of our neighbors." She pulls me through our foyer, my arms flailing as I try to release myself from her death grip.

"Tonya!" I scream as everything above my neck feels like it's on fire. Tears spill down my cheeks.

"Stop calling me that name! I'm your mother, goddammit!" she screeches, finally releasing my hair. But now I'm hurling through the kitchen and fall, slamming my head into the side of the kitchen table.

"Stand up, you fucking klutz!" She's on me again before I know it, I can barely get my knees pulled in to protect myself from her tennis shoe pounding into my side. Air is forced from my lungs as her foot seems to find the right place. Her arms start to swing, punches landing everywhere. I'm still trying to catch my breath when her massive diamond connects with my cheek. I cough and cry out, finally finding my breath.

"Please–" I wail, the taste of rusty blood fills my mouth.

Her blurry figure is above me and I see her fist in the air again, about to strike. Then the doorbell rings.

She immediately composes herself, smoothing out her blouse. "Get up and get to your room now. Show your face out here, and I'll fucking kill you." Her voice is calm, cold, and terrifying.

The bell rings again, and she kicks me on my shin. "Go!"

I scramble to my feet, pain ripping through my stomach. I shuffle to my bedroom down the long hall behind the den, slamming the door shut. As I fall onto my bed in the corner, a familiar voice fills my house.

"Mrs. Durand!" Heath calls out, his voice strained. "Noelle left her hat over at my house, so I thought I'd bring it by."

"Thank you, dear." The words leave her mouth so evenly. "I'll make sure she gets it."

"I'd like to give it to her myself, if that's okay, ma'am."

I moan in pain, rolling on my bed. Blood spreads on my white pillows. *"Please go away,"* my mind screams.

"She's in her room. She's been grounded, thanks to you and your antics. Don't expect to see her for *several* days."

"But she didn't do anything wrong!" he pleads with her. "Neither of us did!"

"I'm sorry, young man. But you need to leave. I'm sure your mother wouldn't appreciate the tone you're taking with me right now."

"But–" His voice is cut off by the door slamming in his face.

I hear footsteps getting louder on the hardwood floors, coming toward my room. I pull my knees into my chest and squeeze my eyes shut. My door flies open, and I feel the baseball hat land on the bed next to me.

"I don't want to see your disgusting face for the next week. Do you hear me, you little bitch?"

I nod in compliance, praying she doesn't punch me again. She peers out the window, straining her neck to see the Wiffle ball field behind Heath's house. She snaps the blinds closed and they drop to the windowsill with a bang.

"And look at the mess you made in here. You're never going to get that blood off of those perfect white pillow cases!"

Stop! Just stop!

"I won't tell your father what *you* did. He'd be livid if he knew you disobeyed me."

I didn't do anything!

I'm afraid to open my mouth at all but I whisper, "I'm sorry."

"I can't hear you, what did you say?"

"I'm sorry," I sob.

"That's more like it. Remember, you're grounded for the entire time your father is gone. I don't want to see your face at all. In your room except to eat. Blinds stay closed."

My door slams shut, and I open my eyes. *She's gone.*

I push my face into my bloody pillow and scream, crying until I'm hoarse.

Daddy, I need you. Please come home.

CHAPTER 4

Heath
Present

THE DRIVER TURNS the town car into my driveway, winding toward the house. It's not as immense and sprawling as some of the other guys' houses, but I don't need as much space as they do. I'm still single, after all. Well, *mostly* single. There is someone I see on a regular basis, but it's more like a friends-with-benefits situation, and neither of us is emotionally attached to the other.

In fact, I should send her a text to let her know I'm home. I pull my phone from my pocket as I step out of the car.

"I'll get your bags, Sir," the driver says, interrupting me, as the the trunk flies open.

"Thanks, you can leave them right inside the foyer." I slide a fifty-dollar bill into his hand and unlock my front door.

As I step inside, a fresh scent hits my nose. *Home.* It feels so fucking good to be here.

Rosie must have been here this morning, getting the house ready for my arrival. There are a few great things that have come out of my odd and somewhat close relationship with Garrett. One of them is Rosie. She's his housekeeper's, Peggy's, best friend. Peggy is also Garrett's aunt-in-law, or something like that. There's a fresh loaf of Italian bread on the counter which means she made her delicious lasagna for me. I open the refrigerator to see that it's been fully stocked and the aluminum-foil-covered-tray is sitting on the middle shelf with the word "lasagna" scribbled on the top in black marker.

I bet she also put fresh sheets on my bed, which reminds me of the reason I took my phone out in the first place. I glance back down at it and type.

Me: I'm home. Want to come by tonight? Rosie made lasagna :)

As I'm about to hit 'send,' my phone rings in my hand. My mother's name appears. I abandon sending the text and answer.

"Hi, Mom."

"I've been tracking your flight all day. I'm so happy to hear your voice, but you sound so tired."

"I slept a lot on the plane," I reassure her. My driver carries my guitar case in, placing it on the floor next to the rest of my luggage. He waves his hand and silently backs out of the door, pulling it closed.

"Well, you need to get a lot of rest to combat that jet-lag I'm sure you're going to have. You know how much I worry about you when you travel."

"I'm good. I promise." I walk to the back stairs off the kitchen and go up to the second floor. My bedroom doors are wide open, and the fresh scent grows stronger. *She definitely washed my sheets.*

"I'm staring at my bed right now," I say. *And it's going to get some good use as soon as I can send that text.*

"Good."

"How's Dad?" I change the subject, realizing I haven't spoken to him in weeks.

"He's busy closing things down in his office in the city. Before I forget, his retirement dinner is two weeks from tomorrow. Make sure it's on your calendar."

"I'm already aware and have confirmed it's in there at least three times since you told me a couple of months ago." She's been dropping 'hints' about how important his retirement dinner is and how much she wants me to be there. She's known our tour schedule for over a year and planned the dinner aware I'd already be home.

"Oh, thank goodness," she says. "You never know if something more important could pop up."

"Really? Something more important than Dad's retirement?"

He's been the District Attorney for Philadelphia for almost two decades, but working in private practice part-time for the past five years. He's been "transitioning" from the DA's office for a while as his replacement was officially sworn in last month. He's happy to just start practicing law, without all of the high profile prosecutions he's usually involved with. His office is in Bucks County, not too far from where I live. He gets pulled into cases every now and then, mostly on a consultant basis. And the national news channels will have him speak about the higher profile, nationally-televised cases. I know he secretly thrives off of those cases. My mother constantly worries about the repercussions of the past, especially when some of the more dangerous criminals he's put behind bars are up for parole hearings.

"We're both so happy you're home, Heath."

"Me, too. I hope our next tour isn't as long as this one." But I know it's already being planned. We were able to get a lot of writing done in Europe, even taking the opportunity to record a couple new tracks during our downtime in London. Stuart is already lining up venues for next year, so our hiatus isn't going to be too long.

"Don't worry, I'll be around for a little while."

"Are you bringing anyone to your father's dinner?" she asks, trying to be subtle. She's been wanting me to settle down for years.

"I'm not sure. I may be seeing someone later tonight, maybe I can ask her?"

"Oh! That's so exciting! Who is she? Have we met her before? How long have you been seeing her?"

"Mom. Calm down. It's nothing serious. I see her every so often, but I'm not in a relationship or anything." I try to let her down easy, but the next question out of her mouth could very well be, 'When are you getting married?'

"Well, I'll need to know by next Tuesday when the final headcount for the caterer is due. Do you think you'll know by then?" Her question is pointed, but can also mean so many things.

"I'll know if I'm bringing a 'plus one,' if that's what you're asking," I respond and can't help but smile.

"Thank you."

"Okay, I gotta run. I need to catch a nap before I do anything tonight."

"Okay, honey. I'm so happy you're home. I love you."

"Love you, too, Mom."

I disconnect and toss my phone onto the bed next to my pillow. I kick off my jeans, stepping out of them and dive onto the bed. I'm asleep before I can pull the covers around me.

I WAKE UP to the sound of banging coming from the first floor. The room is dark, and I reach for my phone to check the time. It's dead. *Fuck.*

The banging continues until I reach the front door, tearing it open. "What the hell?" I ask, Garrett's hand mid-swing, about to bang again.

He looks me up and down, shaking his head as he walks past me into the foyer. "If I have to see another one of you assholes in your underwear, I'm going to punch something."

I shut the door and follow him through my house into the den.

"Where's your shit?" he asks, looking around somewhat frantically.

"What the fuck are you talking about. What shit?" I throw my hands out to my sides.

"Your luggage? Your gear?"

"Why?" The hall clock begins to chime, and I notice it's ten o'clock at night. I've been asleep for almost seven hours. *Holy shit.*

"They sent your guitar to my house, so you must have mine. And I need it."

I shake the cobwebs from my head and look at him. "You need it now?"

"Yes. You know how it is, you start hearing chords in your head and you just need to get that shit down on paper before you lose it."

"G, you have about forty guitars at your house. Why do you need that particular one?"

"Because that's THE ONE."

"What?" Is this a dream? What is this fuckery that's happening in my foyer right now? And why am I still in my boxers?

"It's the only guitar I can use when writing music. None of the others work for me. That's THE ONE," he proclaims again and starts pacing.

"Dude, you need some sleep. And some Xanax."

"I'll leave as soon as you give it to me."

He follows me back into the foyer where the pile of suitcases remains from earlier today. I point to the case that is clearly not mine and wonder how I didn't notice it when the driver brought it in. "There you go."

He pushes the case on its side and fumbles with the combination locks. It pops open and he strokes the black and white American Telecaster with the tips of his fingers without removing it from the case. "There she is," he swoons, and I start to get itchy.

"Are you done eye-fucking your guitar?"

He snaps out of his lusty trance and looks up at me smiling. "All is now right with the world, dude." He shuts the case gently, spinning the locks so it's secure.

"Well then. That was enjoyable." I smirk and walk into my kitchen. "Are you staying for a little while or do you have candles burning at home, awaiting your return with your girl?" I chuckle and pull a cold bottle of water from my fridge. I eye the lasagna and realize I was supposed to do something earlier. *What was it?*

"I'm good. I need to go. Kai is still awake, he was super amped when I got home and Sam texted me when I got here to tell me to hurry back. He wants me to tuck him in, then I'm riding this adrenaline until I can't ride it any longer. I have a long night of writing ahead of me."

"You need to get some rest. Trust me, I feel like a different person now that I've slept for a few hours."

"I don't get it," he says. "Coming back from Europe shouldn't affect you as much as going to Europe. Right?"

I shrug my shoulders. "I have no idea how jet-lag works. I just know either way, I'm a fucking mess for days. On that note, I'm going back to bed."

"Later," he replies as he strides to the front door. He pauses before he leaves. "Come by tomorrow if you can, I'd love for you to hear the music I'm writing for the songs you wrote. I think you're really going to love it."

He closes the door, and I lock it behind him.

Those songs I wrote while we were on the road in Europe were written for one person.

Someone who'll never hear me sing those words.

Someone who's been gone for almost twelve years.

Someone I'll never forget.

Someone I'll love until the day I die.

CHAPTER 5

Noelle
Past
Age 14

MY EYES POP OPEN, my room filled with warm sunshine. I jump out of bed with a spring in my step, tossing my favorite stuffed animal, Mr. Jingles, on top of the rumpled sheets. Today's my birthday and for the first time ever, I'm having a party. I hear a noise outside my window and peek out to see workers in the backyard, setting up a tent with tables and chairs. The pool is being cleaned and all of the umbrellas on the surrounding patio have been opened.

The invite list is extensive at the urge of my father. He wanted me to invite my entire class, boys included. So I'm expecting at least twenty-six of my friends and classmates. My heart beats quickly, and I giggle with excitement. Hanging over my closet door is a sundress cover up with a really cute one-piece plum-colored bathing suit hanging next to it. They coordinate perfectly, and I love them. Tonya actually took me shopping last week and helped me pick them out along with a fantastic pair of dressy flip-flops. She's been really nice lately, quite uncharacteristic for her. I haven't needed to walk on eggshells as much. It's also helped that my father hasn't traveled for a few months and has been home most of the summer with us, working out of his home office. They even took a trip to Napa last month to celebrate their wedding anniversary, and she came home with the biggest cluster of anniversary diamonds on her right ring finger.

Life has been good. And peaceful.

I step into the bathroom that's attached to my bedroom so I can wash my face and brush my teeth. After splashing cool water on my face, I look at myself in the mirror. I've gotten taller over the past year, according to my pediatrician. I talked with her about the changes that have happened to me since I got my first period late last year. My father was really uncomfortable when it happened and Tonya was at a spa weekend with her girlfriends, so he took me to the doctor right away. Thankfully, my pediatrician, Dr. Kathryn, is so easy to talk to. I've been completely avoiding saying anything to Tonya since Dr. Kathryn gave me her personal cell phone to call her with any questions that I had. This has been a tremendous relief, and thankfully, I haven't had the need to call her. But it's so comforting to know she's there if I need her.

After I shower, I pull the bathing suit on, noticing the small buds on my chest. I'm suddenly self-conscious. Thankfully, my dress will cover me, hiding my tiny breasts. Some of my friends are much more developed than me, and I hope my girlish chest will go unnoticed.

Tapping on my bedroom window startles me. I quickly pull the dress over my head and walk through my room to see Heath opening the window before I can reach it.

"Hey!" I scold him. "I was in the bathroom. How about some privacy?"

His cheeks flush as he notices the dress that I'm wearing. "Sorry," he mumbles. "Nice dress."

The dress falls just below my knees, and I flop into the plush chair next to my window. With my bedroom on the first floor, it's a common occurrence for Heath to stop by unannounced. We'll sit just like we are now, him outside the window, me in the chair. We talk about everything, but mostly the Wiffle ball games we still play together several times a week. We've played hundreds of games against each other since I moved in four years ago—our scores diligently recorded in a little notebook that he carries around with him constantly.

"So I guess we aren't playing a game today?" he asks, flipping the notebook through the window so it lands on my lap.

"Obviously. It is my birthday today, after all."

"Oh, I know. How could I forget? You've been talking about it for the past three weeks." He pulls his knees to his chest as he adjusts his position in the well-worn grass outside my floor-to-ceiling window. "It's hot out here today." He looks toward the pool. "Good thing it's a pool party."

"Yeah," I say and start to flip through the notepad. "Did you record yesterday's score? The game I won?" I joke as I search for the record of our game. Months and months of scores scroll by, and I suddenly notice a change in the pattern of notes scribbled. The page after the last game has words scrawled sloppily on it. It looks like a poem. "Hey, what's this?" I ask.

He quickly leans through the window and swipes the pad from my hands. "Nothing," he replies flustered, tucking the notepad back into his shorts.

"Whatever," I mutter. "No reason to act all weird about it."

"It's nothing, okay?"

"Fine," I snap back at him, now I'm uncomfortable.

"What time should I be here for the party?" he asks, changing the subject. His face is still flushed, his ears bright red.

"It said the time on the invitation," I respond, folding my arms across my chest.

"Oh, I don't remember seeing it. I didn't think you sent one to me since I talk to you *every single day*." His eyes lighten up, and a smile spreads across his face.

"It starts at noon." I glance over to the clock on my nightstand. "You have just under two hours to get yourself ready." I smile back, and the awkward tension is no longer in the air.

"Should I bring my Wiffle ball stuff? We could play boys versus girls."

"Sure, that would be fun!" I know my father suggested a couple of things for us to do and he hired a DJ. But I'd rather play ball over dancing any day.

"Great!" He begins to stand up, but bends back down to stick his head through my window. "You look really pretty, Noelle." He blushes again and pulls his head out of my room, taking off across the lawn toward his house.

I lean back in my chair and smile. *I feel pretty today.*

I RUB MY ARM along my forehead, wiping the sweat that has formed. Tears sting my eyes as I attempt to avoid eye contact with Heath, who is sitting across from me at a table by the pool. Some awful music plays loudly from the DJ booth, but the DJ is nowhere to be seen since he disappeared inside the pool house about thirty minutes ago. He's running this crappy music on a constant loop.

"Maybe the invitation had the wrong time?" Heath insists, reaching across the table to grab my hand.

I jerk it away, placing it in my lap. "No, Heath. I saw the invitations myself. It said very clearly that my party started at noon and ended at three." Tears now spill down my cheeks, and I don't attempt to wipe them away. "My birthday party started two-and-a-half hours ago. Where is everyone?"

My shoulders start to shake as I pull my hands from my lap to cover my face, sobbing uncontrollably.

"Hey, there has to be an explanation for this." He gets up and kneels next to me on the hot concrete.

"Everyone hates me!" I wail. "That's the explanation." My excitement from this morning has been replaced with self-loathing and despair. It all makes sense now. Not a single one of my friends and classmates from school mentioned that they were coming. Even though we haven't seen each other since school let out, I do keep in touch with a few through email and texts. Not a single person said a word to me about the party. It's official. They all hate me.

"That's impossible," Heath says and pulls my hands away from my face. "Completely impossible." He takes a napkin from the table and softly dabs my cheeks.

"Then where is everyone?" I yelp. "You would think at least a few of them would have showed up?" I can't control my tears as my sobbing continues. I've never felt so alone in my entire life. Realization sets in that I have no one. My father isn't even here, called away on business about a half hour before the party was supposed to start. He kissed me on my forehead before he left, slipping a small wrapped box into the palm of my hand, promising me he'd be home as soon as he could. And Tonya is nowhere to be found.

"I'm so sorry, Noelle." Heath pulls me against his chest and I throw my arms around his waist, holding tight.

"I just don't understand," I cry, snot dripping from my nose. "What did I do to them? Why does everyone hate me?"

"You don't deserve this," he whispers into my hair. "I'm going to get to the bottom of it."

"God. No!" I exclaim. "I just want to forget this day ever happened. I want it to be over and done with. Maybe everyone is away on vacation?" I'm grasping at straws, trying to keep Heath from intervening.

He nods his head in agreement. "That must be it," he says unconvincingly.

The music suddenly stops and I look up, the DJ begins packing up his equipment. "Is it okay if I leave?" he asks from the other side of the pool.

I wipe the tears from my face and nod.

"Okay, cool. Happy Birthday," he announces awkwardly into the microphone before all sound is cut from the speakers.

I choke back more sobs as I push myself away from Heath. "You should go," I object, weakly.

"I'm not going anywhere, slugger." His hand drops to mine, and he begins to pull me through the fence that surrounds the pool and toward his yard where our Wiffle ball field is set up.

"I don't want to play," I snap, snatching my hand from his. "I'm sorry, but I just want to be alone."

His face drops, his eyes falling to the ground. "I don't want to leave you. It's your birthday."

"Please. Just go."

He steps toward me, hugging me tightly. "Happy Birthday, Noelle."

I turn and walk back to my house, leaving Heath standing alone in my yard. Once I'm inside, I kick my flip-flops off and head toward my room, nearly bumping into Tonya who's blocking my way.

"Sorry," I mutter.

"You should be," she hisses. "After everything I did to make this day special for you and nobody shows up? This is an embarrassment. What are my friends going to think? You should be ashamed of yourself, young lady!"

"I don't know what happened," I sob. "I don't understand why nobody came! You did send out the invitations, right?" My cheek stings as her cold hand slaps my face.

"What are you–"

"Shut the fuck up!" she yells. "Are *you* accusing *me* of not sending out your invitations, you stupid bitch?"

Thwap!

Her other hand stings my other cheek, and I fall back against the wall.

"I didn't say that–" I cough, forcing the air to leave my lungs as she brings her knee into my gut, her hands grasping onto my shoulders, nails digging in.

"How dare you blame me for this unsuccessful party?! Your friends must really hate you for not showing up today."

"I don't understand," I wail as her knee connects with my belly again. I nearly vomit as I try to wrangle myself from her grasp.

"What am I going to say to my friends? How am I going to explain that my daughter is a complete fucking loser who has no friends of her own? Except for that pathetic boy next door that only wants to get in your pants!"

Oh my God. What is she saying?

"Heath isn't like that!" I snap back, trying to protect the one true friend I actually do have.

"He's just like all men. He's a sick, twisted, and perverted teenager. Don't think I don't know what he does after he leaves your room at night!"

"What?" I gasp. She's never told me she's seen him come up to my window. We've always been so quiet.

"When he leaves you, he pleasures himself outside before he goes home. He's vile and disgusting and only talks to you because you can get his rocks off! What do you let him do to you?" she shrieks, punching my breast. Pain shoots across my chest as she punches my other one. "There's nothing to see here! You're not even developed yet. He must get off on your boyish chest. He's probably gay!"

"Stop it!" I scream, flailing my arms in front of me. I scratch her cheek, tearing at her skin and drawing blood. Her eyes widen and she punches me again, this time on the side of my head.

"He's only using you to get off! Don't you see?"

I don't even know what *getting off* is. She's being so hateful and ugly in her descriptions of what Heath does to himself and I don't understand any of it.

"He'll never touch you the way you want. He saves that for the Haley Simon." Haley is in our class and it's no secret she has a crush on Heath, but he's never said anything about her to me. "In fact, I saw him groping her the other night on the side of his house. I bet he did it so you could see that he doesn't even want you."

"No! I don't even know what you're talking about!" I'm sobbing. Picturing Heath doing *things* with Haley makes me sick. I can't listen to her anymore. I'm able to run down the hall and slam my bedroom door, locking it.

"You can't lock me out, you slut!" she screams as her fists pound on the door. "I have a key, and I swear to God I'll make you pay for scratching my face causing me to bleed!"

I cower into the corner, pulling my knees to my chest, preparing to defend myself against her blows.

"I'm coming back as soon as I pay the DJ and the caterer. You're going to regret ever laying a hand on me." Her heels click down the hallway, and I squeeze my eyes shut.

I try to remember the events leading up to today. She asked me to sign my name to the invitations a few weeks ago. Then I sealed them and watched her place stamps on each one, tucking the bundle into her purse. She told me she was going to the post office that afternoon and would monitor all of the RSVPs as they came in. I haven't heard about a single RSVP, but assumed she was taking care of everything.

Could she have done this?

I know she hates me, but why would she jeopardize her own reputation? I pull my knees to my chest and notice something in my chair. The wrapped box, that my father placed in my hands earlier, still sits where I left it earlier. I crawl over to it, wincing in pain from the blows that I took to my chest and belly. I slowly unwrap it and find a note inside.

Noelle,
This was your mother's and I know she would have wanted you to have it.
Please wear it every day, close to your heart.
Know that no one loves you more on Earth than I do.
And more in Heaven than she does.
I love you, Buddy.
Happy Birthday,
Dad

I lift the piece of cotton up and a beautiful necklace sits in the box, a large single diamond at the end of a long platinum chain. It's so long, I don't even need to undo the clasp, it fits over my head and drops down into my dress, settling right next to my heart. This is the most beautiful thing he's ever given to me, and I reach down to wrap my hand around the diamond. I smile through the pain that is shooting through my body, knowing this necklace used to sit next to my mother's heart.

Suddenly, it seems so logical to me that Tonya would sabotage my birthday. She's hated me for as long as I can remember. I must be a reminder of the perfect woman that my father loved for so long, before her. Tonya can never replace my mother in my or my father's eyes. He loved my mother with everything he had, and it still surprises me that he would compromise who he is to be with a wretched woman like Tonya. She hides so much of her vileness from him.

Lately, her behavior toward me has been sweet, and I honestly thought she was moving past her hatred, finally accepting me as her stepdaughter. My father has been so much happier with our relationship, it's been less strained, and even a little pleasant.

Until now.

CHAPTER 6

Heath
Past
Age 14

"WHERE ARE YOU GOING?" my mother asks as I attempt to sneak out the back door.

"I forgot to give Noelle this." I hold the birthday present in the air for her to see.

"Okay," she says. "I'll let Gus know that you're going to be outside." Gus is the head of security and the last time I snuck out of the house, my parents knew before I reached Noelle's window. Thankfully, nobody saw the black car stop in front of her house and one of the security guards, Lou, chasing me across the yard. It would have been funny if I wasn't completely embarrassed. When he caught up to me and I had to tell him exactly what I was doing, he fist-bumped me then brought me back to my house. My father lectured me for a half hour. But all I could think about was that our security detail thought I was going to Noelle's house to hook up with her or something. So gross. Now my parents know every single time I'm going over to see her, because I don't ever want to have that happen again.

"How was the party?" Her face contorts with concern. "Not that I was spying or anything, but I didn't see anyone outside. Was it too hot to cause the party to move inside?"

I shake my head slowly. "Nobody showed up."

"Oh dear!" she gasps. "Why not?"

I shake my head again. "I have no idea. Noelle's really upset, and I don't know what to do."

"She's the sweetest girl. I can't understand why her friends wouldn't show up for her birthday party." My mother looks so incredibly sad and it tugs at my heart. She's saying exactly everything I've felt all day today. Noelle doesn't deserve to be treated like this, and I'm completely surprised that our entire class did this to her.

My cell phone buzzes in my pocket, and I pull it out to see a text from Trevor.

Trevor: I didn't get an invitation. I even asked my mother if she saw one and she said no.
Me: Thanks, T.

I texted a few of my friends and fellow classmates, asking if they received their invitations, trying to find out what the hell was going on. I wanted to get in on the secret and find out why everyone would do this to Noelle.

"Hmm," I say, shaking my head.

"What is it?" my mother asks, and I look up.

"Mom, did you happen to see an invitation to her party? She says they were mailed about three weeks ago?" My mind is swirling with ideas as I try to piece this crazy puzzle together.

"No, but I assumed you saw it first and RSVP'd."

I smile a little. "I don't think it's as bad as she thinks. Trevor didn't get an invitation and I bet the rest of the class didn't either." They must have gotten lost in the mail. *But all of them?* It still seems weird, but at least there's a logical explanation beginning to come together.

"I'm going to go give her this." I shake Noelle's present gently. "And tell her I think there was a mix-up at the post office. If I can get in touch with a few more people, it should explain why nobody showed up."

My mother smiles. "You're a really good friend, Heath. I'm proud of you and the young man you're growing into."

"Thanks, Mom." I blush and rush out the back door, down the stairs of our deck, and across our yards. I hear the sound of the security camera attached to the exterior of our house above my window and turn to see the familiar red light. I wave and mouth "Hi Gus," floating the peace sign in the air.

When I reach her window, there's a faint light coming from her bed. I tap lightly, and the light goes out. There's no movement coming from her room and instead of tapping another time, I lift the window so it opens slowly.

"Noelle?" I whisper. It's at least nine o'clock, the sun setting just a few minutes ago, fireflies swarming in the humid air.

"What are you doing here?" she whispers back. She crawls across her floor, and her face is near mine.

Moonlight reflects on her cheek, and I notice a huge bruise under her right eye. "Oh my God, what happened?"

Her hand flies to her face, and she stammers, "Nothing. We uh–we lost power–and uh–it got so dark that I–uh–I walked into the corner of my bathroom door."

"You did?" I look toward the pool and notice the lights are still lit around it. Our house is also still lit up. "When? We have power, and it looks like yours is still on."

"About an hour ago, but it came back on pretty quickly," she blurts out, turning her cheek away from me.

"It was still light out an hour ago," I challenge her. She's acting super weird. "What really happened?"

"That's exactly what happened," she snaps at me and tries to close the window in my face. I jam my hand underneath it and push it back up. "What are you doing?"

"I forgot to give you this," I say, shoving the present through the open window. She looks around and quickly pulls my arm.

"Get in here, quick," she orders as I jump through her window and into her room. She shuts the window and looks around, both of us on our knees.

"What's going on?" I ask, suddenly confused. She looks terrified.

"Nothing. I mean–it's so hot outside, you shouldn't have to sit out there."

"Okay?" Still weird.

"But we have to be quiet," she whispers. "It's late and I don't want anyone to hear us. I'm not allowed to have boys in my room."

I'm fully aware of this already, and that's why I sit outside her window every time we talk.

"Then why did you pull me in?"

"I told you already. It's too hot out."

Her erratic behavior is very concerning, but I shrug it off. I came here to give her a birthday present and hopefully some good news about all of the birthday party no-shows.

"We need to be really quiet," she says again. "Follow me."

She leads me to a door at the far end of her room and when she opens it, I realize it's her large walk-in closet.

"You're being really weird," I say as she pulls me inside and shuts the door. She turns on the light, and I suck in a breath as soon as I see her face. "Holy shit." I reach out, placing my hand on her swollen cheek. "That is really bad."

She shrinks away from me and backs up against the far wall, leaning into a large pile of stuffed animals. "I'm fine," she mutters softly, her gaze falling to the floor.

She's not telling me the truth, I can feel it. There's no way that the corner of the door could have done that to her face. I open my mouth to challenge her story again, but quickly close it, vowing to get to the bottom of it at some point.

"Why are you here?" she asks.

"To give you this." I slide her gift across the closet floor. We're facing each other, legs folded like pretzels in front of us.

Her glistening eyes light up as she places her hand on the present. "Thank you."

"Before you open it, I have some news," I say, excited.

"Shh. Please. You need to whisper." I see fear in her eyes and I nod, whispering, "I'm sorry."

"It's okay."

"Anyway," I start, "I texted Trevor and he says he never got an invite." She raises her eyebrows and tilts her head to the side. The light above shining on her incredibly bruised cheek.

"And then I asked my mother if she saw the invitation in the mail, and she said no."

My cell phone buzzes with another text message, and this one is from Haley.

Haley: Nope. I didn't get an invite. Why wasn't I invited? Does she hate me?
Me: No! We think they all got lost in the mail. All is good!
Haley: Oh! Thank God! Tell her HBD for me! TTYL!

"What was that?" she asks, straining her neck to see my phone.

"That was Haley. She didn't get an invitation in the mail either." I smile, now that I've figured out the mystery.

"Haley Simon?" she asks, her face drawn and sad.

"Yes. And she says Happy Birthday."

"Whatever." She shrugs her shoulders, and I'm confused by her response.

"Are you and Haley not talking to each other?" I press.

"What? No, I just thought maybe she hated me or something."

"Well, she thought the same thing, and you're obviously both wrong."

"Okay." Her voice trails off, and she shifts in her place on the floor.

"So there's at least three of us that I know that didn't get the invite in the mail." My phone buzzes a couple more times and I look at a few more incoming texts. "Make that seven." I smile, reassuringly.

Relief floods her face, but it's quickly overtaken by a strange, pained look.

"Are you okay?" I ask, concerned.

"Yeah. Just trying to sort something out." She closes her eyes briefly, nodding her head.

"Are you sure?"

"I'm good." A couple tears fall from her eyes, and she quickly swipes them away.

"This is *good* news," I press. "No need to get upset. The post office messed up." I scoot closer so I can squeeze her knee. "Okay?"

She nods slowly, allowing a few more tears to fall. "I'm relieved that our entire class wasn't staging a group protest. I'm happy they don't hate me."

"Never," I promise, leaving my hand on her knee.

"And thank you for checking with everyone. You didn't have to do that, you know."

"I figured there had to be a logical explanation. And I hated seeing you so sad today. Like I said earlier, you don't deserve to be sad. Ever."

She looks up, our eyes connect and she exhales slowly.

"Yeah. I guess." There's still something going on with her that I can't put my finger on. Almost like she either doesn't trust the explanation that I gave her or something more.

"Are you sure you're okay now?" I have this overwhelming need to continue to push her for the truth about the bruise on her face.

As if she's reading my mind, she touches her cheek and drops her hand into her lap.

"Everything is fine," she insists. "I'm just a colossal klutz." A weak smile spreads across her face, and I feel a little relief, but not much.

"Here," I remove my hand from her knee to pick up her present, placing it on her lap. "Happy Birthday."

"Thank you. You didn't have to, you know." She blushes as she opens the card.

I stop her. "You can read that later." There's something inside the card that I want her to read when she's alone. It's embarrassing, and since we're in her closet, it would feel really weird if she reads it in front of me. I suddenly regret scribbling that poem for her. I know she saw it this morning, and I just ripped it out of my notepad and shoved it in her card. It's a sloppy mess.

"Okay," she says and starts to open the wrapping paper gently and quietly. "What is it?" she asks, excited.

"You'll see, just open the box."

She pushes the torn paper onto the floor next to her and removes the lid from the box. When she pulls back the tissue paper inside, she gasps, bringing one of her hands to her lips. "Oh my God, this is gorgeous!" she whisper-shrieks. "Where did you get it?"

She pulls the crescent moon-shaped light catcher from the box, holding it above her head. "It's seriously beautiful." She squints her eyes, trying to see the light from the ceiling in her closet reflecting through the multicolor shapes that fill the inside.

"I'm glad you like it," I say, feeling my face flush. My family spent a week down at Long Beach Island right after school got out, and this was the nicest one in the store. She looks back at me and smiles.

"I don't know what to say." Her eyes glisten again as she lowers the moon, placing it gently in her lap. "I'm going to hang this in my window."

I nod and my butt is starting to fall asleep. I stretch my legs out in front of me, brushing against her bare leg and lean back on my hands.

"This was the second best gift I received today." She smiles and touches a long silver chain that's dangling around her neck.

"Second best? Now I'm insulted," I joke.

She reaches into her dress, and I squirm a little. *What is she doing?*

"My father gave me this." At the end of the long chain she pulls out is a giant gem.

"Is that a diamond?" I ask, in disbelief.

She nods her head. "It belonged to my mother."

She's told me about her mother and how she died so young. She was too young to even know her, only a few months old.

"It's beautiful," I mutter, not really knowing if it's the right thing to say. "It's nice that you have something that was hers."

"I'll always keep it close to my heart." She drops the diamond back into her dress, and her hand falls onto my shin. "And you gave me something equally as beautiful today. Thank you."

Her light touch does something to me, and my leg begins to tingle. "As soon as I saw it, I knew you would love it."

Then she does something completely unexpected. She leans forward and quickly brushes her lips against my cheek, barely making contact.

I freeze in place, my arms are stiff and pushing into the floor behind me. *What the hell was that?*

"Umm," I stammer, unable to speak coherently. *She just kissed me.* My mind is racing. Was that like a kiss–kiss? Or like a friend kiss? Or a 'you're like a brother to me' kiss?

"Sorry, I–" her voice shakes and without another thought, I pull my arm from its support position behind me and wrap my hand around the back of her head, crushing my lips clumsily to hers. I leave them there for a long time, both of us breathing through our noses, not moving at all. My eyes pop open and hers are wide and staring at me, almost alarmed.

I back away from her slowly, first dropping my hand from behind her head, then pulling away my lips that are practically stuck to hers. "Shit," I say, embarrassed. "I shouldn't have done that."

"Is it because of Haley?" she asks.

"What? No. What are you talking about?" Now I'm *really* confused. Why would she bring up her name again? Does she think Haley and I? No. *What?*

"Never mind." She scoots away from me.

"I'm sorry. I shouldn't have done that. I don't know what I'm doing. I mean–" This can't get any more awkward.

"That's okay." Her shoulders drop along with her head.

"I'm not trying to take advantage of you, if that's what you think." So many of my friends have talked about playing games with girls in closets. And here I am. In a closet. With a girl. *Shit.*

"I know," she whispers.

"Seriously. I didn't mean to do that." *Wait.* Yes I did. *Did I? I need to get out of here.*

"I get it."

"You do?" Good. *I think? Shit.*

"It's really late, Heath. Your parents must be wondering where you are." She attempts to stand up and winces, quickly grabbing her side. "Ah," she groans.

"Are you okay?" I ask, forgetting the awkward tension between us and place my hands on her arms. She jerks away as if my touch burns.

"I'm fine. My legs fell asleep."

"You're holding your side, not your legs, and you look like you're in a ton of pain." *What is going on with her?*

She manages to get to her feet and drops her hands to her sides, trying to hide the pain that I still see in her eyes.

"I'm fine. I *swear.*"

"I don't believe you. Did you also fall down a flight of stairs when you 'walked into the door?'" I use air quotes and immediately regret it.

Her face contorts from pain to anger.

"Well, I really don't care if you believe me or not. It's time for you to go." She pushes past me and opens the closet door quietly before turning the overhead light off. We're in complete darkness, faint moonlight shining in through her back window.

"I'm sorry, Noelle. I'm really sorry." I don't know what I'm apologizing for. The fact that I don't believe her weak lie or because I kissed her. *No. I'm not sorry for either.*

"It's okay. Really. Thanks for caring. And thank you for my birthday gift." She pauses and brushes her pinkie finger against mine. "You made my birthday really special, and I'll never forget it."

Without thinking, I loop my pinkie finger around hers, linking them together. Linking *us* together. We walk to her window like this and I break our connection reluctantly, bringing my hand up to her bruised cheek. "Please be careful," I beg, and I'm not sure what I'm even begging her to be careful of. *I'm just so worried about her.*

"I will," she whispers. "Catch a couple fireflies on the way home."

"I'd catch a million for you." Her eyes light up, a smile on her lips. I want to kiss her again. So bad. But all I do is stare into her eyes and back away. I push the window open as quietly as I can and slide out onto the grass.

"Happy Birthday, Noelle."

She smiles as we both slide the window gently along the track, closing it.

She leaves her hand pressed against the window and I immediately do the same, covering hers, only the glass pane separating us.

Her smile is weak and full of pain.

A pain that I would take away from her in an instant if I could.

CHAPTER 7

Heath
Present

HER SQUEALS REACH an octave I've never heard before as she jumps into my arms, wrapping her legs around my waist. "You're home!"

I've never received this sort of welcome from her, her current response to me is off the charts. Haley Simon and I have known each other since kindergarten. Noelle used to swear she had a crush on me a long time ago, but I wouldn't have noticed it if she did. I was too busy being head-over-heels in love with *her* and wouldn't have seen Haley coming riding in on a roaring steam train.

But things are different now. Noelle is gone.

Haley's been a fun 'distraction.' I ran into her several years ago, after we played a local show. She was with a bunch of girls from our old town, they were all screaming and swooning over the band. They used their connection with me to try to meet the rest of the guys. The only one who wasn't attached at the time, besides me, was Garrett. I think he mowed through at least three of those girls before the weekend was out. Of course, that was the *old* Garrett, before Sam.

I don't know what it was about Haley that drew me to her that night. She acted coolly indifferent toward me, not seeming to care that I'd become a mega superstar. She just saw me. Heath Strickland. And that was good. I don't like pretending to be something more than that, even though my name carries more fame these days. I enjoy feeling like I'm back at home, surrounded by my family and the people that truly cared about me.

The first night we reconnected, we talked. A lot. She wanted to know if I ever heard what happened to Noelle. So many stories swirled around our close-knit town. So many theories speculated. Most of which were untrue. Haley and Noelle's friendship throughout high school was strained and odd. Haley's jealously of Noelle was obvious for years, but yet, they were cordial with each other. There was always this weird 'thing' between them when we were kids, something I could never quite put my finger on. One always thought the other one was talking behind her back, spreading rumors. I knew that it had something to do with me, Noelle worried that Haley had a crush on me. It was all such trivial, meaningless, grade school girly bullshit. It went on for a while, until that night that I kissed Noelle for the first time. Our 'sticky kiss' as we used to call it. That's when she realized that Haley was insignificant. I didn't have feelings for her back then. Noelle was everything to me.

Haley brings me back to reality by showering my face in wet kisses. "I'm so glad you're back. I missed you!"

I tense my arms around her. This isn't what we're all about. We don't 'miss' each other. We don't throw ourselves all over each other. We just have sex. Completely unattached, casual, never spend the night, sex.

"Okay?" I say, easing her out of my arms.

She's bouncing up and down on her toes, ready to shoot off like a rocket.

"When did you get home?" she asks.

"The other night." I realize I never sent the booty call text I was planning on sending the night we came home. Then I slept for two days straight. And spent another day in Garrett's studio, listening to the stunning melodies he created for my songs. *Noelle's songs.*

"Oh." Her face drops, and she suddenly stops bouncing. This is exactly what I don't want. Emotions. Feelings.

Fuck.

"This tour really kicked my ass," I admit, reaching out to touch her arm.

She flinches away from me and backs up into her living room.

"I thought you'd be happier to see me," she whines. *Fucking whines.*

I can't do this. My skin begins to itch. She's acting like a girlfriend. Something I haven't had since Noelle.

"I am happy to see you, Haley. But I've slept most of the time I've been home trying to kick this jet lag, or whatever has taken all of my energy away." Her mood is literally sucking the mojo right out of my dick.

"As long as you haven't been avoiding me," she purrs as a sly smile spreads across her face.

My dick shrinks further in my pants.

I don't know what to say to her. She's completely changed since I saw her over a year ago. One of the stops on the American leg of our tour was Philly, and she and I spent two days in bed, enjoying great, satisfying sex. There were no batting eyelashes, no pouty faces. *What the fuck is going on?*

"Haley, I—" I stop myself. I don't want to get into a deep conversation about why she's acting this way.

"Let's relax for a little while," she says, leading me over to the couch. "We need to talk."

Fuck. Me.

I reluctantly sink down onto the couch while she settles into my side, lifting my arm and placing it around over her shoulders.

"I've been thinking. A. Lot," she begins, and I suck in my breath. "For the past few years, when we've been able to see each other, it's fast and furious. We have tons of sex. *Great sex.*"

Exactly.

I don't respond, but sit still and listen. "What are we even doing? Do you have feelings for me?" My shoulders tense, and I wonder if she can feel it.

"Wait. Don't answer that." Her voice lowers, her eyes dropping.

We sit in silence for a few more minutes. "Haley, I don't really have a definition for what this is. But I think you nailed it on the head. We've been casual. *Very* casual. And I've liked that."

"I see." Her eyes meet mine, and they glisten with tears. *Shit.*

"I'm not trying to be an asshole. But I'm also not looking for something long term." *Something binding.*

"Okay. Then let's just keep doing what we were doing." She attempts to shrug off what I just said, but I can tell she's hurt.

"Talk to me," I urge, reluctantly.

"I didn't realize how much I really liked us together until after you were gone for so long. I love our chemistry. I love the fun we have."

Don't. Say. It.

"I think I fell in love with you."

Fuck.

"How is that possible?" I ask. This isn't love. At least not for me.

"You bring me back. You make me feel things I haven't felt for over a decade. The little girl in me loves that we've connected again. When we first hooked up, I was coming out of a really bad relationship. He was controlling and mean and–"

"Did he hurt you?" I blurt out, concerned about what she's going to reveal.

"Not physically. No. It's just, I wasn't free with him. I wasn't me. You changed that somehow, making me feel like I did before I was with him."

"Oh." She's never revealed much about her previous relationship, and now I feel guilty for not asking. For not caring.

"Being with you makes me feel young and happy. Like I can do absolutely anything I want. I'm doing so well, I'm even up for a promotion at work."

"I had no idea," I admit, feeling even worse for not trying to find out anything else about her. I don't even know what she does for a living.

I've been hooking up with the Haley from my youth. The one who had a crush on me for years, stowing it away to build and preserve a friendship with Noelle. The carefree Haley who just wanted to hook up, nothing more.

"It's okay. Really. But I've come alive because of you. You've given me freedom that I hadn't had. To be myself. To be anything I've wanted to be."

"Haley, I didn't give you anything. You did that all on your own." Can't she see that? We weren't really together, how could I give her anything?

"No. You gave me my youth back. You made me forget about all of the bad shit that's happened to me."

I've heard similar words before, but not from her. From Noelle.

The difference is that I *wanted* to give Noelle back her youth. Her childhood. Her innocence. I *wanted* to love Noelle. And I did.

I don't feel that way at all for Haley.

She slides onto my lap, straddling me. Her fingers slip into my hair as she bends forward, lips on mine, tongue stealing past my lips. She rocks back and forth on top of me, trying to elicit a response.

"Heath," she murmurs against my lips. "Make love to me."

My body stiffens beneath her and not in a good way. "Haley–"

She freezes. "Oh my God." Realization sets in and she slides off of me, curling up in the corner of the couch. "I'm such a fucking idiot. Holy shit. What the fuck am I doing?"

"I'm sorry." *It's not you, it's me.*

"I had this whole thing built up in my mind, you know?" she whines, eyes welling up once again. "I thought your feelings grew right along with mine. I had this whole scenario play out in my head, expecting, hoping you'd come through my door and sweep me off my feet. Begging me to be yours forever."

"How could you?" I ask, sincerely. "What have I done to make you think we had anything more?" I'm blunt, but she needs to hear the truth to get her out of the delusion she's been living in for so long.

"Oh don't worry, pal. I hear you. Loud. And. Fucking. Clear. Let me just sit here and feel like an even bigger asshole than I already am."

"I'm really sorry. I'm not trying to make you feel bad about anything. I'm trying to be honest with you."

She sits up straight, her back tight, eyes suddenly clear.

"Why don't you be honest with yourself for a change?"

"What?" I ask, my guard down.

"You're in love with a dead girl. You have been for years. Once you can admit it to yourself, you'll be able to move on and finally open your heart, *for real*, to someone else."

Her words stab me right in the chest, driving deep through muscle and bone, piercing my heart.

"What did you say?" I ask again in disbelief.

"You're still in love with Noelle. And you'll never be happy until you can finally let her go." She shifts uncomfortably in her seat, wringing her hands.

I close my eyes, nodding my head. She couldn't be more right, and I know my heart will never let go.

It's only ever been Noelle.

I'm in love with a dead girl.

CHAPTER 8

Noelle
Past
Age 17

I LISTEN FOR THE GARAGE door to close and wait a few extra minutes. My father and Tonya just left for a long weekend in New York City. Then they have front row seats to the Macy's Fourth of July fireworks on Monday night. So they booked a suite at the Plaza for the weekend. A trip that I respectfully declined. Tonya was as relieved as I was. She hates me, and the feeling is more than mutual. She really did some damage to me yesterday when she wrestled me to the ground, punching and kicking my side. A large bruise is now visible on my outer thigh, and I've been covering it up.

For the first time in a while, I was almost able to overpower her, but then she reminded me of something she could expose that would destroy my family forever. That's when I relented, allowing her, once again, to take control and finish the beating. Over the years, she's learned to avoid my face so my injuries aren't as visible, but it doesn't matter. I can feel the pain for days, and sometimes weeks, after she unleashes her fury on me.

And my father still has no idea. I can see pain in his eyes every single day he's with her. He is being tortured in his own way, underneath her thumb, I'm sure. For him, I take the abuse. For him, I'd die. Even though he's unaware of what she's been doing to me since I was younger. The hell she and her family could unleash on ours is staggering, so I continue to endure her blind rage as best as I can.

EPIC LOVE

Before they left, my father pulled me into his office to remind me of how I should behave while alone for the next four nights. I plan to relax, maybe play some ball with Heath, and explore every corner of our house, trying to find the 'evidence' that Tonya says she has. I need to destroy it, before it can destroy us. His eyes were sad and hollow when he kissed me goodbye. The words *"I'm sorry"* escaping his lips more than once. If he only knew what else I've endured because of Tonya's rage, he would break to pieces. I hugged him tight, told him I loved him, and watched them leave together. Tonya's glare over her shoulder as they walked out the door sent chills up my spine, the bruises and muscle aches still sore from yesterday.

Once I'm sure they are gone, I slip on my flip-flops and the baseball hat I've been wearing since I was a little girl, and jog out the back door. The sun has just set and flashes of light streak across my backyard, indicating that the fireflies are out in full force.

"Hey," I call out to Heath who's already lounging in one of the chairs out by our Wiffle ball field. He's set up a small table with snacks and what looks like a pitcher of lemonade. "I hope you didn't start our game without me."

He stands up from his seat as I leap into his open arms. When he wraps his hands around my waist, I stiffen as a dull ache radiates throughout my ribs.

"You okay?" he asks, concern on his face.

"Yeah, you know me. Super klutz," I lie for what seems to be the thousandth time since I've known him.

"What did you do this time?" he asks, nuzzling into my neck. "You smell good." He presses his lips lightly against my throat, and I giggle.

"Oh, you know. Ever since I got that new bed, I've been walking into the footboard, it juts out so far into my room. See?" I push away from him and tug up the side of my shorts, showing him the giant bruise caused by Tonya's spiked heel. "Walked right into it, like a dumb-ass."

"Jesus, Noelle. That looks awful." His eyes find mine, and he grabs my hand. I can tell he wants to press further, but he should know by now that I won't answer any more of his questions. He's grilled me in the past about my relationship with my father. With Tonya. He's even come right and asked me if I've gotten "smacked around" by either of them. I'm always able to deflect his probing questions, but I know he's not going to continue to let this go. I can go months without receiving a beating from Tonya, and actually the past year, I can only count three times that she really did some visible damage to me, present injuries included. Not that I consider myself lucky, but I've learned ways to avoid triggering her insane rage.

Heath's face hardens. "You know I don't believe you, right? I've never believed any of the crazy stories you've told me about your injuries. If you don't tell me the truth, I'm going to tell my father and–"

"No!" I shout, grabbing his hands. "You can't say anything. Promise me. Please. Swear to me you'll keep your mouth shut." He can't tell anyone what he thinks is happening to me. It will destroy everything. My father would be lost to me forever.

"What the fuck is going on?"

"You need to stop asking. Please, I'm begging you. Please just trust me." Tears spill down my cheeks, and he pulls me against him again.

"I can't keep that promise anymore, Noelle. I can't keep seeing you like this and not do anything." As his arms tighten around me, his warm breath tickles the side of my neck.

My body stiffens as I say the words I know I'm going to regret. "If you say anything to anyone, you'll never see me again."

"What?"

He releases me and leans back so he can look into my eyes. "Exactly what I just said. You need to trust me or this is over."

Heath and I officially became a couple when he asked me to junior prom last year. Although he likes to remind me that he fell in love with me the first time I hit a home run off of him when we were kids. For him, it's been that simple. Stolen kisses in my closet. Holding hands when we walk through the woods together. Our almost nightly talks, through my open window. He's given so much of himself to me over the years and I've only given him what I want him to see, hiding the secrets of my abuse at the hands of Tonya.

"You can't mean that." He looks distraught, scared.

My eyes lock on his, and I'm determined to make him believe me. "I've got everything under control. But, I swear, if you say anything to anyone about what you *suspect* is going on with me, I'm gone. For good."

He shakes his head, breaking eye contact with me to look down at the ground. "I trust you, Noelle, but I can't keep quiet after seeing you beat up so bad. I've seen it too many times. I don't believe your stories anymore and haven't for a very long time."

My eyes widen. "You haven't told anyone, have you? Your mother? Your father?" Fuck. If he hasn't believed me, it's possible his father is already involved and that would be the worst possible scenario. I can't have the District Attorney snooping around my family business.

"No, but if you don't come clean to me, I'm going to talk to my parents."

I start shaking, sobs taking over. "Please. I'm begging you," I cry. "Please let me handle this."

I'm in his arms once again, he's saying my name over and over into my shoulder. "Don't make me regret this," he begs. "I won't say anything, for now. But please don't do anything stupid. If you need help, please come to me."

Relief floods my chest, and I exhale into his ear. "I promise. If I need you, or your father, I won't hesitate to ask for help."

We hold each other in silence for several minutes before he pulls away, his lips find mine and he kisses me tenderly. Sweetly.

We often joke about our first kiss on my fourteenth birthday. A kiss that wasn't really even a kiss, but two pairs of lips stuck together. Every once in a while, he'll plant one of those 'sticky kisses' on my mouth, causing us to laugh hysterically. Remembering the innocence of my youth makes me sad, especially the times before Tonya's rage and beatings began. I was so young. So innocent. In love with life and clueless to the pain that my father endured with her. *Still* endures. I wish I could turn the clock back and relive some of those times, before I had the weight of my father's world on my shoulders.

His mouth leaves mine as he kisses me softly along my jaw line and down the side of my neck. "I love you so much," he whispers against my skin. "So fucking much. I would die if something were to ever happen to you. Please don't let it, okay?" He finds the sensitive skin at the base of my neck, his tongue tracing my vein.

"I promise," I moan into the warm July air. "I love you."

He groans into my neck, pulling me tight against his shorts. "Did you bring your firefly house out?" I can't believe he's thinking about catching fireflies when I'm about to suggest we go back to my house.

"What?"

"We need to catch fireflies. Now," he growls, and I know if I push him, there will be a point of no return. We've been talking about making love since our senior formal. But I've been reluctant recently because I don't want him to see me fully exposed, too many new bruises to explain.

"It's in the pool house," I point out, nibbling on his ear lobe. "But I thought we'd go back to my house. I have it all to myself."

I'm ready. I want to be with him. Tonight. I have it all planned out, and the lights in my room will remain off. I even unplugged the lamp next to my bed in case he tries to turn it on. I want to give myself to him, but he can't lay eyes on my bruised naked body. Ever.

"Fireflies first," he says, taking my lips gently once again. "It's our Fourth of July weekend tradition." He's all about traditions and I love it. He has no idea how much these small little gestures help me preserve that innocence that I'm desperately trying to cling to.

"Okay."

We walk, hand in hand, to my pool house and open the door. The small closet in the sitting room holds pool toys and outdoor equipment. I open it up and see the firefly house that my father gave to me on my eighth birthday. The sides are made of a black mesh material, the top looks like the roof of what I imagine a fairy's house would look like. When I caught fireflies when I was younger, my father would tell me that if I left them in the firefly house overnight, the light from the moon would turn them into fairies and then they would fly out. They would live in my backyard, always watching me, always protecting me. I eventually realized that he opened the house, letting the fireflies escape, but I clung to this wonderful memory for as long as I could. Until the rage of Tonya started chipping away at my innocence and trust.

I love that Heath wants to give that all back to me, little by little. When first I told him about fireflies and fairies, he made me promise that he could help me catch them every year. And here we are, five years into our newest tradition, running through my backyard, capturing firefly after firefly, giggling like the young kids we used to be.

"I'M USED TO CLIMBING through your window," Heath mumbles against my neck. We're standing in the hallway, the back door closed and locked behind us.

"Tonight's special. I didn't want you to have to crawl through the grass," I smile as he spins me around to claim my lips. His tongue softly parts them, gently meeting mine.

I pull away a little, walking him through the back of the house and down the hallway that leads to my room.

He closes the door behind us, locking that as well. I'm not worried at all that anyone is going to surprise us. My father texted me two hours ago saying they were just finishing dinner in the city and were meeting friends of Tonya's for cocktails and a cruise around Manhattan. Then they'll be nestled away in their hotel, and I won't see them again until Tuesday afternoon.

My bare feet sink into my plush carpet, and I feel every single thread between my toes, my senses heightened. Heath flicks the light switch, but nothing happens.

"My lamp broke," I lie. He quickly dismisses it and pulls his shirt over his head. Moonlight streaming through my window accentuates his well-defined chest and abs. I look at the blinds and consider closing them, so my room is pitch dark, but I see the firefly house hanging from the metal pole that's stuck in the ground just outside my window, and I change my mind. It's meant to hold bird feeders, but my father repurposed it, and we hang my firefly house from it instead. Heath and I caught about a dozen between us and they are dancing in their temporary cage.

Heath sees me staring at the fireflies. "Don't worry, I'll set them free when I leave." He closes the distance between us and pulls me against his bare chest.

"Set them free? Then they won't become fairies," I joke.

His eyes brighten, and he reaches out, gently sweeping my cheeks into his hands. His mouth covers mine as a soft moan escapes my lips.

"I love you so much," he tells me for the tenth time tonight. "I want to give you everything. And take away the pain you're hiding from the world. From me."

I can't cry. I won't cry. He's given me so much already, and I can't let him shoulder my pain. I'll become a burden.

"Make love to me," I whisper against his lips. "Please."

"I thought we're waiting until we're both eighteen?" Our birthdays are just days away. His is on the tenth and mine is on the fourteenth.

"I don't want to wait. Tonight is perfect." And it is perfect. We won't have this opportunity to have this kind of privacy again.

His hands leave my face, and he reaches down, slowly pulling my tank top over my head, exposing my lace bra. He drops the shirt to the floor, and it lands on my feet. "Are you sure?" he asks, holding my gaze.

"I've never been more sure in my life," I respond, kissing him deeply.

He reaches around behind me to unclasp my bra, that, too, falling to the floor. He unbuttons his cargo shorts, and quickly removes them and his boxer briefs so all that remains between us are my shorts and panties. His body is no stranger to mine. We've explored each other as much as we could over the past year and a half. Desire swelling. Need building. We've waited as long as we could. Tonight we will complete the bond that we've been longing for.

I drop my hands to the seam of my shorts and start to push them down over my hips. "Wait, let me," he whispers, his mouth leaving mine. His kisses pass over my neck and shoulders, then he pauses to tease my nipples with his tongue. He spends time caressing my breasts, his fingertips barely touching my nipples as they harden.

"Ah," I moan into the dark room. "Heath."

"Shh," he says against my breast, warm breath softening the buds that his tongue continues to tease.

He pushes me back toward my bed and kneels in front of me, slowly inching my shorts and panties off together. His lips move down across my belly, finding my hip. He scrapes his teeth gently across the bone as he pushes my clothes down to my ankles. I'm afraid to make a move to step out of them, in fear of losing the contact his mouth has with my skin. As if he's reading my mind, his hands travel slowly down my legs, reaching my ankles. He gently lifts one and then the other, pushing my discarded shorts and panties to the side. His lips and tongue trace a line down my thigh, over the massive bruise that Tonya inflicted. My breath hitches as he passes over that area.

"Are you okay?" Concern fills his voice.

I nod vigorously. *I'm more than okay.*

He suddenly lifts me off my feet, hands tucked under my naked ass. He holds me against him with one arm as he pulls back the soft comforter, placing me on the bed. His hands trace every curve of my body. Despite the bruises on my ribs and on my thigh, his touch feels wonderful. Soothing. Amazing.

He eases on top of me, resting his elbows on either side of my head, hands caressing my face, lips kissing away the tears that I didn't even know were rolling down my cheeks. "I love you more than life, Noelle. You have to know that. You have to believe it."

"I do," I pant as his mouth covers mine again.

His length presses against my opening and he pauses, his body stiffening. "Should I grab a condom?" We've talked about our first time, and we decided we wouldn't use a condom. I've been on the pill for almost a year, and I have no fear of getting pregnant. I take it at the same time every single day. We're careful. We're both clean. We've never been with anyone else.

"No. I want to feel you. All of you." His eyes darken, and he kisses me urgently, tongue sweeping in, taking mine.

One hand leaves the side of my face and he touches me softly between my legs, sending tingles through every nerve. He knows how to bring me to that place, he's had lots of practice with his fingers and tongue. And he sweeps over my bundle of nerves one more time, sending me right over the edge. He swallows my cries with his mouth, his tongue swirling in time with his fingers. I raise my hips to his hand as he draws the last of my release by pressing his thumb down, applying the slightest amount of pressure, elongating my orgasm. I begin to tremble, signaling that he can stop. I can't take the contact any longer. "God," I moan. "That was–"

"Not finished," he interrupts me, a smile dancing on his lips. "I want you now."

"Yes," I pant, kissing him softly.

His fingers move away from where they were and move lower. He dips them into my opening, curling two in, hitting just the right spot. I relax under his touch and move my hips along with his thrusting fingers. "Are you ready?" he asks, slowing his pace.

I nod vigorously. I've been ready.

He withdraws his fingers, and I feel his tip at my opening. We've gotten this far before, him pressing slightly into me. Just the tip, never more. Now I want it all, and before he can push forward, I thrust my hips up, taking an inch more, then two, adjusting to him. Slowly. So slowly.

I hold my breath. I can feel myself tightening around him. "Relax," he whispers. "Breathe."

And I do. I inhale deeply, relaxing my shoulders. On my second inhale, he pushes several more inches in, almost filling me. His eyes open wide, and he looks scared.

"Are you okay? Did that hurt?"

I feel a slight burning and pulling, but nothing excruciating. Nothing what I imagined.

"No," I say. "It feels–wonderful."

Relief floods his face and he moves slightly, adjusting himself over me. He pushes in deeper, until he's fully inside and doesn't move.

"Are you okay?" I ask, reaching up kissing him gently on the lips.

"I can't move," he says, embarrassed.

"Why?"

"Because it will be over if I do, and I don't want this to ever end. My God, Noelle, you feel so fucking good." His hips stiffen above mine, the dull ache back in my ribs. But I don't care about any of that. I don't want this to end either.

I begin to rock back and forth underneath him, feeling him swell even more inside of me. The burning sensation is gone, and I'm fully relaxed. "Please move, I need you to move," I pant. My belly button tingles with a sensation I've never felt before. "Oh my God, move!" I shout and then cover my mouth, slightly embarrassed.

He doesn't wait for me to say it another time, and he begins to move his hips. His mouth drops open as his eyes squeeze shut. Soft grunts escape his lips, his hips swirling and swirling and swirling.

Cries fly from my lips as our hips move together, the tingling sensation building and building. "Heath!" I don't know what's happening, this is not a feeling I've ever had down there before. "Don't. Stop. Please. Don't. Stop!" I don't even know what I'm saying. I think I mutter "fuck" a few times as our bodies begin smacking together. Building toward a desperate release. I lock my legs around his back, holding his body against mine in the most perfect position. He circles his hips one last time and then pushes into me deeper, with all of his strength, sending us both into a passion we've never felt before. Our bodies tense against each other as he twitches inside of me.

"Oh my God," he exhales and practically collapses. "Oh my God," he says again. "That was–are you–God–are you okay?"

He pulls out of me and slides next to me, his eyes searching my face. "Please tell me you're okay. I didn't mean to be so–forceful."

I smile, a dull ache between my legs, feeling the void, wanting it back.

"It was perfect."

"Really? Are you sure?"

"I can't even describe what it felt like. It was wonderful."

He closes his eyes and kisses me softly. "I know exactly what it felt like. And it was mind-blowing."

I nod, kissing him back. "I've never felt anything like this in my life, Heath. Never. Thank you for giving this to me."

"I'd give you anything. Anything at all. I love you, Noelle."

"I love you," I respond, curling into his side. He slowly eases out of bed, making his way to my bathroom. We've had to clean ourselves up before, but this time there's less to worry about since he came inside of me. He returns with a warm washcloth that he slowly, carefully places between my legs.

"Does that hurt?" he asks.

"No."

He finishes and I see him dab a few spots on the sheets. I'm suddenly embarrassed that he's cleaning up the blood that must have come from me.

"Is there a lot of blood?" This bed has been stained by my blood before, but not the kind that he's looking at. I've bled from the wounds that Tonya has caused.

"Only a few drops. I can barely see them." He disappears again, and I hear my hamper open and close.

He comes back into my room a few seconds later and slides next to me. "I don't want to go home," he whispers into my hair. "I want to stay here and hold you all night in my arms."

I wish. His parents will be expecting him home. He can't spend the night.

"Hold me until I fall asleep?"

"That I can do," he says, pulling me tight against his body, our legs entwining.

"Sleep tight," he whispers. "Know that I'll love you forever."

The moon is shining brightly, protectively, through my window as I fall asleep with a smile on my face.

And I dream of fireflies becoming fairies.

CHAPTER 9

Heath
Past
Age 17

"HEATH, CAN YOU COME down here and help your father?" my mother yells up the stairs. I quickly pat myself dry, running the towel through my hair before I pull on my clothes.

It's July Fourth, and our backyard has become a flurry of activity. Tents, tables, chairs, and caterers running around, trying to get everything set for our annual party. Family and friends have been coming to this for as long as I can remember. It's an annual tradition, and I'm thrilled that Noelle is going to spend the entire day with us, without interference from her wicked stepmother.

"Coming!" I call, jogging down the stairs, practically colliding with one of the caterers.

"He's out back, trying to set up the ping pong table, and he's going to hurt himself," my mom laughs. "I can't imagine why he wants that outside anyway."

"Beer pong, Mom. What do you think?"

"Your father doesn't play beer pong, for heaven's sake."

I chuckle as I walk through the kitchen, out the back door, and down the stairs into the yard. My father is bent over a large table, trying to figure out how to unlatch it.

"Dad, I got it." He looks up as I slide the table across the grass, giving us a little more room to work with. "See this here." I point to a latch on the underside of the table. "You slide it like this and boom, you have a ping pong table." The table opens up easily. "Grab that side so we can stand it up."

Once it's in place, he picks up the bag that contains paddles and balls. "What are those for?" I ask.

"Excuse me?" He looks at me like I'm crazy.

"I thought you were setting this up to play beer pong."

"Absolutely not," he declares. "Just like you have Wiffle ball tournaments with your friends, I have ping pong ones with mine."

"You have friends?" I joke.

He tosses a paddle toward me and I catch it. "Let's play. Unless you're afraid?" He teases me and gets into a defensive ping pong stance.

I laugh out loud. "I'll wipe the table with you, old man."

He serves the first ball, and it goes whizzing past me. "Will you?" he chuckles as he produces another ball, seemingly out of thin air. We paddle back and forth for several minutes, each time, he smashes the ball. He's swinging so fast and hard that I don't even have a chance to return a single serve. My paddle flies in the air like I'm trying to swat a fly.

Within ten minutes, he's won the game and I didn't score a single point.

"You proved your point," I admit, wiping sweat from my brow. "I'm going to need to shower again."

An older woman, who's dressed in a catering outfit, walks up to us and hands us each a bottle of ice cold water. "Thanks," my dad and I say in unison.

"That was a freaking work out, Dad. No wonder you're still in such good shape for someone your age."

He swats me playfully on the back of my head. "Don't be a smart ass," he jests.

We walk to the patio, where a huge fire pit sits, and sink into the new outdoor couches. "How's Noelle?" he asks.

I shift uncomfortably in my seat. I'm so worried about her, but I can't say a word. I know that something is going on in that house next door, and it scares me. She begged me not to say anything to my father, so I don't.

"She's good," I answer vaguely.

"Where is she going to college?" he asks.

"She just made up her mind last week. She's going to Boston College." She was undecided between there and Villanova. She chose

Boston College because I'm going to Boston University's School of Music.

He nods his head, realizing that we're going to be close to each other. "Are you okay with that? Sharing a city with your girlfriend?"

Am I okay with it? I fucking love it. What the hell kind of question is that?

"Yeah. Sure," I say, nonchalantly.

"You're both young. It's great that the two of you have been so close for so many years, but try to keep your options open. Try to give each other some space, room to grow as individuals."

His advice seems sound, but unrealistic to me. We can't stand the moments we're apart. Once we're in the same city together, without her controlling stepmother holding her prisoner, we'll be able to grow together.

"Has she been okay lately?" He drops the question like napalm in the air. My shoulders tense, I don't want to answer him.

"What do you mean?"

"I don't know. I just have the sense that something isn't right over there. Her parents seem, unhappy."

"Tonya's not her mother," I stress, repeating the mantra that Noelle says often.

"I'm aware of that. But she's still a parent figure, no?"

"I wouldn't call her that. She's her stepmother. And I don't think Noelle respects her enough to consider her a parent of any kind." I stop when I realize I've said too much. My father's line of questioning is now starting to zero in on a topic that I need to steer clear of. I don't want Noelle to leave me. "What are you getting at?"

"Nothing, really. I know you care an awful lot for her. And so do your mother and I. It's easy to see the sadness she carries, and I know Tonya isn't the most popular person around, so I just assumed she had problems with her."

Everything he says is spot on. My mother asks me almost daily if Noelle is going to join us for at least one meal a day. The only time she's ever able to come is when Tonya is out of the house, unable to stop her from leaving. You don't need to be too perceptive to notice.

"I don't think they get along, but that's pretty normal, right?" I ask.

"Honestly, not really," he replies. "While second marriages can be hard on the children involved, you don't see too many turn into the type of relationship Noelle seems to have with her stepmother."

What can he see? How does he know?

"Whatever. I just think they're like oil and water. It's not a big deal." I need to shut this conversation down before I say something that I'm going to regret.

"If you say so," my father replies. "But, promise me something, okay?"

"Sure."

"If you notice anything that bothers you, promise me you'll say something?"

I swallow hard, nodding my head. "Sure, Dad," I practically choke. "Don't worry."

His smile is tight, his keen eyes studying me. I'm guilty, and he knows it. I wear it like a criminal, and he can sniff out a crook with his eyes closed.

"When is everyone getting here?" I ask, changing the subject.

He looks down at his watch. "In about an hour."

"Cool." I start to jog away so I can get the Wiffle ball field ready for the mega tournament that's going to happen tonight.

"Heath?" I stop dead in my tracks. *Please don't ask me anything else.*

"Yeah, Dad?" I turn around to face him, pulse racing.

"If you love that girl, treat her right. And take care of her."

"Yup!" I answer and take off for the back of our yard. He's definitely on to something.

And knowing him, he'll get to the bottom of it before I can warn Noelle.

"NOELLE, YOU'RE UP!" I call out, and she shifts in her seat. She looks up, nodding her head quickly. Haley has her cornered and they seem to be deep in conversation.

"I'm sitting out this game," she responds as she brushes a wisp of hair away from her eyes. Haley glances over at me at the same time and then grabs Noelle's hand. *Weird.*

"I guess you're down a player," Troy laughs. "Better for us!" He mocks me, knowing Noelle is one of the best players here.

"I'll still crush you assholes," I boast confidently, taking a few warm-up swings. I need to focus so I can wipe the field with them.

"You tell yourself that."

Troy pitches to me and I miss. His laughter bellows but I ignore it as I see Noelle and Haley huddled even closer, whispers between them. *What the hell are they talking about? I've never seen them this close to each other and my concern rises. Noelle routinely tries to avoid any contact with Haley.*

"Are you even paying attention, dude?"

"Just throw the damn ball," I grunt. This time, I make contact and the ball whizzes past Troy's ear, causing him to fall to the ground. It lands in the grass between Dylan and Ethan. "That's a double!" I call out and hand the bat to my only other teammate, Chris.

I look over and see Noelle still oblivious to the game. She's nodding and smiling politely, Haley's eyes wide and curious. Shit. I hope they're not talking about the other night. My cheeks flush with embarrassment, wondering if Haley is getting all of the details of our private night together. The night I can't stop thinking about. Noelle would never share anything like that. Especially with Haley. *Right?*

A bell rings from the deck, indicating food is being served. Chris drops the bat and joins the others in a sprint for food. I tentatively walk up to the girls and lightly tap Noelle's foot with the toe of my sneaker. "Hey."

She looks up, her smile radiant, perfect. She also looks relieved that I interrupted her conversation with Haley. "Hey, yourself," she says, patting the seat next to her. "I saved you a spot."

"I'm glad you came over here," Haley interrupts. "I'm leaving for vacation next week, and I wanted to make sure I gave you this." She pulls a box out from underneath the wicker couch.

"Happy Birthday, Heath."

Noelle shifts uncomfortably next to me, placing her hand on my knee.

"You didn't have to get me anything," I respond. Why would Haley buy me a birthday present anyway? And give it to me in front of my girlfriend?

"It's nothing, really."

Haley places the box on my lap and instructs, "Open it."

"Now?"

"Yes, of course now," she insists.

I tear the wrapping paper from the box and flip the lid off, tissue paper packed inside. The girls shift in their respective seats as I pull the tissue paper out. Inside the box is a medium-sized picture collage, various photos scattered around. The majority of the pictures are group shots of our friends, most of whom are here today. The one in the center is a picture of me and Haley in third grade. Her arm is thrown over my shoulder, and we're both smiling. The surroundings are familiar—it's from when our families went to Ireland together.

"This is cool," I say, awkwardly

Noelle is completely tense next to me. There's not a single picture of her in the entire collage.

"I knew you'd love it!" Haley exclaims as Noelle clears her throat. "Where are you going to hang it? Should we go upstairs to your room right now and find a spot?"

"No. I don't think so." *What the fuck is going on?*

"Maybe later," Haley says and jumps to her feet. "Great catching up with you, Noelle."

She walks away, leaving both Noelle and I sitting, dumbfounded.

"What the hell?" I ask, shaking my head.

Noelle remains silent.

"Say something," I implore.

She looks pensive, then says, "She obviously wanted to make a production out of giving you that collage."

"It's weird."

"Well, she obviously had a lot of pictures of the two of you together," Noelle says with a twinge of jealousy.

"Haley and I have known each other for a long time," I admit. "And yes, our families have gone away together. But there's nothing more between us than friendship. And these days, even that's a stretch." Haley isn't the same girl I grew up with. We used to have fun together when our families would hang out, but now it's just weird.

She places her legs over mine and leans against the back of the wicker couch. "Forget about it," she shrugs. "Sorry I missed the game," she apologizes, changing the subject.

"It's okay. Chris and I were about to win, but then—food," I chuckle and see the guys on the deck piling hot dogs and hamburgers onto plates.

I lightly run my fingers along her shin, stopping at her ankle. "I was highly distracted, watching you and Haley talking over here. What were you talking about?"

She shakes her head. "I wasn't talking about anything. She, however, was talking my ear off."

"Oh?"

"She's quite full of herself," Noelle declares. "I tuned her out when she went on and on about the number of text messages she has from three different guys."

"You didn't tell her about the other night, did you?" I ask, worried.

She slowly shakes her head back and forth, surprise plastered on her face. "Oh my God. Never. Not that I even had a chance to get a word in."

"Good."

"Let's eat before all of those bozos eat all of the food." Noelle says, pulling me to my feet.

I throw my arm over her shoulder and kiss her cheek, letting my lips linger. "I love you," I whisper against her skin.

"This is the best weekend ever," she says.

We walk hand in hand to the deck where our friends are all seated at two large round tables near the buffet. We fill up our plates and join them.

FIREWORKS IN OUR NEIGHBORHOOD have been a spectacle since I was a kid. The Mason family, who live in the first house as you enter our street, sets off a fireworks display that would rival Macy's any year. Between our annual barbecue and their party, our private cul-de-sac is usually lined with so many cars, we need to hire valets to keep everything organized. It's obnoxious, but we love it.

Noelle starts buzzing with excitement. She and I have watched fireworks together for as long as she's lived here. But for the first time in years, she doesn't have to sneak out to watch them with me. Since her father and Tonya are away for the weekend, she's free to do what she wants. I tense up thinking about when they get home and Tonya makes Noelle's life miserable again. It's been so hard keeping my mouth shut around her. The way she looks at Noelle would make anyone cringe. Hatred and contempt spew from her pores. I've suspected Tonya has been abusing Noelle for years, and I have to figure out a way to expose her for the horrible person that she really is, without losing Noelle in the process.

"Let's get to our spot," she says, grabbing my hand and jarring me from my worried thoughts.

We leave the deck and walk around the house to where all of the cars are parked in the street. We hear giggles and see Haley, flirting with one of the valets. He drops her keys into her outstretched hand, and she slides into her light blue Volkswagen Bug. She sees us turn the corner and waves goodbye.

"She's going to get herself in trouble," Noelle declares, shaking her head. "That guy must be at least ten years older than us. Doesn't he realize she's only seventeen?"

I chuckle. "I don't think he cares."

"Whatever. That's gross."

The sea of cars packed into our street provides the perfect viewing area for the show that's about to start. We weave through them to where my pickup truck is parked at the far end of the cul-de-sac. I strategically placed it there, knowing we'd want the best spot on the street.

I help Noelle into the back of the truck and she gasps. "What have you done?"

The bed of the pickup is lined with soft blankets and pillows. There's a cooler to the side that's filled with bottled water and sliced watermelon. Last year, I snuck out some beer and had to listen to my father lecture me about how much trouble I would be in if a police officer searched my truck. He went on and on about underage drinking and being responsible. I decided not to chance bringing any kind of alcohol out here this year, it's just not worth having to listen to my father rip into me again.

"I wanted it to be more comfortable than it was last year," I say as she settles down against the pillows.

"You've outdone yourself." Her eyes light up, and her lips curl into a sexy smile. Even though the sun has almost fully set, I can see the light in her eyes. She's so beautiful.

I slide next to her on the makeshift bed, and she instinctively wraps her arms around my waist, draping her leg over mine. Fireflies are lighting up the street all around us, reflecting off of the car windows. Several fly over my head and I reach out, softly cradling two in my hand. "Quick, open your fairy house," I direct and she reaches across me to grab it. I'm able to grab two more lightning bugs, and her house begins to glow.

"This weekend has been awesome," she says as she nestles back into my chest. "Thank you."

"No, thank you," I say. "I love you, Noelle."

She tips her head back so she's looking up into my eyes, her lips part and I waste no time covering them with my own. She kisses me back urgently, her tongue diving into my mouth, soft moans escaping her lips. My fingers trace the bare spot on her belly where her tank top has ridden up, and I'm tempted to go further. As I push the shirt higher, so more of her abs are exposed, a loud *boom* sounds overhead. We both turn on our backs to see the fireworks show begin.

Her fingers intertwine with mine, and she rests her head back on my chest. Colorful lights explode above us, one after the other. Faint, patriotic music, plays from the Mason's yard. Several other people have walked into the cul-de-sac, and I notice that others are perched on top of their own cars. It's like a drive-up movie theater, except the theater is the sky. That's when I realize we won't have as much privacy as I had hoped.

The fireworks continue to blast above us, cheers echoing throughout the neighborhood. Noelle stays firmly pressed into my side, and I kiss the top of her head. "The Masons have outdone themselves so far," I comment.

"Oh my God. It's seriously incredible!" she practically shouts, trying to be heard over the loud thundering booms.

A colorful blast of hearts explodes above us, and then a flurry of fast white lights shoot through the sky.

Twenty minutes later, the finale of fireworks covers the sky, blanketing it in red, white, and blue.

"Wow," Noelle murmurs, stretching out her legs next to mine.

"They get better every year," I say, rolling onto my side so my forehead rests against hers.

A small smile plays on her lips. "I will remember this moment forever."

"Me, too."

"I don't think my life could get any better than it is right now. This weekend has been perfect. This moment is perfect." She kisses me lightly and leans back to look into my eyes.

"Every moment is going to be better than the last," I say, kissing her.

"Get a room!" someone shouts from the yard, and Noelle giggles against my lips.

We both look up and see Chris and Dylan laughing from my front lawn.

"Oh God!" Noelle cowers. "I guess they can see us?"

"Shit," I mutter.

"We should go someplace–more private." Her eyes widen, and she scoots down toward the edge of the truck bed.

I quickly follow her, leaving everything in the back of my truck. "Do you want any watermelon?" I ask. I swiped a bunch of it earlier and put it in the cooler, remembering how much fun we had eating it and spitting out the seeds last year.

"No, that's okay."

I grab the firefly house and link my hand with hers as we weave our way through the cars parked in the street.

"I feel like we're on a walk of shame," she says, embarrassed.

I lead her around the left side of her house where nobody can see us. "Don't ever be embarrassed," I say, gently pushing her against the brick wall. "Do you hear me?"

She smiles. "Everyone was watching us."

"It was only the guys, and they're just poking fun."

I kiss her quickly, pulling her chin up so she can look into my eyes. "Let's go someplace where they can't watch us."

She nods quickly, and we walk through the gate, into her backyard. As we pass her bedroom window, I hang the firefly house on the hook.

We make our way inside, walking through the dark halls and into her room. "I want you to stay all night," she says as she shuts the door.

With all of the party guests in and out of my house, I wonder if my parents would even notice if I didn't come home tonight. I wonder if my father's security detail will tip them off. I suddenly don't care and plan to honor Noelle's request.

"I'm not going anywhere."

She falls onto her bed, her hair splayed out behind her and a smile spreads across her lips. "I was hoping you'd say that."

I don't waste any time and quickly remove every article of clothing from the two of us, throwing them on the floor in the middle of her room.

We spend hours making love, creating our own fireworks as the fireflies dance in the moonlight outside her window.

CHAPTER 10

Heath
Present

"HEATH, ARE YOU BRINGING anyone to our party next weekend?" Garrett's wife Sam asks.

I shift uncomfortably on my barstool. Garrett, Dax, and I have been working on music for our next album while Tristan is handling some personal things. I've had songs in my head since we got back from our tour and Garrett can't ever sit idle. The three of us have been able to record basic melodies for at least six of the songs I've written.

"No, I don't think so," I respond.

"Well, if anything changes, just text me."

She turns to Garrett and says, "Don't be up too late tonight." She kisses him, and an impish smile spreads across her face.

"Goodnight, guys," she waves before heading upstairs.

"See ya, Sam," I respond.

"Sweet dreams," Dax says.

"Why aren't you bringing Haley next week?" Garrett asks once Sam is out of earshot.

"Because I'm not." It's none of his damn business.

"You cut her loose, didn't you?"

"Why does it matter?"

"You're an idiot."

"Excuse me?" *What the fuck is his deal?*

"You heard me. You're a fucking idiot. Why would you toss aside a perfectly good thing?"

Here we go. As if my love life is any of Garrett's business.

"Are you being serious?" I ask, annoyed.

He reaches below the bar, opens the refrigerator, and places three more beers in front of us.

"Haley was good for you. No?" He pops the tops off and slides them toward us.

I take a long pull from the beer, hoping by the time I'm finished swallowing, he'll drop his line of questioning. His intense stare tells me that he's not relenting. Dax raises his eyebrows, encouraging me to answer.

"She was good. Until she wasn't," I admit.

"Holy shit. You're more of a douchebag than I thought you were!" He laughs and clinks his beer against mine.

"Listen, I don't need a lecture or anything. Things just didn't work out." She accused me of being in love with a dead girl, and she's right. I can't give myself to her or anyone until I properly put Noelle behind me. It's been years since she died, and I've never stopped loving her.

"Dude. You aren't going to get it any easier than Haley. You got to fuck her whenever you wanted. No strings. No heartache."

What he doesn't realize is Haley *did* get attached. There were strings. Strings I didn't see.

"It's not that simple. She wanted more than I could give her."

"Will you let up a little, G?" Dax jumps in to defend me. "He doesn't need to explain why he isn't into a chick, to you, or anyone."

I lift my chin at Dax and nod my head. *At least he gets me.*

"Seriously, though. Weren't you cool with things?" Garrett asks, mellowing his tone a bit.

"Yes, I was. But she suddenly thought she loved me." I instantly regret blurting this out.

"What's wrong with that?" Dax asks. *I thought he was on my side.*

"Everything," I mutter and take a swig of my beer.

"He was having a good time. I guess love isn't part of the equation," Garrett says, and now my head is spinning.

"Aren't we supposed to be getting work done tonight?" I ask, desperately trying to change the subject.

"Maybe you and Haley need to go to Mexico. It worked wonders for Dax and Giselle." Garrett tosses his empty bottle into the recycling container behind the bar.

Dax smiles and nods. "Mexico was perfect. And everything that happened after was, too."

"*Almost* everything," Garrett reminds him. "You can't forget about the tabloid that almost destroyed it all."

"But it didn't, and *that's* what matters," Dax replies.

Dax and Giselle's whirlwind romance took everyone by surprise, but mostly Garrett. "Stop being so cute," Garrett laughs.

"Listen, if it didn't feel right, don't kill yourself," Dax says.

The problem is, for a while, there was nothing wrong with Haley. But as soon as she wanted more from me, I choked. Maybe Garrett's right. Maybe I am an idiot.

"I don't know. I think there are things that I need to deal with before I can commit to anyone else." I shrug my shoulders and shake my head.

"Does it have anything to do with the chick you wrote all of these songs for?" Garrett blurts out. I knew I shouldn't have said anything at all to him that last night in Europe.

"What chick?" Dax asks.

"It's nobody," I state, not wanting to get into this any further. Hell, I don't even know what I'm feeling anymore. There have been too many reminders just popping up here and there, drawing my memories of Noelle to the forefront. It's almost like I can *feel* her near me. Maybe she's trying to tell me something.

"Some girl he knew when he was younger. His 'first love.'" Garrett uses air quotes. It pisses me off that he's replaying our private conversation and making it seem trivial.

"Enough. Alright?" Anger boils inside me.

"Chill, dude," Garrett instructs. "I'm just filling Dax in."

"You don't have to tell me anything," Dax replies, once again trying to be the good guy.

"Thank you," I reply.

We all sit in awkward silence for a few minutes. I finish my beer and stand up. "I gotta run."

"Seriously?" Garrett asks. "I wasn't trying to be an asshole. I'm sorry." His demeanor changes drastically, and I believe him.

"It's okay. Really. I'm just dealing with a lot of crap in my head, and I need to straighten some things out."

"Just do what feels right," Dax interjects. "If things with Haley didn't gel, then you have to walk away before anyone gets hurt."

That's the problem. She's already hurt. She fell in love with me when I hadn't even considered love to be an option. *Is it an option?*

"Maybe you could just take a little time to figure it all out?" Garrett says, trying to redeem himself after the gossip he tried to start. "Who knows? By our party next week, you and Haley could be good as gold."

Dax shakes his head, laughing. "The last thing he needs to do is force something that isn't there. And I'm sure he won't do it just to have a chick on his arm for your party."

My mind is reeling. *Is something there?*

I've known Haley since kindergarten. We were friends long before Noelle moved next door. Our mothers are good friends, and I remember spending many summers with her family on vacation. When I was eight, our families went to Ireland together and I'm constantly reminded of photobombing Haley while she was kissing the Blarney Stone. There are years of memories. Years of friendship. I even remember Noelle telling me that she thought Haley had a huge crush on me, but I didn't see it. We were close, but I never had any feelings for Haley. *But do I have feelings for her now?*

"You okay?" Garrett asks.

"I'm good. Like I said, I just need to figure out my shit."

"Take your time," Dax says.

"I'm sure Haley will accept your apology once you realize you fucked up," Garrett chuckles. *And the dick is back.*

"Shut up, asshole," I blurt out.

"Trust me, when you look back at what you just walked away from, you're going to kick yourself in the ass. And then thank me for making you think about it." Garrett swipes the rest of the empty bottles from the bar, tossing them in the recycling bin.

Dax turns to me. "Give me a call if you want to talk."

I take a deep breath. "It's all good. I'm going to take off."

Garrett and Dax stretch out their arms, and I bump fists with them both. "Later," Garrett says.

"Later," I reply.

I try to keep my mind from racing as I walk up the stairs and through the quiet first floor toward the front door. Sam and Kai must be asleep–all of the lights are dimmed. Once outside, I inhale the warm July air. Dozens of fireflies flash their lights in and around the driveway and my heart pulls.

Noelle is here. She's trying to tell me something. *But what?*

I slide into my car and immediately open the glove compartment. The light catcher that I gave Noelle for her fourteenth birthday is resting inside. I lightly swipe my fingers across the colorful crescent moon and so many wonderful memories flood my mind. She was so fragile, yet strong. She was so delicate and beautiful. She was tragic and perfect. My stomach lurches with the familiar feeling of regret. Why didn't I do something to save her? Why didn't I tell someone my suspicions of her abuse? I blame myself for so much. I should have done something. *Anything*. She might be alive today if I did.

After I leave Garrett's driveway, I pull over so I can take out my cell phone. I find Haley's number to send a text.

Me: Are you awake?

A few seconds go by before she responds.

Haley: Yes. Why?

I can hear her tone loud and clear.

Me: Can I come by?

Haley: OK.

Me: I'll be there in twenty.

I drop my phone onto the passenger seat and pull back onto the road. It's late, but I can't go the night without talking to her.

"HEY," HALEY SAYS, opening her door. "I'm not sure why I agreed to let you come over." Sadness fills her eyes, and my guilt grows.

"I'm glad you did."

"Come in before my neighbors get too nosey. I haven't seen Nina in a few days, but you never know who she has spying for her." Her townhouse is the end unit and is somewhat private, but one of her older neighbors always seems to catch me coming and going, no matter what time of day. She's told Haley that "her secret is safe with her."

I step into her foyer, and she quickly shuts and locks the door behind us. Her Yorkshire Terrier, Keiko, rushes to greet me, bouncing up and down on his hind legs. He expects me to pick him up and carry him through the house like I usually do, so I oblige. His little dog grunts cause him to vibrate in my arms as we walk into Haley's living room.

"So, what's so urgent that you had to come here at almost midnight? Or are you here for a booty call?" she huffs, folding her arms over her chest.

I sit and place Keiko on my lap. He immediately rolls over onto his back, demanding a belly rub.

Her stance stresses me out. I want to have a relaxed conversation with her, without the attitude. Although, I honestly can't blame her for how she's feeling right now.

"Can you sit down?"

She drops her arms and reluctantly walks over to the couch, settling next to me. She pulls her knees up in front of her and turns sideways, her feet touching my thigh. "I'm all ears."

"I'm really sorry," I say, the words getting stuck in my throat.

"That's it?" she asks, annoyed.

She's glaring at me, and I realize I started off all wrong.

"I wasn't prepared to come home and hear that you're in love with me."

"I wasn't prepared to fall in love with you. But I did." She looks away, locking her eyes on something outside the window.

"You said something the other night that really stuck with me. Something that I haven't been able to get out of my head."

"I said a lot of things the other night."

"I'm not trying to get you any more upset than you already are," I implore.

"You're perceptive," she snaps. "How could I *not* be upset?"

I stop rubbing Keiko's belly so I can place my hand on her foot. She tenses underneath my touch and Keiko grunts, demanding my attention.

"Listen, I realize you're upset. I get it. But you touched on something the other night that we need to talk about."

The tension starts to leave her body, my touch softening on her foot. "I'm not sure I want to hear the truth," she sighs.

"I'm not sure I believe the truth myself," I admit.

Her eyes widen, and her face falls. "So you *are* still in love with Noelle. After all of these years?"

I close my eyes and nod slowly. "I don't know how to stop loving her," I admit. My heart pounds in my chest over this admission.

"I don't get it. She's gone. And I'm here." Her shoulders start to shake as she covers her face with her hands. "I'm still freaking here. And I have been for years."

Shit. What have I done?

"Haley–"

"Don't. Please don't say something you think I want to hear."

"I'm trying to ask for help. Yes, I fully admit I love her, but I need help moving on."

"I refuse to be used to help you forget about her. You can't put me in that position. I need you to be with me because you *want* to be with me. Not so you can forget Noelle." Tears cascade over her cheeks, and I can't do anything about it. Keiko is still sprawled out on my lap, and Haley pulls her knees tighter against her chest, closing herself off from me.

"I'm not asking you to help me forget. I'm asking you to *remember* her with me." I desperately need to talk about Noelle. I need to hear if Haley feels the guilt that I do. Did she also have her suspicions about Noelle's abuse?

"What do you want me to say?" she asks.

"Did you see what I saw? Did you ever have the suspicion that she was being abused?"

She gasps and covers her mouth with her hand. "What?"

I immediately realize the mistake I made by bringing up this topic, but I continue. "She was constantly injured. Bruises all over her body. She always claimed she was a klutz, but I couldn't help but think she was lying. Covering up for someone."

"You don't think her father—"

"No! I don't think that at all. I think it was her stepmother."

"Tonya?"

"Yes."

She shakes her head. "No way. Tonya was nothing but kind. My mother played Mahjong with her almost every Friday. She spent so much time with us, and my mom was one of her best friends. I don't see it at all. There is no way Noelle was abused by Tonya."

I'm shocked by this admission. While Haley and Noelle weren't very close, Haley would have noticed something. She always did. "Are you serious?"

"Yes," she replies defensively. "How can you, after all of these years, accuse someone of abuse when you have no proof? Noelle is dead. She's gone. Stop blaming others for it and move on already."

Her sudden coldness sends chills down my spine. Keiko jumps off of my lap after I tense up with anger. "How could you *not* see it?" I demand. "Tonya treated her like shit!"

"I never saw anything like that."

I shake my head. Of course Haley didn't notice anything. She wasn't Noelle's friend. Ever. *I feel like I've betrayed Noelle in some way by sharing these private things.*

"I shouldn't have come tonight," I admit. I stand up and look down at her. "I'm sorry I wasted your time."

She jumps to her feet, toes touching mine. "You're going to leave?" Anger rises in her voice.

"Either I'm crazy, or you and I saw very different sides of Noelle— and her family."

Her eyes lock onto mine. "We certainly did see different sides of her, which is exactly why you can't let her go. You were in love with her. You saw things you wanted to see. You spent every single night at her window, professing your undying love to her. Sneaking kisses. Making up goddamn fairy tales. Dreaming about spending your lives together once you both left for college." She backs away from me and begins pacing through her living room. "I watched all of this. Jealous of the connection that you had. Her life was perfect *and she had you*."

Holy shit.

"What the fuck, Haley?"

"It's been over ten years, Heath! How can you still be in love with her? Why can't you move on?" She's begging me for answers, her anger still heightened. "I'm standing here, right now, in the present. I'm willing to do anything to keep you, but you can't even look at me without thinking about her!"

"And suddenly all of this matters, now? For the past few years, I've been nothing but honest with you. You knew that I wasn't in search of a relationship. We were having fun. I'm sorry that you had another expectation. I'm sorry you thought we could be more than we were."

"Are you serious? Everything matters, Heath. Everything matters because I'm in fucking love with you. I have been for years. Longer than you will ever know. I was in love with you before she ever showed up. She's. Dead. You can't get her back. And I can't understand why you won't let her go." Her eyes are wide, and she looks possessed. Like someone I don't even know.

I can't return her feelings. I'm not capable. But hearing her talk about her long term feelings for me and her jealousy of Noelle makes me realize that Haley's definitely not the person to rationalize with right now. Or ever. She can't see past her own feelings to try to even understand why I can't let Noelle go. My guilt is strong, and Haley doesn't believe the theory that Noelle was abused.

Selfishness oozes from Haley at the moment, and I can't believe I never saw it.

"I'm really sorry, Haley. I wish things could be different, but they can't." She needs to understand that I'm not here to grovel. I'm not here to fix things. I came here for help. Help that Haley is completely incapable of giving. She's too caught up with what could have been and what should have been. She feels no guilt over Noelle's death. She was so consumed with herself, years ago, that she didn't see what was right in front of her the entire time.

"Get out," she orders, sensing that I'm about to unleash my pent up anger on her.

I walk toward the front door but turn around before I leave.

"I fully admit that I've been fucked up for years over what happened to Noelle. I feel intense guilt for not talking about my suspicions. I wish to God I would have said something to someone. She was getting beat up by her stepmother, whether you choose to believe it or not. That girl was tortured. I saw it in her eyes every single day. I confronted her on more than one occasion and she threatened to leave me if I told anyone anything I suspected. If that doesn't tell you that she was hiding something, I don't know what does."

Haley's eyes widen, but she makes no move to speak.

"I blame myself for her death. I should have spoken up, and I didn't. The guilt I carry outweighs any other feelings that I have. I haven't been able to move past that guilt and I mistakenly thought you might feel the same way. Man, was I wrong."

"Don't you dare try to pull me into your vortex, Heath. Are you trying to make me feel guilty? Feel bad? Well, fuck you!"

Keiko starts barking, moving his head back and forth between us. He doesn't know who to believe or protect.

"I loved you, Heath."

I can't listen to this anymore. I open the door and walk out. Keiko barks tentatively as I close it behind me.

I'm shocked at how this conversation progressed. Haley's unwillingness to see and absorb what I was trying to say was staggering. Selfishness oozed from her.

I'm validated by my decision to end things with Haley. I've wasted so much time in a void. In a "relationship" that was really more about her than me. Almost three years of a no-strings-attached fling that was really riddled with barbed wire and hooks.

Garrett was right.

I'm a fucking idiot.

CHAPTER 11

Noelle
Past
Age 17

"NOELLE, WHERE THE fuck are you?"

I hold my breath, backing further into the corner of my closet. I'm surrounded by all of my old stuffed animals that I've had since I was a child. They've been in a pile in the back of my closet for as long as I can remember. I haven't had the heart to throw them away, attempting to maintain some of the innocence that used to be my childhood. My favorite summer dress hangs in front of me, hiding me. I clutch one my cherished plush toys, Mr. Jingles, against my chest. He's a stuffed puppy that I've had forever, and he's been with me through thick and thin. Even longer than *she's* been living here.

"NOELLE!" Her screams are getting louder, closer. I remain as still as possible as I hear her opening doors and slamming them. She's in the hallway outside my room and about to kick in the door.

My bedroom door flies open, and I squeeze my eyes shut. *Please don't find me. Please don't find me.*

"I'm going to give you one chance to come out from wherever you're hiding," she hisses. "If I find you–when I find you, I'm going to make you wish you came out on your own." Tears sting my eyes, my heart racing. She's going to kill me this time. *I don't want to die.*

"Three..."

"Two..."

"I'm here!" I yelp and jump up before she can see the intricate camouflage I made in the back of my large, walk-in closet. I glance behind me and see the small wooden door that leads to the crawl space behind my closet. She doesn't know about that door. *I should have gone in there.*

The closet door flies open and she walks in, rage in her eyes. "One!" she yells as her fist flies through the air, connecting with the side of my head. Pain shoots behind my eyes, and my vision blurs. My arms fly out to my sides, trying to grab onto anything that will stop my fall. I grasp onto dresses and shirts, pulling them from their hangers. Another fist is buried in my gut, forcing the air to leave my lungs. I gasp for air, doubling over and falling to my knees.

"Get up, you piece of shit!" she screams and grabs my hair on the top of my head, yanking me to my feet. I still can't breathe. I'm choking and dizzy, her face two inches from mine. "I'm going to ask you for the very last time, where is your father's safe?" Her mouth is open, her teeth look like they could tear through my flesh.

"I don't know!" I choke. Tears stream down my face, and I know I'm about to get punched again. There's nothing I can do to stop her right fist from hitting the side of my head. Her screams are drowned out by the ringing in my ear, but I can still hear my own moans and sobs.

"Don't lie to me, you little shit. Before we left for New York, I know he told you!" Until recently, I didn't even know this secret safe existed.

"I swear to God, he didn't tell me anything!" I scream, begging for mercy.

Everything is spinning now. Her face is blurry, and I whimper. "Please. Stop. I don't know." I tell a partial lie. My father didn't tell me where it is, but I stumbled upon a hidden switch in his office last week and when I flipped it, a key pad appeared from underneath his desk drawer. It was recessed into the wood, so you couldn't feel it if you ran your hand over it. I don't know the code to the key pad, but I assume it opens the safe she's looking for.

My knees buckle, and I fall to the floor as she kicks my shin with full force. "You better figure out really quick where it is, or you're going to regret it!"

The ringing in my ears gets worse. I can barely see.

"Tonya, I don't know–"

"Mom! Call me Mom, you fucking bitch."

This woman is not my mother. Cancer took my real mother a few months after I was born. My father married Tonya when I was two. And until recently, they seemed to be happily married. But Tonya has become more desperate, more violent, trying to find whatever she's been looking for.

I don't understand all of the details, because I've only heard bits and pieces of conversations and arguments, always about money. Sometimes they talk about the "accident" but I have no idea what they're talking about. I've heard them arguing over some other documents and only my father knows where they are. She's begged him to give them to her. She also said something recently about her family coming after me and my father if anything were to ever happen to her, or if those "documents" were to ever see the light of day. I can't stand that she's holding something over him and has been for years.

"Do you hear me?" she screams, jerking my hair harder. I feel her hot breath on my nose, and I squint through my tears.

"I'm sorry, *Mom*," I apologize with as much sincerity as I can. But I know I'm not fooling her. She knows how painful it is for me to call her Mom.

"Apology not accepted." My cheek stings as she slaps me as hard as she can with her open hand. She releases my hair, my scalp tingling from her grip. Warm liquid fills my mouth, and I realize I'm bleeding. *Did I lose a tooth?*

She backs up, assessing my injuries. Her eyes are wide when she sees the shape I'm in. It's summer break, and I officially graduated from high school last month. So my injuries can be hidden from the public, since I don't leave for college for another month. She's not worried about me having to go to school on Monday with visible injuries. No. She's doing the math in her head, counting the days until my father comes home from his current business trip.

"Noelle, time is up. Where is that fucking safe?"

Blood drips from my mouth, and I attempt to catch it in my hand. I run my tongue along my teeth and they feel like they're all in place. That's when I realize my lower lip is split wide open. *Definitely a visible injury.*

She makes a fist again and I shake my head, pleading, "No, please–"

The doorbell chimes loudly, and I exhale. Her eyes dart down the hallway and back to me again. "Keep your fucking mouth shut. And don't leave this room." She punches me square in the chest, and I fall backward into my closet. She adjusts her blouse as she walks out of my room and down the hall. A few moments later, I hear our front door open, and her voice has changed. She sounds cheerful and happy. "Girls! What a surprise!" she cackles, laughter traveling throughout the house.

"It's game night. We wouldn't miss it for the world!" Heidi Daley says. She's one of the teachers from my school and is part of Tonya's traveling game group.

"That's right," Tonya giggles. "I almost forgot."

"The rest of the girls are on their way," Heidi says. "We brought wine and cheese. Laura is on her way with chips and dip."

"Fabulous!" It's amazing how Tonya can go from crazy to cheery in a matter of seconds. "Come on in."

Her friends come inside, and I flinch when the front door closes.

They can't see me like this. Tonya would kill me if I went out there, covered in blood and bruises. My chest tightens, and I cough up warm blood. I stare at what looks to be a large blood clot and can't believe that just came out of me. *Holy shit, I'm bleeding internally.*

Laughter fills the house as her friends become comfortable. The wine is going to start flowing soon and I begin to dread the moment her friends leave tonight. Her inquisition of me is hardly finished. Maybe I'll be dead before that happens.

I've got to get out of here.

I grab Mr. Jingles from the floor and notice he is stained from the blood that was dripping from my lip. I try to wipe the blood away, but it only smudges, turning the faded blue fabric an odd shade of crimson-purple. I limp over to my first-floor bedroom window and open it; pain rips through my knee and ribs at the same time. My bare feet hit the ground and I panic, my heart pounding in my chest. *Where am I going to go?*

My father's in Europe on business and won't be home for another week. How can I stay away from her while avoiding the place where I think his safe is?

Heath. I need to get to him. Now.

Tonya's laughter drifts through the open kitchen window, and I drop to my knees and army-crawl through the grass. I don't want her, or her friends, to see me out here. I can't embarrass her in front of them. My elbows dig into the grass as I make my way to the other side of the yard. My ribs are screaming in pain; my knee throbbing. I need to reach the far end of the yard where the wooded piece of our large property begins. There are several walking trails that weave through the trees, and I can disappear without her noticing. My lungs constrict again, and my chest feels even heavier. Breathing is becoming difficult as my eyes begin to blur.

My arms won't move anymore. The throbbing in my side is getting worse, and a stabbing pain grabs me. *God, please don't let me die out here.*

"Noelle?"

My eyes pop open, and I exhale slowly, moaning in pain.

"Noelle?" The voice is more urgent now, but my eyes are blurry. Feet rustle in the grass, rushing toward me. *A familiar voice.*

I look up and see a shadow bending over me, and I immediately begin sobbing in pain and embarrassment.

"Can you help me?" I choke as grass tickles my cheeks.

"Jesus, what the hell happened?" Heath asks, worry in his voice.

I look back and see that I'm no longer in the line of vision of our back kitchen window. He reaches down and grabs hold of my hand. "You're bleeding!"

"I know," I admit weakly, as he pulls me slowly to my feet. I wince, trying to disguise the immense pain that I'm in.

He holds me firmly against him. "I'm getting you inside."

"No!" I shout, gasping in pain. "Please don't take me there." Warm tears begin to slide down my cheeks, and his eyes widen with concern.

"Don't worry, I'm taking you to my house," he pauses. "Who did this to you?" he demands. "And this time, you need to tell me the fucking truth!"

"I fell." The lie hits the air, and I immediately regret saying it. Every step I take reverberates in my skull, reminding me of the crushing pain from her punches.

"I don't believe you. I'm calling the police." His arm is wrapped around my side, and his fingers dig into my bruised ribs.

"Ah–" I wince as his grip on me tightens.

"I'm so sorry." He loosens his hold on me a little as he continues to guide me.

Sobs take over, and my shoulders shake. My head throbs harder, and I wonder how big the bruises are going to be on my face. She punched me at least twice. Three times? I lost count.

I inhale deeply and my lungs burn, causing me to cough uncontrollably, more blood spewing from my lips. "You need to get to a hospital," he orders, and I immediately shake my head.

"No!" I can't catch my breath; it hurts to breathe. I wince, grasping my tender ribs where one of her punches landed.

"Noelle, you need help. Please tell me who did this to you." He's frantic. Worried.

The ringing in my ears is back, and I can't focus on his face. *Is he really here?*

My knees are weak again, standing upright is becoming nearly impossible. "Just leave me here."

"What?" he asks, wrapping an arm around my waist. "I'm getting you inside."

"Don't take me home," I beg again. It's hard to breathe, my chest is so tight it feels like an elephant is sitting on it.

My knees buckle again and I gasp for air, nearly blacking out. "Stay with me," he begs, worry filling his voice. My bare feet are no longer on the grass as I feel myself being carried. I can no longer speak as nausea takes over. Soon, a warm, plush carpet is suddenly beneath my toes. "You're safe," he whispers in my ear.

I'm not safe. I never will be. Pain emanates throughout my body, like pain I've never felt before. I think she's done enough damage to kill me this time.

Then I collapse and everything goes black.

CHAPTER 12

Heath
Present

THE SUN SLOWLY RISES over the horizon as I wipe the sleep from my eyes. The sound of crashing waves woke me up from my restless slumber a few minutes ago, reminding me that I'm in my car, where I've been asleep for the past few hours.

When I left Haley's, I was too amped and angry to go home. Her attitude and admissions shocked me, and I still can't shake the feeling that she never even cared about Noelle. The more I think about it, when Noelle disappeared, Haley barely mourned. It was almost like she was glad she was suddenly gone.

Haley's jealousy of Noelle is now more obvious to me than ever. I never witnessed Haley doing anything overt to upset Noelle, but every once in a while, she would take a dig at her, making fun of her clumsiness, pointing out her awkwardly long legs or skinny ankles. These are things that would normally have gone in one ear and out the other, but for some reason, the memories are flooding back. After listening to Haley talk tonight about Noelle, it's astounding I didn't pick up on the cues when we were younger. She was envious and when I told her we couldn't be together, her defenses took over and ugliness spewed from her mouth.

I'm startled by two surfers who breeze by on their skateboards, surfboards in hand. They're heading toward the inlet, a popular place to catch the waves as they break against the jetty in the distance.

The jetty that Noelle plunged to her death from.

Before I open my door, I look into the rearview mirror. My hair is a mess, sticking out in all directions, and I'm sure my breath is kicking.

I find a pack of gum in the dash and shove two pieces into my mouth. That should do it until I can get to a real bathroom. Speaking of, I have to take a piss. I step out of my car and see the beach bath houses are just opening up. I make a beeline for the men's room and relieve myself. Then I splash some water on my face and look at my reflection in the mirror. I'm twelve years older than that boy who lost the love of his life. I've muddled through the better part of the past decade wondering if I was ever going to find someone like Noelle again.

I hooked up with a few different girls in college, but threw myself into my music. I wasn't with a girl for more than a few weeks before my aloofness drove them away. It wasn't until I reconnected with Haley when I began to yearn for more companionship, but certainly not in the way that Haley needed it. The casualness of our relationship was what I craved. I didn't have to think deeply. I didn't have to wonder if I was doing anything wrong. How was I supposed to know she'd been in love with me for decades?

My eyes are drawn and tired. I feel like I'm re-living the days and weeks surrounding Noelle's disappearance. I came here to try to put this all behind me. To say goodbye to Noelle so I can finally move on with my life and attempt to open my heart to allow someone else in.

I hold onto the light catcher that I gave to her, the one that they found on the jetty. Her father gave it to me after the police released it from evidence. Memories flood back to me as I walk out of the bathrooms and toward the jetty as I can picture that day so vividly in my mind.

"Prominent local businessman, Tom Durand and his wife Tonya, said goodbye to his daughter today after the Coast Guard officially called off their search early this morning. Noelle Durand was last seen on August sixteenth, before she disappeared from the jetty at the mouth of the Point Pleasant inlet, leaving behind a grieving father and stepmother, and this, a crescent-moon-shaped light catcher."

The screen flashes to video taken earlier today when a police officer is shown holding the light catcher that I gave Noelle so many years ago.

"Authorities found this piece of evidence nestled between two large boulders, her father quickly identifying it as Noelle's. Her boyfriend, Heath Strickland, son of District Attorney, Palmer Strickland, was heavily questioned about her disappearance. Their family attorney quickly squashed any rumors that there was trouble in paradise between the two young lovers. Strickland was escorted from the police station by his parents and declined any comments. The Durand family has been very guarded about her mental state before her disappearance, but our investigative team became aware of a

recent home invasion where Noelle and her stepmother were brutally beaten. Is her disappearance somehow connected? Does the boyfriend know more than he's telling? We'll be back at eleven with our investigative reporter, Monica O'Malley, as this story develops."

I switch off the television and throw the remote control against my bedroom wall, causing it to shatter into pieces. Why is this happening? Why, Noelle? I want to scream her name into the air, throughout our yards, hoping she can hear me. Haley thinks she committed suicide, but I can't believe in a million years that Noelle would ever do this to herself. Maybe it was an accident? I know she loved going to Point Pleasant when she was a kid. Her father's boat was at the local marina. She told me that she drove herself out there, just after she got her driver's license a little more than a year ago. She took her father's car and spent the night on his boat. That's the first place that Mr. Durand looked when they realized she was missing. After scouring the area for days and then conducting a search of the inlet and the ocean, they stopped looking. The Coast Guard believes that her body washed out to sea.

When the police questioned me, I had to explain to them I was the one that found out she was missing. They grilled me for over two hours, trying to get me to admit that I did something to her. That I killed her. They were skeptical of my whereabouts and wondered why I had such easy access to her bedroom window. After my father got involved, our security team provided video surveillance of outside our houses and have been cooperating fully with the police. It's obvious I had nothing to do with this, but my father explained to me the boyfriend is always the first person they place on an 'interested party' list. I'm not exactly a named suspect, but I couldn't help but feel that way since we left the police station. Why aren't they investigating Tonya? Why is she allowed to roam free when I know she's been hurting Noelle for years?

Mr. Durand came by the house about an hour ago to extend his apologies to me and my family. My father told him not to worry about anything, we all know I'm innocent and have nothing to hide. Her father then pulled me aside to give me the same light catcher they were showing on the television. He explained that they weren't processing it as evidence and gave it back to her family. Her father knew I gave it to her and wanted me to have it to remember her by. I didn't even know what to say. I shoved it into my pocket and came up here to my room. My mother suggested we hang it in the kitchen nook, alongside her light catcher collection, but I want it all to myself. I don't want to hang it in the window as some sort of memorial.

She can't be gone.

She just can't be.

I walk onto the rocks and look out at the ocean. The waves crash violently into the jetty that juts out from the inlet. The surfers from before rush out to catch the tremendous swells. Concern surges inside of me as I watch the two teenagers bounce in the waves and wonder if they're experienced enough to handle the rough waters.

Was Noelle a strong enough swimmer to handle these waters? I look down from my perch, and I'm at least twenty to thirty feet above the water level in the inlet. The water below is rough and deep. The current just beyond the cove is strong, which is what's causing the waves to crash so forcefully against the rocks. How long did it take her to go under after she fell? Was she unconscious? Did she know what was happening?

I back away from the edge, nervous of my own footing. Something just isn't sitting right with me about this whole scenario and it never did. I distinctly remember the day she disappeared. I picked her up from her physical therapy appointment and dropped her off at home. She was acting erratically. Strange. She was constantly shifting in her seat, fidgety. My first thought was she took too many pain meds or something like that. I'd never seen her act the way she was. I wish I had said something to her at that moment, or at least stayed with her after I dropped her off. She was clearly impaired and if she drove out here and stood where I'm standing now, she could have easily fallen.

Or she could have been pushed.

CHAPTER 13

Noelle
Past
Age 17

"NOELLE?" MY FATHER'S VOICE sounds like it's a million miles away. "Can you hear me?" He's worried. *Why is he here?*

My eyelids are stuck together, making it hard for me to find the face that goes along with the voice. "Daddy?" I croak, and I feel a tight squeeze around my hand.

"Easy, now. Take your time," he urges while maintaining a firm grip on my hand. My coughing fit continues.

Where am I?

When I'm able to open my eyes, my vision isn't clear, the room around me is blurry, figures hovering around the bed that I'm lying in. A beeping sound coming from behind me speeds up as I try to lift my head. "What's going on?" I manage to ask, and my father lets go of my hand to gently press my shoulders back into the bed.

"Take it easy," he says and kisses my forehead. "You don't have to get up right away."

The room starts to come in to focus and I see my father, looking tired and worried. He's wearing one of his custom-tailored business shirts, his undershirt clearly visible. He's disheveled, and I can't remember the last time I saw him without a tie. His face has razor stubble, and he has dark circles under his eyes.

"Daddy?" I ask again, my heart racing. I take a deep breath, causing pain to radiate through my abdomen. The incessant beeping once again speeds up.

One of the blurry figures in the room comes into focus and a nurse is at my bedside. "Can you take a deep breath for me?" she asks, as I watch her adjust a bag of fluids to my right. Her cool hand squeezes mine, and I attempt to do as she asks. My lungs burn as if a small fire erupts in my chest, and a crushing pain settles on my sternum. My eyes tingle, tears spilling over. "It stings," I gasp.

"Good, that's a good sign." The nurse smiles. "You're going to be just fine. The anesthesia is wearing off and what you're feeling is completely normal. Take a couple more deep breaths, just like that." She adjusts my bed so I'm no longer lying flat. *Anesthesia?*

My father settles into the chair next to me, his voice less tense. "When I heard about what happened to you, I came home as soon as I could."

"I don't understand," I say.

"You don't remember anything?" he asks, sounding almost relieved.

I squeeze my eyes closed, trying to remember something. Anything.

"No. And you're scaring me." I try to see who's in the room with us. "Where's Heath? Is he here?"

Whispers come from across the room, and I open my eyes, seeing two more people come into focus. My heart races when I see her. Tonya is speaking with a police officer who is feverishly scribbling notes on a pad.

My eyes widen, and memories flood my vision. My entire body trembles as I attempt to fill my lungs with much needed air. *She* did this to me. *What the fuck is she doing here?*

"Calm down, sweetie," my father says, smoothing my hair. "After Heath found you outside, he was able to get you to safety. Tonya told the police everything. You don't need to say a word."

My mind is screaming, words unable to escape my lips. What could she have possibly told them? Why isn't she in handcuffs? *Where's Heath?*

I open my mouth to tell him everything that sadistic bitch did to me, but all I can do is gasp for air. The nurse quickly slides an oxygen mask over my face. "Just breathe, Noelle."

My father's face is once again filled with worry. "Listen to the nurse," he urges. "Take a deep breath."

My heart is beating so fast it causes the pain in my chest to intensify. "I can't," I choke.

"This will help her calm down a bit," the nurse says, injecting something into the bag of fluids that is attached to my arm. Within seconds, I exhale deeply. My arms and legs suddenly feel like jelly, the room blurry once again. "I'll be back to check on her in a little while. Get some rest." She seems to float out of the room as I'm left alone with my father, Tonya, and the police officer.

"Do you think you can answer a few questions for me?" the policeman asks, approaching my bed.

Oh, I'll answer your questions.

Tonya steps in front of him. "Tom, I think she needs to rest," she says to my father.

"My wife already answered all of your questions," he tells the officer. "I think you have everything you need."

What?

I open my mouth to stop the officer from leaving the room, but nothing comes out. "Thank you and feel better," he says to Tonya. *What?*

The door closes behind him and Tonya is now standing next to my father. She takes my hand from his and I can't move.

"I didn't want you to have to relive what those horrible men did to us," she lies, squeezing my hand tightly. *Us? Men?*

"But–"

"Shh," she purrs and squeezes harder. "Your father already knows everything that happened." That's when I see her face. Her right eye is black and blue, swollen shut. The cheek below it multiple shades of purple, her lip bloody and stitched. "If it weren't for you, those men would have killed me," she lies. "You saved my life, Noelle." Sobs escape her lips, fake tears stream down her face.

What the fuck is going on? She did this to me. *She* beat me to within an inch of my life. She's lying. I need Heath now. He's the one who found me and can back up my story.

"The police are doing everything in their power to track these men down. Palmer Strickland already has an idea of who did this." Mr. Strickland is the District Attorney and Heath's father. Surely, he must know what really happened.

The bitch who did this to me is standing in this room! RIGHT NOW!

"I don't understand," I say and manage to pull my hand from Tonya's icy grip.

"I told them everything," she says and walks to the far end of the room.

My breathing is more even, the medicine given to me is taking its desired effect. I feel like I'm going to slip back into unconsciousness. And I'm so confused. After she beat the shit out of me, her girlfriends showed up to play some stupid housewife game. *Why aren't they here? Are they in on this charade?*

"Shortly after they arrived, Heidi got a phone call that her daughter was sick, so we canceled game night. About twenty minutes after they left, that's when it happened." Her lies are almost believable as her new timeline aligns with when I think Heath found me in the backyard.

"What happened?" I ask, urging her to continue her elaborate lie.

"The doorbell rang. I thought it was Heidi because she left her Mahjong game in the den. When I opened it, two men wearing ski masks pushed through the door, demanding to know where *our* safe was. When I tried to stop them, one of them did this." She points to her lip as tears fall down her cheek. Nausea spreads through my chest.

"Then you came out from your room. Don't you remember?" she asks.

"I don't remember anything you're saying," I say. "Stop lying–"

She interrupts me to continue her farce of a story. "I don't know much of what happened next, but you attacked the big one. The one that was punching me. If you hadn't showed up when you did, he would have killed me." She sobs louder, and my father lets go of my hand to comfort her. "Tom, if you would tell me where the safe is, neither of us would have gotten hurt." *What the fuck?*

I can't believe all of this has to do with the damn safe. It's hidden for a reason and ever since I found it, Tonya has sensed that I know something. When we built the house, Tonya scoured over the blueprints and plans, but she's yet to be able to find it. I know how much she wants whatever is in it, and she wants it bad. "I don't see how that matters, Tonya. And this isn't the place to discuss the safe, or what's in it," he says while turning his attention back to me.

"Those men were big," she lies. "They hurt me and your daughter very badly. Look at her!" she points to me and I feel like I'm sinking deeper into the bed. "They almost killed her."

"Thank God they didn't." My father kisses me on my forehead and sits back down in the chair next to me.

"I don't know how you were able to get out of the house," Tonya continues. "After what I saw them do to you–*both of them*–you are so lucky. Oh my God, it was horrible!" Her act continues and I have no strength to correct anything she's saying. She knows damn well that I was the one trying to escape–her.

"You need to get some rest," my father says. "And so do you," he says to Tonya.

"You're right, dear." Tonya backs up and makes eye contact with me, nodding her head. Her eyes tear through mine, sending a chill down my spine.

She disappears through the door, and I exhale.

My father grabs my hand once again. "My God, Noelle, I don't know what I would do without you. I'm so relieved you're going to be okay." His voice is calm. Tears roll down my cheeks. "They had to repair your lacerated spleen. You also have stitches behind your right ear along with at least four bruised ribs. One with a hairline fracture in it. My God, if that rib snapped, it would have punctured your lung. Do you know how lucky you are?"

I need to tell him what really happened. *Will he believe me?*

"Daddy–"

"Shh, you heard the nurse. You need your rest." He rubs my hair again.

The pain in my chest is dull, my heart slower. Sleep is about to take me, but I don't want it. I need to tell my father everything.

"Noelle, you're such a gift to me. You're everything. Please rest so you can get out of here."

I open my mouth, but no words come out.

He settles next to me, relaxing in the chair. "I remember the day we found out your mother was eight weeks pregnant. It was Christmas Eve and we both cried tears of joy. She was able to carry you full term, and you were born perfect and healthy on July fourteenth. Your mother was already so sick, riddled with cancer. But you were a breath of life into our lives. Our gift and Christmas miracle. Christmas in July. When your name left her lips for the first time, I knew it was perfect. Our Christmas angel, *Noelle*." His voice drifts as his hand rubs my arm up and down. "You were perfect in every way. You gave your mother so much strength those last few months of her life." His voice breaks as if he's fighting back his own tears.

I sink further into the bed as my body fully relaxes, even though my mind is racing with murderous thoughts of my stepmother. *What did the nurse give me?*

"Close your eyes," he orders. "Rest and heal. We need you home."

I manage to nod as I begin to drift off to sleep.

"I love you, Noelle. More than you can ever imagine."

His words don't comfort me as they should. He's my father and I love him, but I can't help but think how he's blind to the monster that is his wife. She's out to destroy him. And she wants me dead. *How could he not know this?*

"Sleep well, my precious angel. I'll be here when you wake up."

As much as my father claims to love me, he can't protect me from her.

It's about time I do it myself.

CHAPTER 14

Heath
Past
Age 18

THE MOON DANCES OFF my ceiling, and I can't wait any longer. I need to see her. It's been a rough couple of weeks since Noelle's attack, and she's been fighting back every single day, getting stronger. I glance at my clock and it's after midnight. I've been expecting her text for over four hours.

Something's not right.
Where is she?
I grab my phone and send another text to her.

Me: Hey. Where are you?
Me: If you're tired, I understand. But I want to see you to at least say goodnight.

A few minutes go by, and there's no response.
Twenty more minutes and still no response.
My heart pounds in my chest. I'm beyond worried.
She was acting so strangely after I picked her up from the physical therapist's office today, the memory still fresh in my mind.
I pull up in front of the medical building, Noelle is waiting outside.
"I was expecting to hear from you at least forty-five minutes ago," I say as she slides into the passenger seat. "Everything okay?"
"Everything's fine. My session just ran longer than expected today." She fastens her seatbelt, and I notice her hand is shaking.

"Are you sure you're okay?"

"Yes," she answers quickly.

"Wow, almost two full hours of physical therapy. You must be so sore," I note, and she nods her head vigorously.

"Totally."

We turn the corner and head toward the county road. When we pass a parking garage next to a new office building, she cranes her neck as if she's looking for something. Someone.

"Noelle?" I ask, curious why that particular garage is so interesting to her.

"What?"

"Everything okay?"

"Yeah. Sure. Yeah." She's now looking over her shoulder, trying to catch a glimpse of the building getting smaller and smaller behind us.

"What's going on?" I ask, concerned.

"Nothing. It's nothing." She's wringing her hands in her lap.

"Are you okay? You're not acting like yourself." She hasn't been herself for a while now, ever since the attack. Maybe even longer.

"That's my father's new office building," she says. Now it makes sense why she was craning her neck.

"Oh."

"I thought I saw his car. Did you see his car?" Her nerves seem heightened, and her behavior seems even more odd.

"No, I didn't see his car. Listen, you're not acting right. Tell me what's going on."

"I'm fine. I'm fine. I just thought I saw my dad. That's all." Her voice trails off, and she rests her head against the passenger window.

"That's cool that your dad's office is so close to home now. Right?"

"Yeah. I guess."

I make a few more turns and soon we're in our subdivision, private, gated homes lining the streets.

"What are you doing tonight?" I ask, and she inhales sharply.

"Nothing. I'm doing nothing. Why do you ask?" Her voice shakes, and she's incredibly nervous.

"What the hell is going on with you?" I demand, raising my own voice inadvertently.

She exhales, trying to calm herself down. "I'm fine. I promise." But I don't believe her.

I place my hand over hers and squeeze. "You're really worrying me, Noelle."

She squeezes back. "Don't be worried. Please."

She shifts a little more in her seat and winces through some pain. I know her ribs are still badly bruised, and her incision from the surgery is very uncomfortable.

"I love you," I say, needing to hear her tell me the same in return.

"I love you, too." A weak smile spreads across her face as we pull into her driveway.

"Do you want me to come in for a little while?" I dread spending any time in her house when Tonya's there, but I also feel the need to be with her constantly. Protecting her.

"No!" she blurts out, startling me with her abrupt response. "I mean. I need to shower and lie down for a little while. I'll text you later?"

I'm concerned that she's really tweaked from all of the pain meds she's been on. Her behavior is really erratic.

"Okay," I resign, reluctantly. "I'll text you in about an hour?"

"That's good. That's good. I think," she mutters.

"Noelle?"

She turns to face me and practically leaps across the seat into my lap, her hands wrapping around my head, fingers tearing into my scalp. Her mouth devours mine violently. Her hips press into mine as moans escape her lips. Moans of excitement and of pain.

Her tongue dives into my mouth as her hands hold my face in place. I carefully wrap my arms around her waist, trying to slow her down. "Hey, take it easy," I mumble against her lips.

"God, I love you so much," she pants, her mouth covering mine once again. Her kisses are urgent, desperate. "Please don't forget that. Ever."

Her pain finally catches up to her, and she winces in my arms, favoring her ribs. "I'm sorry," she says, trying to catch her breath. "I'm so sorry."

"You need to take it easy," I say. "I want to be with you so fucking much, but you need to heal. And we can't do this here." She's folded over me, still on my lap, no room for either of us to move. "As much as I would love to be with you right now, we can't. You're still injured."

Tears roll down her cheeks, surprising me. "Please don't cry, Noelle. You know I want you so damn much."

She nods against my forehead and pushes away from me. "I don't know what got into me," she whispers.

"We have plenty of time. Give yourself a few more weeks to get better and I promise, when the time comes, I won't be able to keep my hands off of you."

Tears flow again and I gently pull her against me. "Just breathe," I say into her ear, letting my lips linger.

"What if we don't have time?" she asks, and I stiffen against her.

"What?" I push her away so I can look into her eyes. They're darting all over the place and now I really think she's on something.

"Never mind. Forget I said that."

"No. What do you mean by that?" I press.

"You're right. I'm not myself. I just need to get some rest."

"Noelle?"

"Seriously, I'm exhausted. I need sleep. I'll call you later?" She opens the driver's side door and gingerly places her feet on the ground. Before she slides off of my lap, she kisses me tenderly on the lips. "I love you, Heath."

She walks away from my car, and I watch her go into her house. I sit there for several minutes, expecting the front door to open, Noelle emerging. But it doesn't. And she doesn't.

I back out of her driveway and drive through the cul-de-sac and pull into my own, all the time watching her house, hoping I'll see her run across the lawn to my car.

Her goodbye was strange. Unsettling.

I do everything in my power to stop myself from running to her house and busting down her door.

My text messages remain unanswered. Now my heart is pounding harder in my chest.

Maybe she fell asleep? Maybe she can't hear my texts?

I call her phone, and it goes right to voicemail. Relief floods through me when I realize her phone must have died. She's probably upset that I haven't called, and she may have no idea her phone is even dead.

I'm going over there. I need to see her now.

Before I leave the house, I let Gus know where I'm going. It's still almost a nightly occurrence, but if I don't tell him or the security team where I'm going or they aren't aware, all hell could break loose.

Her house is eerily quiet when I approach, and my heart sinks. I realize I haven't captured fireflies for her tonight when I see the empty firefly house hanging from the hook outside her window. *There won't be any fairies tonight.* I've broken an almost perfect string of firefly magic for her. I look around to see if I can catch a few before she notices that I'm here, but it's too late, there aren't any in sight.

When I tap on her window, I notice the light catcher isn't there. *That's strange.*

That light catcher has been hanging in the same spot for over four years, since her fourteenth birthday. I tap lightly on the window again before I slide it open. Her room is completely dark, and I whisper her name, "Noelle?"

There's no movement from her bed at all.

"Noelle?"

No response. I push the window open wider and step over the sill into her room. That's when I see her bed is empty.

What the hell?

I see her phone is on the night table next to her bed, and I walk across the room to grab it. It's dead.

Her bed is still made neatly, no sign of anyone sleeping in it at all tonight. It's now after one in the morning, where the hell is she?

The room is completely silent, no sounds coming from anywhere in the room or even the house.

I turn and walk toward her bathroom and notice the door is open and the light is out. I enter the bathroom anyway, my heart in my chest. "Noelle?"

Nothing.

Her bathroom is also empty, no sign of her at all.

The only place in her room that I haven't checked is her closet. The place where we shared our very first kiss. Our "sticky kiss". I don't see any light shining from underneath the door, and my heart burrows deeper in my chest. I slowly open it and immediately turn on the light.

Everything is in its place. Nothing disturbed. She's not in here either.

Worry rises again as I frantically look around her room, hoping to find anything that will tell me where she is. She wouldn't ever fall asleep anyplace else in this house; she's always locking herself in here, waiting for me to arrive. She would have expected me hours ago, so we could have our nightly talk through her open window. Stealing kisses. Talking about leaving for school in a couple of weeks, sharing dreams of our future.

This isn't like her at all. She definitely wasn't herself earlier today, and now I'm terrified that it's all connected.

My eyes fall onto her bed and notice something missing.

Mr. Jingles.

He's normally propped up against her pillows, sitting like he's waiting for her to return. He's always on this bed. Always.

Bile rises in my throat, and I make a mad dash out of her window. So many things about tonight are wrong.

Everything about her room is wrong.

Her light catcher is missing. Mr. Jingles is missing.

Noelle is missing.

I run as fast as I can through her yard, over the fence and into mine. I take the back steps three at a time as I rush through the door, flipping on the den then kitchen lights.

"Dad!" I yell into our silent house. My parents have been asleep for hours.

"Dad!" I yell again as I dash through the foyer and up the stairs.

"Heath?" my father's groggy voice meets me at the end of the hallway. "What's going on? Is everything okay?"

My mother emerges from behind him, fastening her robe around her waist.

"No. Everything is not okay," I pant.

He opens his phone and presses one button. "Gus, get to the house. Now." He snaps his phone shut and says to me, "Calm down and tell me what's going on."

My mother looks worried. Terrified.

"It's Noelle," I gasp.

"She's gone."

CHAPTER 15

Heath
Present

"GOOD MORNING," NOELLE says as she slides up my body, her naked breasts pressed against my chest. "I can't believe you're still asleep."

I smile and kiss her forehead. She's cool, so I pull her tighter against me. "You're so cold, babe."

"You'll warm me up, like you always do," she purrs. Her lips kiss a path from my shoulder to my jaw as she slowly moves her right leg over me. Her perfect body slides on top of mine as she continues to softly kiss me in the places she knows get me ready for her. "I love you so much," she says as her tongue trails down the center of my chest. I suck in my breath, anticipating where she's going, and I can't speak. "Tell me what you want," she moans, kissing, sucking, biting her way down even further.

"You," I gasp. "Now."

She pulls the blankets down with her body as she makes her way lower, soft sounds escaping her lips.

"Look at me," she demands as she wraps her hand around my length.

She's never talked like this before, and I'm suddenly rock hard, her warm breath teasing the tip of my dick. She's ready for it. I'm ready for it.

"Look at me," she orders again.

She wants me to watch.

I pop open my eyes and lift my head from the pillow to watch Noelle perform. Suddenly, her hand drops away and her warm breath turns ice cold. When she looks up at me, her eyes are hollow and look frozen. I suck in my breath as I see her once gorgeous hair muddled with seaweed and dead fish. Her body is draped in moss and filth.

What the fuck is happening?

I try to yell, but nothing comes out of my mouth. This isn't Noelle.

My heart is pounding in my chest, pain rips throughout my entire body. I hear waves crashing around us, but we're in my bedroom. None of this makes sense. I'm terrified.

"Look at me," she says again, her voice sounding further and further away.

I can't speak. I can't scream. I'm frozen in place as the seaweed covered corpse writhes on top of me.

I'm gasping for air, trying to breathe. Trying to do anything to get away. My arms are pinned next to me, my legs paralyzed.

I open my mouth to try to yell, but only air comes out. Cold air freezes between us, forming a shield between me and her.

Her face contorts, her wrists suddenly tied in front of her. Her mouth is now closed, eyes scared and pleading with me. She begins sliding away from me, sinking into the floor. Her tied hands outstretched above her head like she's slipping into the depths of the ocean.

"Heath!" she calls out.

I try to reach her, but I can't move. I'm fighting to save her. Fighting to break free from the invisible chains that have me tied down to my own bed.

She sinks further and further away from me, eyes wide open and terrified. And there's nothing I can do to help her. Nothing at all.

BEEP BEEP BEEP.

I sit up with a start, covered in sweat. Was that a dream? What the fuck was that?

The sun is shining into my room, and Noelle's not here with me.

My heart is still pounding in my chest, the vision of her sinking into the ocean is still vivid in my mind.

"What the fuck?" I shout out loud as I try to catch my breath.

I swing my legs around the edge of the bed and realize they're shaking. I'm shaking all over. I've had intense dreams in the past, but this one was insane. What the hell did it mean?

After I got back from Point Pleasant last night, I had a few beers and went to bed. I was mentally and emotionally exhausted. Visiting the place where Noelle took her final breaths was more difficult than I could have imagined. I pictured her emerging from the water, completely unscathed and beautiful. Exactly how I remembered her.

But the vision of her in my dream became grotesque. Rotting. Dead.

Am I finally beginning to heal? Is this what happens when I spend days on end thinking about her, wishing she was still here?

My phone rings from my nightstand and I swipe it immediately.

"Dax," I say, slightly out of breath.

"Did I catch you at a bad time?" He laughs.

"No, just waking up."

"Dude, it's almost eleven. Late night?"

"Yeah, something like that."

"I hadn't heard from you so I thought I'd check in. I guess it's safe to assume you and Haley worked things out?" He chuckles into the phone.

"No. We didn't."

"Oh, sorry. I just figured since you were up so late and you just woke up–"

"Don't assume, Dax."

He huffs on the other end of the line. "I'm sorry," he says again.

"It's okay. I've just had a rough night."

"Anything I can do to help?"

"No, I just need to clear my head."

We're both silent for a little while then he speaks up again. "I'm sorry Garrett and I got in your business. We didn't mean to pry about Haley. Whatever you two are going through, I'm here for you."

"Thanks. But we're not going through anything because there is no *us* or anything to go through. I ended it for good, and she's accepted it. I think."

"You think?"

"It was a rough conversation. She showed me a side of her I never knew existed. So yeah, I'm done."

"Cool. Well, glad to know you're alive and breathing. Glad she didn't try to kill you or anything." He laughs nervously.

"What? Why would you think that?" I ask, startled. What would ever give him the impression that Haley would do something like that?

"I'm kidding, bro. You seem to forget that we've met Haley before. She can be–intense. When we didn't hear from you yesterday, Garrett and I joked that you were either having incredible make up sex, or you were at the bottom of the ocean with a brick tied around your waist."

My head begins to pound, my heart racing again. Visions of Noelle in my dream come flooding back, and I feel like I'm going to puke. "That's not funny," I say weakly.

"Hey, are you meeting us tonight at my place? Garrett, Sam, and Kai are coming over. We're going to grill some stuff." Quick change of subject. Good.

I'm used to going to various functions alone. Haley was never an arm piece for me and I hate the concept of it. Dax and Giselle were nice enough to invite me to their little party with Garrett and his family, but for once I'm going to bow out.

"I don't think so," I mutter. "I got a shitty night's sleep, and I'd like to just chill, if that's okay with you?"

"Totally cool, man. If you change your mind, you know where we live."

"Thanks."

"Later," he says.

"Later."

I hang up and I'm about to toss the phone onto my bed when I notice how disheveled my sheets and comforter are. They must also be completely filled with sweat. I tear them off the bed and roll them into a ball, tossing them into the corner of my closet. I have a spare set of sheets and an extra comforter on the shelf and I take them out and place them on the bed. *I'll make the bed later.*

The room is warm, and I need to shower. I look around one last time, searching for signs of Noelle, searching for something that would have triggered that horrible nightmare. Her light catcher is sitting on the nightstand where I just placed my phone. I've carried it around with me for years, trying to preserve our memories. Our love.

"Noelle, I wish there was something I could've done to save you," I say out loud, knowing there will be no response.

I've carried so much guilt around for too long. I suspected abuse for years and never told anyone. I should have. Maybe she'd be here with me today instead of these grotesque dreams that remind me of the pain that I could have prevented.

MY SHOWER DIDN'T REFRESH me at all. My body is still tingling from the nightmare I had, fresh memories of Noelle vivid in my mind.

I did make a decision, though, while I was showering–to stop carrying the light catcher with me everywhere. It needs a permanent place in my home, rather than in my pocket.

I hold it up in front of me, watching it reflect the light from the kitchen window. Colorful patterns reflect off of the walls, and I imagine Noelle's eyes lit up. She loved my mother's collection that hung in our breakfast nook back home. She was always mesmerized by how unique each one was and the level of light they reflected.

EPIC LOVE

I don't have a kitchen nook like my parents do, but I have a deep set window above the sink. There's an empty hook already in place because wind chimes used to hang there. I took them down a few months ago because they annoyed me.

I reach up and hook the fishing wire that holds the light catcher over the hanger, letting it fall gently from my hands. As it settles, it twirls in place, reflecting every color of the rainbow onto the walls and ceiling in the kitchen. From this perspective, it's amazing, and I can fully understand and appreciate why Noelle loved these so much.

"That's beautiful," a soft voice says from behind me, startling me.

I turn to see my housekeeper, her eyes glistening. "Hey, Rosie."

"I'm sorry, I didn't mean to surprise you. I thought you heard me come in."

"That's okay."

"Did you get that overseas?"

I turn to look at the crescent moon hanging in my window. "No. It was–an old friend's."

"It certainly complements your kitchen and home, beautifully. Like it always belonged there."

"Yes it does," I mutter.

"I didn't expect you to be home. You're usually gone by now."

"I had a late night, so I slept in today."

"Good for you. You need rest."

"Oh. I'm sorry, I took all of the covers off of my bed and tossed them into my closet. I'll bring them down to the laundry room for you." I feel bad. I'm embarrassed that those sheets are a sweaty mess.

"I'll take care of it, don't you worry. Have some breakfast and relax," she orders, disappearing up the back stairs.

Rosie is great, and I don't know what I'd do without her. She is always thinking one step ahead of me, anticipating my every need.

I pull the English muffins out of the bread drawer and pull apart two of them, dropping them into the toaster. Once I have a couple of eggs scrambled, I drop the English muffins onto a plate, dividing the eggs on top of them. I squirt some ketchup on each and inhale my breakfast.

My phone rings from the counter, but I ignore it. My mouth is full, and I wipe ketchup from the corner. These egg sandwiches could have used some bacon and cheese, but they hit the spot anyway.

Now I'm thirsty. There's container of orange juice on the table next to me, and I swig it right from the bottle, quenching my thirst.

My phone rings again, and I look at the Caller ID. It's an unfamiliar number and it says it's coming from Massachusetts. Not many people have this number and I certainly don't know anyone from there, unless it's Stuart calling from Boston. Is he even up there?

I swipe to answer, "Hello?"

I hear light breathing on the other end of the line, but nobody responds.

"Hello?" I say again, annoyed.

Still nothing.

"Look, I don't have time for–"

"Heath?" a hauntingly familiar voice interrupts me. I swallow hard, the hair on my arms suddenly standing.

"Who is this?" I ask, already knowing the response I'm going to get.

The voice returns and I wonder if I'm still dreaming.

"Heath, it's me. It's Noelle."

CHAPTER 16

Noelle
Past
Age 18

MY BODY ACHES. I just finished a strenuous physical therapy session, and each time it seems to get harder and harder. My strength is slowly returning, the visible signs of Tonya's beating slowly fading. But it's still so fresh in my mind.

I walk through the doors of the medical building about to text Heath to let him know I'm finished, and I'm surprised to see my father's car waiting for me. The window rolls down, and his face is serious. The past few weeks have been rigorous, trying to nurse my body and my mind back to health. Tonya's lies were not found out. She stuck to her story of two masked men pushing past her into our home, searching for our safe and subsequently beating us both to a pulp. Me, obviously more than her. She visited me in my hospital room the day after she told the police her version of events, threatening to expose the secret she's been keeping for years if I didn't keep my mouth shut. A secret I still don't know, but she assures me it will destroy my family. In return, she promised to keep her hands to herself. She told me she was seeking help for her anger issues. I don't believe a word she says and I vow to remain guarded around her until I can do something about it.

Heath has been by my side almost as much as my father has. Every single night, the firefly house is placed on my windowsill, dozens of beautiful lightning bugs glowing into my room, aided by moonlight. I know it's Heath, but he just shrugs his shoulders and smiles. He says they are there to make more fairies to watch over me and protect me. He hasn't brought up what happened again, and for that I'm thankful. He's let me heal at my own pace. He's also been my main chauffeur to physical therapy, which is why seeing my father is so surprising right now.

"Dad?" I ask, approaching the car.

"Hey, Buddy. Want to go for a ride?"

"Where's Heath? Is everything okay?"

His lips tighten as the back door of his car opens. My Uncle Ronald, who is also our family lawyer, slides over to make room for me.

"What's going on?" My heart begins to race. I haven't seen my uncle for at least a year. He never makes a trip out of the city unless it's important.

"We'll explain in due time. Please get in the car." My father's voice tightens. I tense up so much, a random bystander would think I was getting kidnapped.

"Okay," I say and hesitantly slide into the back seat next to my uncle. There's another man in the front seat who turns around, nodding his head at me. He looks like he would be Secret Service if my father were the President.

"What the hell is going on?"

My father slowly accelerates, driving us from the physical therapist's office.

"I know what Tonya did to you," he declares, and I choke.

"What?"

We drive in silence for a while, before he pulls into an underground garage and parks the car. A door opens to the building in front of us, and we all get out.

"Daddy?"

He grabs my hand and squeezes. "It's going to be okay. I promise. *Everything* is going to be okay." His voice breaks as he releases my hand.

"Uncle Ronny? What's happening?"

"Your father will explain as soon as we're inside."

The other two men stand guard on either side of the door, allowing the three of us entry into the building. We walk into an open elevator, my father pressing the button to the eighth floor. When the door opens, we walk into a large office. We're the only ones here.

"Welcome to my new offices," my father says, arms outstretched. I had no idea he had office space this close to home.

"Nice?" I say, still suspicious of why we're here. He would never be so secretive about showing off new space.

We walk through the vast office and into a conference room surrounded by ceiling-to-floor glass walls. The door shuts behind us, and my father presses a button on the wall, causing the clear glass to become frosted, hiding us from our surroundings.

"Cool effect," I state, falling into a large leather chair. "Now can you tell me what the hell is going on, and what you said about Tonya before?"

My father drops his head, shoulders shaking. He breaks down, sobbing like I've never seen him sob before. Tears fall down his face as he pulls a handkerchief from his suit pocket. I get up to console him, but my uncle holds his hand out, indicating that I should stay seated. I nod and let my own face fall into my hands.

"Daddy, please tell me what's happening," I cry. "You're really scaring me."

He chokes on his remaining tears and makes eye contact with me. "I'm so sorry, Buddy. You have no idea how horrifying it's been for me to learn you suffered at her hands. This is all my fault, and I should have done something to protect you sooner. It's time." He dabs his eyes with the damp cloth in his hands. "I'm so sorry and hope you can forgive me someday."

"What are you saying? You knew? You knew what that bitch has been doing to me for years? Beating me to a pulp? Nearly killing me?"

His eyes widen. "Been doing?"

"Dad, she's been beating the shit out of me for years. Since I was twelve years old. This last time was the icing on the cake. She nearly killed me."

"What? I thought it was just this once!" he cries and looks at my uncle, alarmed.

"Yes, it all started with a slap here and a punch there. It started escalating when I was about fourteen. Every single time she laid a hand on me, you were away on business."

"I had no idea. I had no idea," he repeats, shaking his head, his tears return. "I can't imagine you'll ever forgive me for putting you in so much danger."

"How could you have known if I didn't tell you?" I try to let him off the hook a little, but this entire conversation is making me sick, bile rising in my throat.

My father nods to my uncle and says again, "Ronny, it's time."

My uncle slides closer to me, opening a series of folders as I try to keep from puking all over the table.

"Your father has signed papers to fully release your trust fund to you, as of close of business today. Once you sign this document, it will be considered fully executed. The money in the accounts your mother set up for you is now completely yours. You've just inherited your mother's fortune to the tune of eighty-six million dollars."

My eyes widen, and then I puke. My mouth full of bile and my lunch, threatening to spill out of my lips as it burns my nose. My uncle pulls his own handkerchief from his pocket, quickly handing it to me.

I turn and spit the contents of my mouth into the rag, tears stinging my eyes.

"What?" I stammer, trying to breathe deeply so I don't throw up all over the table.

"Your inheritance. It's yours," Uncle Ronald reiterates. "Are you okay?"

"I don't understand why–how–this is happening?"

My father looks back up at me. "I want you to take it all. And disappear."

The room starts to spin, and I can't think. This can't be happening.

"Noelle, take a deep breath and listen to me very carefully," my uncle says, getting my attention.

I close my eyes and inhale deeply through my nose. I must be asleep–dreaming. This can't possibly be real.

"For your safety, we're going to keep some of the details to ourselves, but Tonya and her family are extraordinarily dangerous. Your father was blackmailed into marrying her when you were a baby. At the time, it seemed like he'd be able to get out of the deal after a few years. But then other things surfaced, and her family threatened everything your father loves and holds close to his heart."

I sit in silence, the room spinning around me. None of this makes sense at all.

He continues. "Your father found evidence that Tonya murdered her first husband and locked it away as leverage. She and her family realized that they couldn't do anything to either of you until that evidence was found and destroyed."

"The safe," I mutter, bringing my fingers to my lips.

"Yes, the safe. He used it as a diversionary tactic, building an elaborate safe in your home, keeping her looking, guessing, hunting. The real evidence has been copied, recorded, and locked away in more than one location. If anything happens to you or your father, I have permission to blast it to the world. Tonya's family may be dangerous, but they're protective of their own. Several of her brothers have already perjured themselves protecting her. They would all stand to go to jail for a very long time."

"What do they have on us? What are they holding over my father's head?" I demand.

My dad makes eye contact with my uncle and nods his head.

"Before you were born, when your parents were young and in love, your mother made a very big mistake. A grave mistake. She got behind the wheel of a car and drove drunk. Your father was the passenger and their friends in the back seat. The conditions were terrible, an ice storm coating the roads. That, paired with the fact that your mother shouldn't have been driving in the first place, contributed to a horrible accident, injuring both of your parents and killing both of their passengers. Your father pulled your mother from the car and told the police that he was driving. However, his blood alcohol was minimal, so the police wrote it up as just what it was, a terrible accident."

"So? It was an accident? How is this blackmail material?"

"Because it was your mother behind the wheel. And the people she killed were Tonya's brother and his wife."

I suck in my breath, the room spinning once again.

"My mother's dead. I don't understand why we have to worry about this now?" I can't believe I want my dead mother to take the blame for an accident from so many years ago, but if she did it, doesn't the crime deserve to fall on her shoulders?

"I won't allow that!" my father yells from his perch at the head of the table. "I refuse to let her memory to be tarnished in anyone's eyes. She doesn't deserve it. It was an accident." He stresses the point, and I can tell he won't budge.

"But Dad, think about it. If you let the truth come out, then we're all free and you can put Tonya and her family away for a lifetime."

"It's not that easy," he sighs. "For any of us. Her family is still dangerous and has far reach. They'll make us pay for hiding the evidence we have on Tonya."

"They should cut that crazy bitch loose from their lives. If she murdered her husband, she deserves to pay for it."

"I completely agree, Buddy. But like I said before, if she gets indicted, so do her brothers. That's the last thing her family wants. It would destroy their business."

"How did you get involved with her family in the first place?" I press, angry that we're even in this predicament.

"They funded the startup of my company. With dirty money. It goes really deep, Noelle. Too deep for me to turn it around."

I shake my head, and my heart pulls seeing the pain my father is in.

"So you want me to disappear? This is your answer to fixing things?"

My uncle chimes back in. "Noelle, this is the only way we can guarantee that you stay safe."

"But what about him?" I point to my father. "Tonya may be a certifiable lunatic, but she's not stupid. She'll figure it all out, and then what? They kill him and hunt me down?"

"Tonya won't know. She has no idea about the trust fund that your mother left you."

"Is that money dirty, too?" I ask, needing more answers.

Uncle Ronald shakes his head. "No, that money is cleaner than clean. It came from your mother's family entirely. It never mixed with anything your father ever used to run his various businesses. She made sure of that and so did her family."

"But, if my mother was so freaking rich, why couldn't *she* invest in your company? Why did you have to borrow money from Tonya's family?"

"I didn't want your mother tied up in my business in any way. And she didn't know."

"So you lied to her? From what you've told me about my mother, she was a wonderful person. Don't you think she would have helped you? Helped us?"

My father nods his head slowly. "Yes, she would have. But like I said, I didn't want anything from her. I wanted her to stay as far away from my business dealings as possible. I thought I was keeping her safe."

"Well you certainly dug us into a huge hole, haven't you?" My anger rises, fist slamming against the table. "You've accomplished the one thing you've been trying to avoid for eighteen years. You're about to lose the only family you have left."

Uncle Ronald raises his hand. "I'm not going anywhere. I'm going to make sure we get through this, protecting your father and you as best as I can."

"Sorry, I didn't mean to imply that you don't matter, Uncle Ronny."

"Noelle, if I could go back and change the way I did things, I would. I think. I–ah–I just don't know." My father's exasperated. Tears threaten to fall again, and he chokes them back. "All I want is for you to be safe, and you leaving is the only way to make that happen."

"Will I ever see you again?" I ask, my voice shaking.

"I hope so," he says as my uncle shakes his head.

"I'm sorry, Noelle, but you have to consider this a permanent solution. Tonya's family is too dangerous. Their reach is wide. The Constantinos are known for violence from coast to coast."

"I can't do this," I cry. "You can't make me do this."

I'll never see my father again. I'll never see Heath. All of my friends. My fireflies.

"Please don't make me do this."

My father looks away as my uncle pushes the pile of papers in front of me and hands me a pen. "Sign where the yellow arrows are pointing. This will be over soon."

Tears fill my eyes as I scrawl my signature on page after page. When I'm finished, my uncle closes the folder and takes a deep breath.

"The funds are being transferred into an account offshore. Here is the name on the account as well as a new social security card and ID. When you get to your destination, you'll find a bank where you can access and draw as much at a time as you need to establish yourself, anonymously. You won't be able to contact your father, or any of us. You need to understand that now. You're disappearing. People are going to think you're dead. You need to stay dead."

I feel like I'm about to pass out. All of this becoming too real. Too preposterous. I feel like I'm suddenly in the middle of a mob movie, having to hide to stay alive. We all know how those movies turn out– the hero or heroine running for their lives. The bad guys always find them.

"This isn't going to work," I mutter. "It's not going to work."

"You have to trust us," my uncle says. "Tonya will have no reason not to believe that you're gone for good."

"Then she'll get too comfortable in her life with my father and she'll slip up. She *has* to. She'll get sent to jail, and I can come home." I'm rambling, hopeful.

"You have to stay away," my uncle insists. My father's eyes are now hollow, the life is being sucked out of him every second that we sit here, planning my disappearance. *Planning my death.*

"I can't do this," I bawl. "Please don't make me do this."

My father stands up and walks across the room, falling to his knees in front of me. He wraps his arms tightly around me, pulling me close, sobbing into my hair. "I never wanted it to come to this. I can't say goodbye. I never thought I'd ever have to say goodbye to my daughter." My tears join his, and we cling to each other, not wanting to let go.

"When?" I ask, relenting.

"Tonight," my uncle answers quickly. "You'll go back to physical therapy and call Heath, letting him know you ran later than you expected. He'll come pick you up and take you home like nothing has changed."

"Does Heath know? Is he in on this?" I'm hopeful. Maybe he'll run away with me.

My uncle shakes his head. "He has absolutely no idea, and it needs to stay that way."

"But his father can help us, he's the District Attorney for God's sake!" I contradict my own thoughts. Thoughts that raced through my head a few weeks ago when Heath was pressing me for information about my bruises. At the time, I begged him to stop trying to guess what was going on with me. I begged him to believe me that I was okay. The thought of his father knowing anything scared the crap out of me. Now, I feel differently. Maybe we can get him to help us?

My father releases his grip, placing his forehead against mine. "That's exactly why he can't know anything. Palmer Strickland cannot get involved or we'll all be dead."

"Oh my God. How far does this go?" I whisper.

"You now know everything. We've told you far more than we should have," my uncle admits.

"Dad, I can't say goodbye," I cry, tears pouring out of my eyes. I can't leave him or Heath.

"You have to, Buddy."

He stands up and leaves the room. Was that it? Was that the last time I'll ever see my daddy?

"Uncle Ronny?" my voice shakes. "There has to be another way."

"Noelle, you need to get it together now. We need to move quickly if we're going to make this work."

My hands shake as he shoves my new identification and bank credentials into my hands. Words swirling in my head, instructions about what to do, what to say. Steps I need to take to disappear.

He asks me to find something meaningful, something those close to me will know I would never leave behind. I need to take that with me tonight to the location he jots down on a piece of scrap paper. The stage will be set when I get there, I just need to leave this one thing behind and vanish into thin air.

I'm numb as I go through the motions, nodding when he asks me to confirm specific details. I wring my hands together on my lap.

I'm convinced that I'm going to fuck up. I'm going to do something to put everything in jeopardy.

"Your father wants you to have this," my uncle hands me an old worn, leather messenger bag. It looks like it's decades old, the leather smell faded long ago.

"What is this?" I ask.

"I'm not sure what's in it, your father didn't tell me. But he insisted you don't open it until you're safe and settled."

"Okay," I whisper, fastening it over my shoulders.

"Text Heath now. I'll get you back to the physical therapist's office right away."

"Okay," I nod, trying to maintain my composure. "Can I say goodbye to my father one last time?" I beg.

He nods his head. "He's in his office. You have five minutes."

I stand up, pulling my phone from my pocket.

Me: Hey! My appointment ran late. They messed up their schedule. Can you come get me in twenty minutes?
Heath: God, I was worried about you! I should be able to get there in twenty. It may be thirty, if that's okay?
Me: No problem. Sorry to worry you.
Heath: No worries. I love you.
Me: Love you, too :)

I walk across the floor toward the muted lights in the corner. His door is half open, and I hear him sobbing inside. I hesitate before I push the door open further. "Daddy?"

He jumps up and rushes to me, pulling me into a huge hug. "I'm so sorry to do this. I can't believe we're saying goodbye. I'm not ready."

"Neither am I," I cry. "I don't want to go."

He kisses me and hugs me one last time, composing himself. "I never meant to put you in any danger. I need you to know that I swear I would have done something sooner had I known she's been abusing you for years. You have to believe me that I didn't know."

I nod and inhale deeply. "I know, Dad. I believe you."

"I promise I'm going to do everything possible to make sure we can see each other again," he croaks weakly. He's trying to make me believe his lie, but I don't.

"Okay."

"You need to go. Now."

I turn and walk slowly out of the room. "Goodbye, Daddy. I love you."

"Goodbye. And I love you more than you will ever know. Please be careful."

I don't turn around when I hear his breathing hitch. I can't look into his eyes for the last time.

I need to pull myself together before Heath sees me. He can't know what's going on. He has to think I'm fine.

This is the biggest lie I'm ever going to tell.

And it's going to destroy me.

CHAPTER 17

Noelle
Present

"THANKS, UNCLE RONNY," I say into the phone. "I'll see you soon." The last time I spoke to my uncle was the day I disappeared. The day I died.

I hang up and I stare at the phone number scrawled on the notepad in front of me. I've been in contact with my uncle for the past few days, since receiving some overwhelming information. When he called me on Sunday, it was the first time I've spoken to anyone in my family for almost twelve years. His news shocked me, and I'm still trying to process it all. But, his phone call prompted me to ask for a favor, which he just fulfilled.

My heart races as I fold and unfold the worn piece of paper that I've carried with me since the day I left home. The words of a teenage boy are scrawled on it, frozen in time.

Take me back to two weeks ago.
My blue oil lamp painting
the fireflies dancing in the ink night sky
of your backyard in amber rose mosaics.
When the moon is asleep I will
find a way to rescue you.

Take me back to two nights ago.
Your eyes afire again with the tales
your father told.

I know his promises taste like a lie
or a line or paper stack of let downs.
When he has forgotten I will
find a way to rescue you.

Take me back to two moments ago.
Setting fairies free to twirl
under the watchful moon, back with her
unwavering glow, moving the tides of
unruly seas and your smile pulled at the
corners of your mouth like a forgotten
treasure.
When all is forgotten you find
new ways to rescue me.

Heath's poem. Heath's song.
I need him to rescue me–again.
My hands shake as I dial the number my uncle just gave to me.

Before I lose my nerve, I hit send. Nobody answers. *Shit.* Heath's voicemail message plays through the phone, "I'm not here. In fact, I don't even know where I am. Leave a message. If I don't call you back, call Stuart. If you don't know who Stuart is, then I don't know you, which means I probably won't call you back." A long beep sounds and I hang up, terrified to leave a message.

I rest my forehead against the cool tile on my kitchen island. I've been living on Chappaquiddick Island, part of Martha's Vineyard and off the coast of Massachusetts since I "disappeared." My home is quaint and unassuming, despite the size of my bank account. I live on a small beach with only two neighbors. I chose this place because it's a remote location, the ferry being the only way on and off the island, unless you have your own boat, which I don't. Of course, you can also charter a private plane onto Martha's Vineyard, but I've never flown and I'm terrified of planes. With only a few hundred residents, it's private, and I've been able to keep to myself for many years.

I've ventured to the mainland only a handful of times since I moved here. One of those times was a trip to visit Boston, the city Heath and I were supposed to go to college together. My friend, Dahlia, got tickets to an Epic Fail concert and after much prodding, I agreed to go with her. It was a nerve-wracking trip, I was looking over my shoulder practically the entire time, worried that Tonya or her family were following me. I had been sequestered on Chappaquiddick for so long, the bustling of a large city was too overwhelming for me.

I also agreed to go because I knew that I'd be able to see Heath, if only from a distance. I'd been following his life since I left home. Google is a wonderful thing. I'd been a fan of Epic Fail for several years, and when Alex Treadway left the band, I couldn't believe that Heath replaced him. I always knew his poetry was mind-blowing, but only heard him sing a handful of times. I couldn't believe how incredible he was, and to see him playing guitar as well was surreal. It's like he was a different person, singing songs that night just for me. But he had no idea I was even there.

And until the other day, I hadn't had any contact with my family since I left. The conversation with my uncle was nothing I would have expected, which prompted my request to find Heath's phone number. I need to talk to him.

I need to explain.

I need his help.

I dial his number again, my heart beating wildly in my chest. I feel faint and wonder if this is even a good idea.

He answers this time.

"Hello?"

I try to calm myself, taking deep breaths. My dizziness subsides.

"Hello?" he asks again, quickly, sounding annoyed.

I'm about to respond when he blurts out, "Look, I don't have time for–"

"Heath?" As his name leaves my lips, I tense up. What am I going to say?

"Who is this?" he asks.

It's now or never. My finger is hovering over the 'end call' button on the screen of my phone.

"Heath, it's me. It's Noelle," I say softly, wondering if he even heard me.

I hear a gasp on the other end, and then he states, "Impossible."

I cover my mouth to stifle the sobs escaping.

"Who the fuck is this, and what kind of sick joke are you trying to play?"

"I'm sorry," I apologize, about to hang up. "But this isn't a joke."

"Noelle's dead. Haley, if this is you fucking with me, I swear to God, you're going to be sorry."

Haley?

Are they still friends? Or more?

Shit. This is such a bad idea.

"Heath, it's really me. Noelle," I say awkwardly. "I'm not sure what else to say to make you believe me, but I–I'm not dead."

His breathing hitches, and it seems like he's pacing. He says a few things I can't understand, and then he mumbles into the phone, "This can't be real. This has to be a dream still."

A dream? He dreams about me?

"This isn't a dream. I promise you."

"I don't understand," he states.

"There's so much to explain. And I swear, I'll tell you everything. But first, please tell me that you believe me," I plead. I need to hear him say it. I need to know he believes that it's me.

He's silent, and I can only imagine the crazy thoughts running through his mind.

"Heath?"

"I want to believe you. But, she–you–died. I saw the inlet, the jetty. There's no way someone could survive that fall. There's just no way…"

There's so much pain in his voice, guilt overcomes me. I've been carrying this lie for years, hiding in this remote community, pretending to be somebody that I'm not.

"I left you something on the rocks. Something I knew would wind up back in your hands. Something that means more to me than anything on this Earth," I say. I know the light catcher was found because I watched the news coverage. I also know that it was given back to my father, who would have immediately given it to Heath.

He sucks in his breath. "Holy shit. This can't be happening. Noelle?" His voice is pained, and I can tell he's about to cry. I don't think I can listen to his tears without comforting him, holding him.

"I'm so sorry," I cry.

"*Sorry?* Where the hell have you been all of these years?" His anger is back, and I brace myself for what's coming. "I thought you were dead! We searched for you! How could you do this to everyone? To me?"

I've been preparing my response to this for longer than imaginable. From the moment I came to Chappaquiddick, I thought of ways to try to explain my disappearance and my faked death. It's so hard for me to wrap my own mind around everything, much less try to get Heath to understand.

"Can I see you?" I ask, preferring to explain things in person. Face to face.

"What?"

Does he not believe that I'm alive?

"I can be in Pennsylvania by tomorrow night." If I time the ferries just right, I should be able to be on the mainland before noon and I can make the drive in just about six hours.

"You're coming here?"

I'm not afraid to be in public anymore, and I need to explain everything to him.

"Yes," I pause and take a deep breath. "I need your help."

When all is forgotten you find new ways to rescue me.

CHAPTER 18

Heath
Present

I'VE BEEN PACING throughout my first floor for the past few hours, watching the clock like a hawk. None of this seems real, and I have no idea what the fuck is going to happen when Noelle gets here. I didn't sleep at all last night, afraid that yesterday was a dream, a crazy continuation of the nightmare that I woke up from yesterday morning.

Hearing her voice was insane. No explanation given as to why she's even alive or where she's been for twelve years. She sounded older, her voice so much more mature than I remembered. If I didn't have that dream the other night, I don't know if I'd still remember what she looks like. I'm so confused as to what's real and what's a dream.

One thing I do know is how real my anger is. Intense, nearly blinding, anger.

How could she do this to everyone? Why didn't she tell me she was alive?

I'm fuming, clenching my fists and pacing. What am I even going to say to her after all of these years? This isn't going to be some star-crossed lovers' reunion. No fucking way. She ran away and pretended to be dead. I demand–I deserve– an explanation. An apology.

And then, I can finally move on with my life.

I made the decision the other day at the inlet that I would try to get past what happened. That I would attempt to move on from my memories of Noelle. I've been stifled in my life for far too long, settling for the status-quo. I haven't been able to give my heart to anyone. Once she explains herself, I need to move on. For good.

I look at my phone for the hundredth time in the past fifteen minutes. It's seven-thirty. She should have been here by now. *Maybe this all really is a dream. Or maybe I'm just going crazy.*

The doorbell rings, and I freeze in place. After all of the pacing I've done over the past few hours, I suddenly can't move.

Beyond that door is my past. A past filled with so much love, heartache, and loss.

The doorbell rings again, prompting me to walk toward it. I grasp the doorknob with my hand, briefly closing my eyes. My heart pounds in my chest and fear rises. Fear of the unknown and what's going to be staring at me beyond this door.

I pull it open and all reality fades away. I've been brought back in time, staring at the most captivating woman I've ever seen. Noelle is even more beautiful than when we were younger. Her eyes are bright, sharper than I ever remember them to be. When she was a teenager, they were always drawn, worried. Dark circles and sometimes bruises shadowed her face. That has disappeared and her eyes now look alive, bright.

"Oh my God," I say, unable to gain control of my emotions.

She drops her car keys to the ground and takes a hesitant step forward. Then she rushes into my arms, diving her head into my chest, grabbing me and holding me tight. She doesn't say a word, but her body shakes uncontrollably in my grasp. Soft sobs begin to escape her lips and I pull her snug up against me. "I can't believe you're here," I say, kissing the top of her head, squeezing her. "Is it really you?"

"It's me. It's me," she repeats over and over again.

We hold onto each other, afraid to let go.

After a few minutes, I loosen my grip on her. "Come inside." I release her, bending down to pick up her keys.

"Okay," she says weakly.

She follows me through the foyer and into the den. Before she got here, I rehearsed this moment in my head, imagining where we would sit and who would talk first. My nerves are heightened once again, and I gesture for her to sit on the couch. When she does, I settle into the chair across from her.

I try to calm myself down and say, "You need to explain to me what's going on. Why you're here. How you're not dead."

Her eyes fall to the floor, and she nods her head. "I'll tell you everything."

I brace myself and wait for her to begin.

She closes her eyes and inhales deeply, wringing her hands together in her lap. I have no idea what she's about to tell me, but I can tell it's paining her to keep it in.

"Before I begin, you have to know how sorry I am for leaving the way I did."

As incredible as it is to see her here, *alive*, I'm not sure forgiveness is on the agenda at the moment. "I need you to tell me what happened."

She inhales deeply and begins. "You were right. You always knew something was going on with me. I made you swear that you'd never tell anyone. But you were right all along. Tonya mercilessly abused me for years. It began shortly after we moved to Pennsylvania, but her verbal abuse started many years before."

I clench my fists, anger coursing through my veins. So many years of abuse could have been stopped if she only let me help her. "Why didn't you tell me the truth? Why did you hide it from me?"

"I had to. I didn't have a choice. Even my father didn't know until it was too late."

"I don't understand," I state, trying to calm down.

"Tonya was blackmailing my father and had been for years. Although I didn't know the exact nature of what she had over him, she continued to prey on my father's weaknesses–me and the memory of my mother. I eventually found out that she had evidence about my mother that my father wanted to keep secret, to protect her. If I did anything to disrupt the facade of their relationship, of our family, she would have tried to destroy my father. She held a secret over all of our heads, and we bowed down to her, let her run our lives."

I'm in disbelief that one woman could hold so much control over a family. "How is that even possible? How could your father let your abuse go on for years?" While I was held powerless to do anything about it, surely her father could have tried to stop it.

"He didn't know. I hid it from him along with everyone else."

I don't understand this mentality at all. "If I saw it, your father should have!" I raise my voice, unintentionally.

"Heath, it's so hard to explain. But you have to believe me, that as a young girl, as a teenager, I wasn't in the right mind to speak up for myself. I was terrified of the repercussions. Terrified that nobody would believe me. Terrified of losing the only family I had left. I've learned a lot about abuse over the past few years, and I've been through more therapy than anyone could even imagine. I was a victim, and apparently, I played right into her hands, allowing her to take advantage of my mental state. To take advantage of my fear. She controlled me, and I'm embarrassed to even admit that."

She bows her head and wipes tears from her eyes. My heart sinks for her, and I realize I've been too hard. Too angry.

"I'm sorry," I say, trying to comfort her.

"There's so much more about Tonya you don't know, and that's why I had to disappear."

She doesn't realize that I *do* know, and I speak up.

"I know all about Tonya and her family," I blurt out.

"What?" She looks surprised.

"After you disappeared, I went insane. I begged my father for help. I told him what I knew, what I suspected was happening with you. I wanted him to open an investigation into your death."

"Oh my God," she utters, holding her hand against her mouth. "I had no idea."

"My father told me what he knew about Tonya's family. The Constantinos are apparently known from here to Portland, Oregon, and a few cities in between. She has some very dangerous cousins and uncles, apparently. Many of them are in jail for crimes like prostitution and murder," I say as she nods her head.

"My father found out about what she did to me–what she tried to disguise as a home invasion. That's when he made the decision to save my life and aid in my disappearance."

"What? You mean to tell me that your father *helped* you disappear?" She nods again.

"Yes. He helped me escape. He thought it was the only way to keep me safe and get me as far away from her as possible. He wanted to handle things on his own and keep me out of danger. So he and my uncle planned everything, and I had less than five hours to come to grips with what was going to happen. And I had to say goodbye to everyone forever." I can tell she's filled with sadness and grief. Tears threaten to spill down her cheeks, and I feel compelled to comfort her. To hold her.

But I need to know more.

"Tonya went to prison years ago when she was convicted of conspiring to murder her first husband. So why couldn't you come back then? Why are you now suddenly able to rise from the dead?" I realize my words are harsh, but her sudden appearance still makes no sense to me.

"Because I'm not afraid anymore. She can't touch me again. She can't hurt me or my father." She drops her head into her hands, and through her sobs she cries, "He's dead. My father's dead."

I jump up and rush to her side sitting on the couch next to her, cradling her against me. "I had no idea."

"It's okay. I only just found out on Sunday." That was several days ago, and I wonder why I haven't heard from my parents about this. They usually know everything that's happening.

"How?" I'm suddenly worried for her safety again, wondering if he was murdered by Tonya's family. But I think I would have heard about this though, so I try to put my suspicions to rest.

"A blood clot traveled to his lungs. He died from a pulmonary embolism."

"I'm so sorry," I console, pulling her against me tighter.

She shakes her head. "I've wasted so many years afraid, worried that if I resurfaced, I would cause trouble for my father. And now he's gone."

I have to agree with her that her disappearance seems pointless. She should have been here. With her father. *With me.*

"I said goodbye to him twelve years ago. But I always had hope that one day he'd send for me. He'd tell me it was safe to come home. I had no idea he had so little time left."

I'm at a loss as to why she would even stay away, especially if she knew Tonya's family couldn't hurt her any longer. "This is all too hard for me to understand."

"I knew what was going on with Tonya. I knew she'd been put in jail. But my father's and my uncle's words never left me. They warned me about the Constantinos and how vengeful they could be. They made me promise that, no matter what, I would stay away. That I would never come home."

"Then why did you?" I ask in disbelief.

"Uncle Ronny called me to tell me he was dead. I lost it. The fact that I wasn't here completely destroyed me. I was angry that they kept me away for so long. I demanded to be able to come home to properly say goodbye to my father."

I can't believe her father wouldn't even try to contact her after Tonya's trial and conviction. Was he worried that something else might happen?

"Are you safe now?" I ask, worried.

"I don't care if I am or not." Her words grab me hard. Why wouldn't she care?

"Don't be foolish," I demand. "Strutting around, out in the open, is just asking for trouble. Don't do anything stupid."

She shrugs her shoulders. "I can't worry about these things anymore. There's nothing else that Tonya and her family can take away from me. My father is dead." She pauses for a moment and then clarifies, "I do have a small security detail that I hired a few years ago. They monitor my surroundings and blend in so I'm not even aware that they're near." *Thank God.*

We sit silently, Noelle leaning into my side, my arm tucked protectively around her shoulder. Everything about this feels so comfortable. So right. But it also feels unreal, like I'm going to wake up from another dream.

"When you called me yesterday, you said you needed my help." I remind her of the reason why she's surfaced, curious for her motivation for coming to find me.

"Yeah. That," she admits, hesitantly.

"What is it? I'll do anything," I state, yearning for penance for allowing her abuse to continue for as long as it did.

"My father's wishes were to be put to rest with my mother. I don't want to do it alone."

"Of course," I state immediately. "I'll be there for whatever you need."

"That's where it gets tricky," she says.

"Tricky?" I raise my eyebrow.

"Her ashes were spread at the Grand Canyon, the place where my parents ended an incredible road trip across the country just after they were married."

"I'll book us a flight right away," I mention, reaching for my phone.

"No!" she says, nervously.

"What? Let me take care of it. It's the least I could do."

"Sorry. I should've been more specific. I don't fly."

I sit back so I can look at her and can tell she's being serious.

"You don't fly?"

"No. I never have. And I'm petrified. So, no I don't fly."

"Well, how are we going to get to the Grand Canyon then?" I ask, perplexed.

"I'd like to take a road trip. And I'd like you to come with me."

So much has happened in the past twenty-four hours. Old memories and feelings have resurfaced. I can't believe Noelle is here, alive and well, asking me to drive with her across the country. I can't quite grasp everything that's going on, but I answer, "I'll take you to the Grand Canyon."

For the first time since she walked into my house and back into my life, she smiles. A vibrant light illuminates her eyes, just like the light catcher hanging in my kitchen window.

And I realize that taking her on this trip so she can put her father to rest will give me the opportunity to earn her forgiveness for not protecting her back then. For letting her abuse go unnoticed, unpunished.

I have thousands of miles of open road to talk about the past and what got us here, and I don't plan to waste a second of it.

When the moon is asleep I will find a way to rescue you.

CHAPTER 19

Noelle
Present

I PULL MY CAR into a spot in the parking garage attached to my father's office building. The last time I was here was twelve years ago, the day I said goodbye to him forever, even though I was hoping I'd be able to see him again. Unfortunately, my hopes and dreams did not come true.

"Miss Durand, good to see you," one of the security guards says as I enter the building. He's unfamiliar to me, and I'm curious how he knows who I am. "Your uncle is in your father's office. Do you need me to show you where it is?"

I shake my head, even though I've only been here once, the layout is forever burned into my brain. I walk past the conference room where I found out all of the sordid details about my mother and the accident that killed Tonya's brother and wife.

Uncle Ronny is sitting at the large mahogany table in my father's office. When I walk into the room, he immediately gets to his feet and sweeps me into his arms. "My God, it's so good to see you, Noelle." He squeezes me tight, like he never wants to let me go again.

"You, too," I admit.

"Let me look at you," he says, letting me go and taking me all in. "You've grown into such a beautiful young woman. The spitting image of your mother." I've seen many pictures of her growing up and have several more that my father made sure I had when I left twelve years ago.

"Thank you."

"Sit down. We have so much to go over and so many things to make right."

I have no idea what he means by this, but I slide into one of the large leather chairs across from him.

"What do I need to do?"

"First, we need to get your name legally changed back to Noelle Durand."

I'd been living under my mother's middle and maiden name since I left town. My mother's full name was Melanie Sawyer Duncan, so I became Sawyer. It was strange living with that name for so many years, not using the name my parents gave me. My neighbors on Chappy know me only under that name, my real name never being uttered anywhere.

"Is that going to be hard?" I ask. "I mean, I'm dead, right?"

He shakes his head. "No, technically, you're not dead. Your father never filed a legal death certificate, and we were able to grease a few palms to make sure that never happened. Don't ask me who or how. Just know that you're not dead." He winks and smiles nervously.

"Thank God for that," I say sarcastically.

"But if you wish to live as Noelle Durand again, we'll need to get your name legally changed back. You want to do that, don't you?"

I nod vigorously. "Yes, I mean, unless someone is looking for me?"

"You don't need to worry about the Constantinos. With Tonya rotting away in prison, her family has bigger fish to fry. Your father turned over the evidence he had years ago, which led to her conviction. If they were going to retaliate, they would have done so back then. Your father wouldn't have lived through her trial if that was going to happen."

"Then why didn't you contact me? Bring me home?"

"He didn't care what they would try to do to him. He was adamant about letting you live your life safely and in peace. He was worried that if he allowed you to come home, they would have done something very bad. They would have made him pay for what he did to Tonya by taking it out on you. I think we're well past that danger now, and your father made me promise I would contact you after he died."

"But I thought his death was sudden? He had a pulmonary embolism, right?"

"Yes, it was sudden. I was the one who found him, right here in this office." He hangs his head, and I can tell he doesn't want to relive the scene. I look around the large room, wondering where he fell. Did he know what was happening? Was he scared? Did he see my mother waiting for him as he took his last breaths? I try to imagine a beautiful scene where my mother comes down from Heaven to take his hand. I'll keep that vision in my mind forever, hoping it's true.

"Then how did you know what he wanted?"

"He had a plan. We talked extensively about what was to happen to all of his assets and what would happen in the event of his death. Everything was worked out and executed. But one of his wishes was that you would come home when he was gone, providing I felt that it was safe enough to do so. I think the time is now right, and you're back where you belong."

I've become comfortable in my quaint home in Chappy. I've enjoyed the privacy. The anonymity. The safety. While I've definitely looked over my shoulder on more than one occasion, like I did when I was in Boston, my life grew there. I planted roots. What am I going to tell the people that have come to know me? What will I tell my friends?

My closest friend, Dahlia, has never pried into my background. I work in her flower shop once or twice a week. She thinks that I came to the island to escape an abusive relationship. She assumed I was abused by a man, and I never corrected her. It keeps her off of my back about the lack of men in my life and defensive for me when she sees me in an uncomfortable exchange with anyone we don't know. She comes from tons of money and never had to work a day in her life, but chose to start up a small flower shop to do what she loves doing. I'm most worried about explaining everything to her, but I'll deal with that when I have to. Right now, it's all about fulfilling the rest of my father's wishes.

"This is going to be difficult, Uncle Ronny. I have a life back in Chappaquiddick. I have friends."

"I can't force you to do anything. Your legal name is Sawyer Duncan and if you'd like to keep it, that's up to you."

I never thought I'd be faced with this decision, and I shrug my shoulders. "I'm Noelle Durand. That's the name my parents gave me. So I want it back."

He nods and starts to open a folder in front of him. "We also have a lot of other paperwork to do, so if you're fine, I'd like to have you sign as much of this as possible today."

All of my father's assets are transferred into my name, including the two houses, all of his cars, and various bank and brokerage accounts. I have no idea how much everything's worth, and I don't care. I've been living off of the interest that my mother's estate is worth, my own fortune well over one hundred million dollars now.

"Is all of this necessary?" I ask. "Maybe we could just donate everything?"

"Your father was a tremendous philanthropist and has already designated a large portion of his estate to various charitable organizations."

"Okay."

After everything is signed, he sits back in his seat and furrows his eyebrows. "Your father has already been cremated," he states.

"What?" I had no idea what to expect when I came home. Was there going to be a memorial service? A funeral? Was I going to have to get up on a podium and say some final words about my father?

"Your father wanted everything done before you came home. He didn't want a large service, drawing attention to his death or to you. We'll have a small, private service, just for you, at the house. Time for you to say goodbye."

"You mean to say goodbye, *again*," I stress. "I said goodbye to him already, twelve years ago."

He nods reluctantly. "This time, it will be on your terms."

"Really? This doesn't feel like my terms at all. In fact, it feels like I have yet to make a decision throughout any of this," I snap, immediately regretting taking my anger out on him. "I'm sorry."

"You never need to apologize to me. Ever. Your father and I have put you through some trying things. We turned your life completely upside down. Not to mention what you had to put up with from *that woman*."

"What happens when she finds out I'm alive?" I ask.

"If she finds out, there's really nothing she can do. Trust me, we've taken precautions, and we know you're the least of her family's worries. Plus, she's serving a life sentence without the possibility of parole. The head of the family is also behind bars, while other key kingpins are dead. I don't believe you'll ever have anything to worry about. But just lay low, if that's okay. And please make sure your security is aware of everything."

What I really want to do is visit her in prison. Show her how strong I've become, physically and mentally. I've gone through so much to build up my self-esteem and realize that I never did anything wrong to provoke her prolonged abuse. I shouldered too much as a child and teen. I tried to keep my father safe, and it wasn't fair for me to have to do that. I've always regretted never speaking up and clueing my father into what was happening. So many things would be different today. But, I'm done blaming myself.

There's only one person to blame, and she's behind bars.

"I didn't realize my father owned another house," I admit, changing the subject.

"He bought a house in Point Pleasant about a year after you left."

"Why?"

"He wanted to spend as much time near where you last were. Since his boat was at the marina there, he was able to spend a lot of time there, alone. Tonya was already in prison when he purchased that house."

"Is there anything else I need to know?" I'm overwhelmed by the plethora of information I've been given in the past hour. I don't know if I can handle any more.

"Yes, as a matter of fact. You know your father's wishes were to be laid to rest where your mother is. His remains are at the funeral home, and I can pick them up tomorrow for you so you can spend some time with them before you begin your trip. Do you want to meet me at the house first thing in the morning? Father Baker can meet us there and can say a few prayers with you as well."

"I'd like that," I state. I know my dad respected Father Baker and regularly supported the church.

"It's getting late. You should get going so you can get a good night's sleep. Are you going back to the house tonight?"

Heath insisted that I stay at his place tonight and I think I may just do that. I don't want to go back to an empty house, especially alone.

"I'm staying with Heath."

My uncle knew how important it was for me to tell him everything.

"Please send him my regards. He's a good man, Noelle."

"I'm going to take off." I stand up and kiss my uncle on the cheek. "I'll see you in the morning."

As I drive back to Heath's house, I feel strange. On one hand, I'm sad that my father is gone. I've yet to properly mourn his death, but I said goodbye to him so many years ago, and I don't feel like saying goodbye is going to be the same.

I also feel strangely invigorated.

I'm in the process of reclaiming my life. A life that was, for so long, filled with fear.

I don't know what the coming days and weeks are going to bring, but if they can bring me closer to my parents, then the long trip is going to be worth it.

When he has forgotten I will find a way to rescue you.

CHAPTER 20

Heath
Present

I'M LYING IN BED, staring up at my ceiling, the moonlight shining through my window. I've been wide awake for hours, unable to sleep, my mind racing. Noelle's return is nothing short of miraculous–and confusing. I can't believe she's alive after all she's been through. I'm angry that I wasn't in on the 'secret' of her disappearance, but given who my father is, I can understand their rationale for keeping me in the dark. I'm sure many laws were broken or overlooked while making sure she was able to hide without being found. They were able to keep her safe, so I guess that's what's most important.

But I still missed out on over a decade of knowing her. Who is she now? What does she like? Is she in love with someone else?

So many questions without answers swirl in my head, and I have no chance of falling back to sleep tonight. Tomorrow is going to be another long day.

I gave Noelle keys to my house and told her to come back whenever she was done with her uncle. I heard her come in a little after midnight, but I didn't get up to greet her. We have to get an early start tomorrow morning, so I figured it would be best to stay right here. We'll have days to talk. Days to catch up. Days to get to know each other all over again.

But that was an hour ago, and I'm still lying here wide awake. Noelle's in the guest room across the hall, and it feels so strange knowing she's in my house, alive, sleeping in a separate room from me. We would spend almost every night together when we were younger. I used to sit outside her window as we talked about almost everything. The Wiffle ball game we played earlier that day, our plans for college, our mutual love of fireflies and everything they symbolize.

In those days, I yearned to take away the pain and darkness that surrounded her life. She hid so much behind her smile, always seeming to be on guard, especially around Tonya.

The hallway outside my room is silent, so I decide to run downstairs to get a glass of milk. Maybe that will help me fall asleep.

I quietly open my door and turn right to take the back set of stairs, avoiding walking past Noelle's room. Once downstairs, I walk through the dark kitchen and open the refrigerator, the milk nestled on the shelf in the door. Without thinking, I remove the cap, putting the gallon carton to my lips, and begin to chug. The cold milk quenching a thirst and will hopefully aid my sleep.

"Do you always drink your milk like that?" Noelle's voice startles me, and I practically choke on a mouthful. She's sitting in the den, legs curled up to her chest.

I put the container away and close the door, wiping milk off of my bare chest with my hand. That's when I realize I'm only in my boxer briefs and nothing else.

Her eyes quickly scan my body, then she smiles and says awkwardly, "I guess milk does a body good."

I laugh out loud while looking around for a towel, or something, to help clean the rest of the milk off of me.

"Why are you still up?" I ask, uncomfortably.

"I could ask you the same question."

"I heard you come back well over an hour ago, I figured you would be asleep by now."

She shakes her head and stands up, walking toward me. "Too much going through my mind. It was an overwhelming day."

"Do you want to tell me what happened?" I don't mean to pry, but if she's awake, I might as well try.

"I'll spare you all of the sordid details, but I'm now the proud owner of two more houses, six cars, and a boatload of cash."

"You can't be surprised by all of that, right?" I ask. Her father was a successful businessman, and I know their house next door to my parents' is worth at least four or five million. Maybe even more.

"None of that matters to me though," she admits, her face sad. "I would give it all back–everything–to have my father here again."

I nod in understanding.

"So, what's the plan?" I ask. We haven't yet discussed the long drive ahead of us.

"I figured we could map out our route from the road."

I've been on tour buses countless times and have made cross country trips more than once. But I've never been the driver, and I've never had to figure out the best routes.

"Wing it?"

She smiles. "GPS will guide us."

"Glad to see you're prepared," I say sarcastically.

Her smile falters as she lowers her eyes to the floor. "I haven't been prepared for any of this to happen. I honestly thought the day I was able to come home, I'd be able to hug my father. Instead, I'll be holding his urn."

I take a step toward her, unsure of what to do. "I'm sorry."

She covers her face with her hands. "None of this makes sense," she cries. "I can't even believe that I'm even here."

I close the distance between us and pull her against my chest, her sobs muffled. I haven't held her in years and having her in my arms feels like I'm re-learning how her body feels against mine. It feels right–but not yet comfortable.

"I'm glad you are," I say, kissing the top of her head.

"You smell like milk," she giggles into my chest, but doesn't pull away. Instead, she wraps her arms tighter around me. "I've dreamed of this moment for so long, Heath. I've wanted to be back in your arms for years. I just wish–"

"You wish what?"

She tilts her head to look up at me. "I wish it wasn't like this."

She's reading my mind. It's been so strange the past two days. But now is not the time to talk about why we're here and all of the crazy things that kept us apart.

"We need to get some sleep," I urge, letting go of her. "We have a very long couple of days ahead of us. And I still need to pack."

"I'm so sorry I'm dragging you into this–"

"Stop," I demand, placing my finger to her lips. "I'm here for you, no matter what. I'm glad you came to me."

She turns and I follow her up the stairs. She walks into the guest room and smiles before she closes the door. It's so weird having her in my house, under my roof, without being close to her. Without holding her next to me.

I slip into my own bed, kicking my legs out under the covers. I'm already restless, trying to imagine what the next few weeks are going to be like. Is it going to be a struggle to get to know each other all over again? Will we even like each other when all of this is over?

There's a light knock on my door, and then it opens. Noelle's silhouette comes into my view, her hair cascading down past her shoulders. A long t-shirt coming to just above her knees. "Heath?" she asks softly.

"Is everything okay?" I ask, leaning up on my elbows.

"Are you seeing someone? I mean–is there anyone in your life right now?" She seems nervous, almost afraid of my answer.

I've been waiting for this question since I first heard her voice. Waiting to tell her that the only person I've ever thought about was her. I've been in love with her for years, unable to let her go. Unable to move forward and connect with anyone else.

"No," I respond. "There's no one."

Haley was a distraction. And for a while, being with her was easy. I can't imagine what's going to go through her mind when she finds out Noelle is alive. Things are going to get very complicated and confusing, very quickly.

"Thanks," she says, turning to leave. "Sorry to bother you."

She shuts my door, and my room is once again dark. I wanted to stop her from leaving, but I don't think either of us is ready for that. We have so much more learning to do. So much more growing to do before we can reconnect on any other level.

Too much time separates us from the people we were, the *teenagers* we were, twelve years ago.

We need to find a way to bridge that time.

We need fireflies and fairies.

CHAPTER 21

Noelle
Present

AUGUST 20: I'VE BEEN AWAKE for hours, staring at her sleeping, perfectly content. Mel's the most beautiful woman I've ever laid eyes on. Her perfection goes beyond her looks. Her heart is warm, kind, and selfless. There isn't another person in this world I could imagine spending the rest of my life with. I hope God gives us time. So much time we won't know what to do with ourselves. I also hope he gives us children. Tons of them.

We arrived in Columbus, Ohio, late last night. It's the first leg of our trip across the country. Because of how things have been busy with my company and Melanie's various philanthropic endeavors, we delayed our honeymoon for almost six months. Now it's just the two of us, our convertible, and the open road. We're planning our trip city by city, not sure of where we're going next. And I couldn't imagine anything more perfect. As long as we're together.

Today, we're going to the Columbus Zoo—a destination she's wanted to visit since she was a little girl. I'm looking forward to watching her explore and have fun. I also hope we can bring our children here someday.

I don't want to wake her up, though, she looks so peaceful.

I close my father's journal, slipping it into my backpack. This was in the satchel that my uncle gave me the day I disappeared. I haven't been able to bring myself to start reading it until recently. I'm only a few entries into it, but the irony doesn't escape me.

I'm in the same city that he and my mother began their honeymoon. So close to them, but light years away.

"Are you okay?" Heath's voice pulls me from my trance.

"Yeah," I admit. "Want to go to the zoo?"

He laughs and says, "Of course. Lead the way."

We got here late yesterday after driving for just about eight hours. We didn't get as early of a start as we wanted to in the morning since we were both up so late the night before. We didn't even eat dinner; we were both exhausted. He had a suite booked for us and we both slept soundly in our own rooms.

We're trying to figure out the landscape between us. We're both still strangers, time molding who we are today. I hope when all of this is over and I've laid my father to rest, we can find a way to reconnect. Maybe find a way back to each other.

I take out my phone and pull up the page for the Columbus Zoo. "It's actually not that far from where we are now. Do you want to drive or take a cab?" I ask.

"Oh, you're serious," he says. "I thought you were joking."

"You don't want to go?" I ask, slightly deflated.

"Yes, let's go. But I seriously thought you were kidding. It's all good." He places his hand on my lower back and gently pushes me toward the door of our room. "Let's take a cab. I don't think I'm up for driving just yet. We'll save that for tomorrow."

We ride the elevator to the first floor in silence. Heath reaches the bell station before me, while I grab city guides and brochures from the concierge. He already has a taxi waiting for us by the time I walk outside.

Once inside the cab, I start scrolling through the various attractions at the zoo. "What made you want to go to the zoo?" Heath asks.

I look up, placing my hand on my backpack. "My parents came here. A long time ago. I guess I just wanted to experience something they did together."

His eyes light up, a smile spreading across his face. "I'm glad we stopped here then." He looks out the window and then states, "It's kind of like a living memorial to both of them."

"Yes," I admit. I only wish my mother could have lived long enough to fulfill my father's wish to come here with me. I have a feeling my heart is going to break many times today. Many times during the course of this trip.

"Columbus Zoo!" the taxi driver exclaims. Heath pays for the fare, and we slide out of the back of the car.

"Thank you," I say as he drives away.

We make it into the zoo and take a look at the map. "Where do you want to go first?" Heath asks.

"Let's head over to the right to see the animals of North America and Asia."

We take our time exploring the various habitats of some of the most beautiful animals in the world. There are many families with small children running around enjoying themselves. I'm envious of the innocence that these little kids have, some seeing these animals for the very first time.

"I wish I could have come here with my parents," I admit.

Heath throws his arm over my shoulder. "My parents had a membership to the Philadelphia Zoo, but I think I only went once or twice when I was a kid. I barely remember it." He's pensive, almost sad that his memories have faded.

We make our way to the back of this section of the park where the African animals are showcased. A pride of lions lay, basking in the hot sun. "They're beautiful," I state as I watch one of the females as she cleans herself and the large male next to her.

Did my parents stand here and do the same thing? Are these lions the offspring of the ones that they saw so many years ago? Maybe these large, adult lions were cubs back then. Standing here triggers something that I saw earlier when I was looking through my father's journal. I open my backpack to remove it, opening it carefully.

There's a picture nestled behind the page that I read earlier this morning.

"What's that?" Heath asks as I hold the photo up in front of us.

"It's my mother," I say, tears filling my eyes. She's beautiful. Wearing a floral sundress and a floppy hat on her head. She's shielding her eyes from the sun, the lions' den behind her in the distance. The animals are blurry, but the shot is gorgeous.

"She's standing right where we are now," Heath observes.

So much life was ahead of her. So much happiness. All of which was robbed from her too young.

"I want to know everything about her. So many things I would love to ask her."

"Tell me one thing you want to know," Heath says.

My mind races with the unexpected request. "I'd ask her what drew her to my father the first time she met him."

Heath nods his head. "Your father was a distinguished man," he states. "He was always focused on doing what was best for your family. Providing for you to keep you comfortable. I bet she saw this in him and realized what her future may be like."

I realize he's worded his response carefully. He mentions nothing about keeping us 'safe.' My father changed after my mother died, the man that she saw wasn't the man that I grew to know. Grew to trust.

"I want to know all about the life they had together before me. Before she died. When my father was happy and not afraid of what Tonya and her family could do to us."

"I wish I had a time machine," he says.

"So do I."

I'M SHOWERED AND READY for dinner just an hour after getting back to our hotel. Our day at the zoo was fun, but super hot. There's nothing like being at a zoo in the middle of August, with all of the various smells from the animals coating you along with your sweat.

Heath and I had a great time. Although the reason for our being there hung over our heads, we didn't let it get us down. I found several more Columbus Zoo pictures of my mother and my parents in my father's journal. Heath even had me recreate one of them while I posed in front of the white-handed gibbons' cage, with the beautiful animals swinging on vines behind me. Of course, I wasn't wearing a sundress or a floppy hat, but Heath captured the moment spectacularly.

I scroll through my phone, smiling at the various pictures we took throughout the day. One selfie in particular grabs me. Heath is behind me, his cheeks blown out like the puffer fish we'd just seen. His eyes are closed, and I'm mid-laugh. I chuckle as I make the photo my background wallpaper on my phone.

"What's so funny?" Heath asks, emerging from his room, freshly showered.

"This." I turn my phone around so he can see the picture.

"I didn't think you'd keep that one!" He laughs and swipes the phone from my hand.

"Don't delete it!" I yell. "It's my favorite!"

He thumbs through several more photos, and his expression changes.

"Who's this?" he asks, turning my phone around so I can see it.

It's a picture of me, Dahlia, and Blake, Dahlia's twin brother. Blake is a good friend, but has also been interested in me, romantically, for years.

"Friends from ho– I mean Chappy," I say. I stop myself from calling Chappaquiddick my home, although that's what it's been for the past twelve years.

"I'll ask you the same question you asked me the other night. Is there someone else in your life? Someone you're in a relationship with?"

In the picture, Blake is kissing my cheek while Dahlia is photobombing us from behind. Blake and I have hooked up a couple of times, but nothing serious. He's been persistent more recently, but I've been able to keep him at arm's length–except for this picture.

"There's no one."

"It's weird seeing you with people I don't know. You look really happy in this picture," he notes. His eyes fall to my phone as he hands it back to me.

"I have a happy life there. I've gotten comfortable and feel safe. It's a quiet town, and people have generally let me stay to myself. But, yes, I've found happiness there." It's so strange seeing Heath look through a window into my current life. A life I've managed to make happy and comfortable without him. I can tell it pains him to witness it.

"I'm glad you've been able to find this place," he says. "What do you do, if you don't mind me asking?"

"You mean for work? Like a job?"

He nods his head.

"Well, it's nothing as glamorous as you, Mr. Rock Star." We have yet to talk about his career and how wildly successful he is. I was actually surprised that no one at the zoo today recognized him for who he is–the lead singer of one of the biggest rock bands in the country. "We need to talk about Epic Fail," I demand.

He smiles. "This isn't about me. I want to know about you."

"I don't work. I mean, not really. Dahlia owns a small flower shop that she runs on her own. I help her out a few times a week, but I don't take a paycheck from her. It's really just for fun."

"So you lounge on the beach all day?" he jokes.

"Sometimes," I smile. "I don't have to work. When I left, my father made my trust fund available that was from my mother. I'm very comfortable." I'm embarrassed talking about my money and the fact that I don't contribute to society in any way. Although I do enjoy reading and writing, and of course, helping out at the flower shop.

"That's nice," he states. "I'm glad you have your friends–and the beach."

"I volunteer quite a bit," I admit. "But not as much as I'd like. It requires trips to the mainland, which I tend to avoid."

"What's 'Chappy' like?" he asks, using air quotes.

"It's quiet and quaint. Many of the people who live there have owned houses or property for a long time. Lots of old money. It's a tight-knit community, but people still keep to themselves, mostly."

"Was it hard to assimilate?" he asks.

"Not really. I'm actually surprised that I was able to move in, virtually unnoticed for a while. I bought a small house on a large piece of waterfront property. I didn't meet any neighbors for months. One of them admitted that they thought the house had been abandoned. A lot of assumptions were made about me, but the story that they all believe is I moved there from the city, inheriting money from my family. They think I'm an artist and all I do is paint portraits of the ocean."

"Really?" He laughs. "I've seen your drawings. You? An artist?"

I swat at him, smacking the side of his arm. "Be nice!"

"You have a lot of people fooled, apparently," he says, still laughing.

"The house that I bought came fully furnished. I found two dozen paintings in the attic, and I may have told a few white lies to people who've come to my house." I grin widely. The paintings, I found out, belonged to the woman who owned the house. She passed away a few months before I moved there and her hobby had been painting the landscape around her house. I reached out to her daughter, who didn't want the paintings. She said they were mine to keep or do whatever I wanted with.

"So, what are we going to do for dinner?" Heath asks, looking at his watch. "And more importantly, what time do you want to get on the road tomorrow?"

I shrug my shoulders. "I'm up for anything."

"Why don't you look in your father's journal to see if there's someplace he and your mother may have eaten?"

My heart flutters in my chest, his thoughtfulness overwhelms me. "That's an incredible idea!"

He hands me my backpack, and I pull out the journal, flipping to the pages detailing the time that he and my mother were here in Columbus.

"Lindey's!" I exclaim. "His notes say it's in German Village. They ate on the patio."

He grabs my hand, pulling me to my feet. Our noses practically touch before he backs away. "It's pretty hot outside, but I'll brave dinner on the patio with you." He smiles and doesn't let go of my hand as he guides me toward the door.

I'm overcome with so many emotions. Sadness and excitement wrestle inside my chest. On one hand, taking this trip down memory lane, eavesdropping on my parents' honeymoon, is so upsetting. I wish things were different. I wish they were alive, personally walking me through their adventures. But I'm here, experiencing these things with Heath. The only other person on earth that I would ever want with me on a trip like this.

I'm excited to live their lives through my father's words.

I squeeze Heath's hand as we descend in the elevator. The upcoming days are going to be some of the most difficult and exciting, and I get to share that with him.

Once again, Heath's giving me back my past, my innocence. All while we make new memories. *Together.*

When all is forgotten you find new ways to rescue me.

CHAPTER 22

Heath

Present

"HEATH, WAKE UP," Noelle's soft voice sounds like it's a million miles away. "We're here."

My eyes pop open, and I'm staring at the roof of my SUV.

"How long was I asleep?" I ask, groggily, shifting my seat back into a sitting position. We left Columbus first thing this morning, and I drove the first few hours. But my eyes became bouncy and Noelle offered to drive the rest of the way. I don't even remember passing out.

"About two hours," she replies. "And you were snoring so loud I had to turn up the music. I can't believe you slept through the Foo Fighters blasting throughout the car."

"I can't believe I slept through that either. I must have been totally out of it."

"Yup. And you were right, we made it in just under seven hours," she notes as she turns off the ignition and hands me my keys.

We're in St. Louis, Missouri. The next stop on her parents' cross-country trip.

Last night when we got back from dinner, I suggested we look through the journal so we could get ideas on where we should stop along the way. I want her to experience as much of her parents' trip as she can, at least until we reach the Grand Canyon.

A valet knocks on the driver's window, and I hand the keys back to Noelle. "They'll take care of the car." I chuckle as I open the passenger side door. I honestly don't think I've ever ridden shotgun in my own car before and it feels weird exiting from this side.

As soon as my feet hit the ground, several flashes go off.

Fuck.

"Heath! What are you doing in St. Louis?"

"Is it true Epic Fail is on a break?"

"Are you going solo?"

Shouts from the crowd of paparazzi gathered in front of the hotel quickly snap me out of my post-sleep fog. I raise my hand in the air, trying to block their photographs, but it's no use.

"Who's the girl with you?" one of them shouts as Noelle rushes around the car, darting into the hotel.

"Just a friend," I state and walk past them, shoving my hands into my pockets.

Thankfully, hotel security blocks them from following me in.

How the hell did they even find me?

"I'm sorry, Mr. Strickland. We tried to divert them, but once someone got wind that you were staying here, more and more paparazzi started showing up," the hotel manager apologizes, stepping out from behind the front desk and walks toward me.

"I certainly didn't publicize that I was coming here, so I have no idea how on earth they would even know. You need to check into your staff, Mr. Doyle," I state, looking at his name tag. "Someone ran their mouth, and I'm willing to bet that someone is here."

I look around, Noelle is nowhere in sight.

"Your travel companion has already been shown to your room," Mr. Doyle states. "Again, I'm so sorry for this experience. Please let us make it up to you."

"Just tell me where I'm going," I demand, annoyed. I realize it's probably not his fault, but a crowd is now gathering in the hotel lobby, and I need to get out of here.

"The Presidential Suite. This key will give you access to the floor." He hands me a key card, and I walk to the elevators.

When the elevator opens on the top floor, I walk down the end of the hall where our room is.

"Noelle?" I say as I enter. "Are you here?"

She comes out from one of the bedrooms, wide-eyed. "Sorry, they rushed me up here as soon as I got inside."

"It's okay. I'm really sorry you had to deal with all of that downstairs."

"How did they know you were coming here?"

"Probably some staffer started running their mouth. Although, I rarely travel under my real name, so Stuart must have messed up when he booked this hotel for me."

"You keep talking about Stuart," she notes. "Who is he?"

"He's our manager. Our right-hand-man. He basically handles everything for us."

"Oh," she says, nodding her head.

"Seriously, I'm really sorry. None of this should have happened."

"It's okay. I suppose you're already used to it. But, I'm not comfortable with all of the pictures."

I tense up, clenching my fists. I didn't even think about the ramifications of her being publicly photographed with me or anyone else for that matter. Will this put her in danger? Will Tonya's family come looking for her now that her picture is going to be all over the place?

"Shit. Let me make a few phone calls," I mutter, fumbling for my phone.

"No. Don't worry about it. Nobody knows who I am, remember? Let's keep it that way."

She's right, to a certain extent. But I don't want people prying and trying to dig too deep.

I'll give Stuart a call later or send him a text. I'd like him to try to do some damage control and maybe buy off a couple of the photographers, if he can. I also want him to make sure he books me under another name for our next stop.

"Why don't we book the hotel rooms under my name?" Noelle suggests.

"What? No way. We don't want to draw any attention to you. You're a ghost, remember?"

"I mean my legal name. Sawyer Duncan."

"Sawyer Duncan?" I ask, confused.

"Yes, it's the name I've been living under since I left. It's my mother's name, Melanie Sawyer Duncan."

"It's a beautiful name. But it's not you," I state. "I'm sorry, but I'm being honest."

"I know. It's been weird living with her name. It's what my friends call me. They don't know my real name." She looks sad and guilty at the same time.

"Regardless, we aren't using any of your names. We'll use my fake name from now on."

Her eyes light up, a smile playing across her lips. "Which is?"

"If I tell you, I'd have to kill you," I joke and immediately regret choosing those words.

Thankfully, she laughs it off. "I can keep a secret."

"Dominic Hayes." Stuart chooses each of our names because he has some sort of funny fascination with pseudonyms.

"That sounds like a perfectly normal name," she giggles.

"Exactly why I use it as much as I can, especially when I travel."

"We'll keep that in mind when we make it to the next city," she states as she sits on the large couch in the living area.

"Which is?" We hadn't read that far into her father's journal, and I'm curious where the next stop should be.

She finds it in her backpack and fans through the pages. "Tulsa, Oklahoma."

"That's a great city. I know a few places we could go," I say, remembering the time we stopped there during our last tour. Dax and I had a great steak dinner at this place in the heart of the city. "But first, we need to figure out what we're doing here. Although, now that my cover is blown, it's going to be a little difficult moving around."

She flips back a few pages and removes a picture from the book.

"What's that?" I ask.

"It's my parents, standing under the Arch together."

I walk over to the couch and sit next to her. She hands me the picture and the first thing that strikes me is how purely happy they look. Not a concern or worry in either of their eyes–their entire lives ahead of them. I've never seen this look in Noelle's eyes, and I yearn for it. She never looked this happy to me. Irrational anger bubbles up inside of me toward her father. He should have known the pain that she was experiencing when she was younger. He should have done something to protect her. To remove her from the situation that was poisoning her life.

"What's the matter?" she asks, sensing my change.

"Nothing," I shrug it off. I can't let her know how angry I still am at her father. *Her dead father.*

"Are you sure?"

"I want to bring you there so you can experience the same thing they did, but we're going to have to wait to sneak out much later. I don't want us to be followed."

"Okay," she agrees.

"We should order dinner in, if that's okay?" I feel terrible that we can't venture out much more, but I think it's best at this point.

"Perfect. I want to relax anyway."

We place a room service order and she sits quietly, reading the journal.

"What did he say about St. Louis?" I ask.

She looks up at me with a questioning look in her eyes. "You want me to read it to you?"

"I'd love that," I say, settling into the couch next to her.

She flips back a few pages and begins.

"August 22: St. Louis is nothing like I imagined. There's so much remarkable culture here, hidden throughout the city. After we visited the Arch today, Mel and I found an incredible place, right on Broadway. A small club where local musicians played the blues for hours and hours. At one point, Melanie actually got up on stage and sang a few verses with a band. It was marvelous to watch. Electrifying. She lit up the room, her smile went on for days. And her voice! It was angelic. She sounded like she'd been rehearsing with them for decades, fitting right in. When she finished the song, she practically floated back to our table, her brow a little sweaty. She said she was 'glistening' from all of the fun she was having. And she couldn't have been more beautiful if she tried. We stayed there until well after 3AM. We danced for hours and didn't want to leave. Tonight I fell more in love with Melanie, which I didn't think was even possible."

Tears fill her eyes and she sighs. "Wow," she says.

"Yeah," I reply. It's odd getting this glimpse into her parents' lives. Living through his words.

"It's the little things about her that he loved and was surprised about. He never told me she was a singer."

"No? I would think he would after witnessing her singing her heart out here in St. Louis."

"He did tell me she used to sing me to sleep every night when I was an infant. I guess for as long as she was alive." Her head drops, and I hear her inhale deeply.

"I'm sorry," I state, for what seems like the thousandth time.

"I'm enjoying this. I really am. I just wish I could have learned about these things in a different way."

I know what she means. If only they were here.

"I know," I say. "But to experience everything this way is so special. There's so much meaning here." I tap the journal and then run my hand over the top of her head, smoothing out her hair. Touching her feels so natural. So normal. But I can't help but feel that we're still strangers.

"Thank you," she murmurs, leaning her head back into my hand and settling against me.

There's a knock on the door and a muffled voice, "Room Service!"

I reluctantly remove my arm from Noelle and get up to answer the door. Our dinner is quickly set at the table in the dining area, and the attendant disappears.

"It smells good," Noelle says, sitting down.

Our plates are uncovered, revealing burgers and French fries.

"I figured we'd have bar food, since we're missing the bar scene tonight. I'm always up for a good burger, you?"

Her eyes widen, and her face falls. "I'm a vegetarian now," she states.

Shit.

"I'm sorry. I should have asked what you wanted and not just assumed." I feel like an asshole. She's a vegetarian? Since when?

She suddenly bursts out laughing, picking up the large, juicy burger on her plate. "Kidding!" she jokes and takes a huge bite.

"Not funny." I shake my head. "You're gone for over a decade and suddenly you're a vegetarian? Not funny at all."

"This is delicious," she says, trying to make up for her little white lie.

The phone rings from the table in the living room. "Who could that be?" Noelle asks, curious.

I jump up, shrugging my shoulders. I answer. "Hello?"

"Mr. Strickland, it's Marty Doyle, the hotel manager. How are you tonight?"

"Good," I answer, hesitantly.

"We are truly sorry for the mishap when you arrived today. We promise to make it up to you. Is there anything we can do?"

I think for a minute and then say, "As a matter of fact, yes. We'd like a private car, preferably leaving undetected, to take us to the Arch tonight. Late."

"We can absolutely do that. Come down to the garage tonight, basement level. We'll have a car waiting and take you wherever you want to go."

"Great. We'll be there at midnight," I say and hang up.

I make my way back to the table and sit down.

"What was that about?" Noelle asks, curious.

"We're going to the Arch tonight. And anyplace else you want to go."

Her smile is huge. "Really?"

"It's all taken care of. We should be able to get out of here without a problem."

She drops what's left of her burger on her plate and claps her hands in front of her. "Yes!"

Seeing her so excited and happy fuels my motivation. I'm determined to make this trip positive and fun.

I need to do this for her.

For us.

IT'S JUST AFTER MIDNIGHT and Noelle is standing under the Arch, her hands stretched out above her head as if she's trying to hold it up from the ground. "It's amazing!" she exclaims, twirling around, her smile huge. I snap a picture of her with my phone when she's not looking. I'm trying to capture these moments for her, just like her father did of himself and her mother so many years ago.

"What are you doing?" she asks as she whips around just after I take the picture.

"Capturing a spectacular moment."

Her smile radiates from her, and she twirls once again under the Arch. "Get in the picture with me!" she calls out, gesturing for me to join her. "Let's take a selfie!"

I walk over to her and she stands in front of me, her back to my chest. "Here, take my phone. Your arms are longer." I shove my phone into my pocket and grab hers. My arms outstretched on either side of her shoulders. I'm a bit taller than her, so I need to bend down so our heads are close together and in the frame. I angle the phone so the Arch is clearly seen behind us and take the picture.

"I wasn't ready!" she exclaims and stays between my arms. "Do it again."

We settle on a shot she's comfortable with and I take a couple of pictures, so she'll have at least one that she likes. Before I step away, I quickly kiss her cheek.

"What was that for?" she asks, turning to face me.

"Do I need a reason?" I hope I didn't step out of bounds by kissing her, but it was a friendly gesture, nothing more. *Or was it?*

She starts giggling. "Oh my God, do you remember the first time we kissed?" She covers her mouth with her hand and tries to control her laughter. She purses her lips and puffs out her cheeks, just like I remember us doing so long ago. It was our "sticky kiss."

I nod my head, smiling. "How could I forget?"

"What did we think we were doing? Our lips were touching, but we didn't even move–like our lips were stuck together!" Her laughter is contagious, and I join her. This feels so good.

"I was apparently more experienced than you," I admit sarcastically.

"If kissing like a puffer fish is experienced!" She continues laughing and falls onto a nearby bench, kicking her legs out in front of her. Her expression changes, her face relaxing a bit. "I miss those days so much."

I'm surprised by this, knowing a trip back in time would be a trip back into the house where she was mercilessly abused by Tonya. "Really?"

She nods her head. "I sometimes wish I could go back and change things. Show more strength when I was younger, so I didn't seem like an easy target for *her*."

I sit next to her and place my hand on her knee. "I would hate for you to go back in time and experience all of that all over again."

We sit silently for several moments when she leans against me, her arm outstretched again with her phone. "Let's take one more selfie."

We lean against each other, our cheeks touching. Just before she snaps the picture, she turns and places her lips on my face, puffing out her cheeks. I laugh as the moment is captured on her phone.

She laughs again, trying to move past the moment remembering her abuse. Then she stretches. "We should get back to the hotel," she yawns.

"Are you sure? We're incognito now, we can go anywhere we want." I look at my watch and it's after one in the morning.

"Tulsa is about a seven-hour drive. If we get to bed soon, we can get a much earlier start."

"I suppose," I reply. "Or we can find that blues bar on Broadway and catch some tunes."

Her eyes light up with my suggestion, and she jumps to her feet. "Okay, maybe just for a little while." She reaches her hand out and pulls me off of the bench.

"Are you sure you're up for it?" I ask.

"Yes! Let's do it!"

We find our driver who's been parked on the main road for over an hour. The hotel loaned him to us for the night so we should take advantage of the ride while we can.

Seeing Noelle so happy and free right now is perfect.

I don't want this night to end.

THE BAR IS DARK and mostly empty. Noelle and I are able to walk right in and grab a small table in front of the makeshift stage. A waitress immediately shows up, placing cocktail napkins on the table in front of us.

"What can I get you?" she asks.

I turn and look at the bar to see what taps I recognize while Noelle looks over the drink menu.

"I'll have a Cosmo," she states.

"Eastside Double IPA for me."

The waitress leaves and Noelle's eyes are wide. "I can't believe this is the place where my mother sang."

That's the beauty of places like this. They're so unassuming but filled with character. "Right there on that stage," I respond.

Our drinks are placed in front of us and Noelle quickly reaches for hers, carefully lifting it into the air. "Kind of hard to toast with, but thank you for taking this trip with me. You have no idea how much this means. Cheers." I raise my pint and lightly tap the rim of her martini glass. She takes a sip from the top and places it back down on the table. "Wow, that's strong!"

I smile and place my hand over hers. "I would do anything for you, Noelle. This trip is a gift–for both of us."

She briefly looks down and then back up to me again. "I don't know what to say." Her eyes are glassy, and her lips quiver for just a moment. "When I called you, I didn't know what to expect. I prepared myself for the worst, readying myself for anger and denial. The fact that you're here with me is nothing short of a miracle. I promise I'll make it up to you someday, Heath. As long as you'll let me."

"You don't have to make anything up to me. You being here, alive, is all I need." I squeeze her hand tightly, never wanting to let go.

The band walks past us and onto the stage, their instruments already set up. The singer speaks softly into the microphone and says, "Hey. We're going to play some blues." And with that, the most incredible music begins to fill our ears, invade our senses. The bass is deep, so deep you can feel it in your veins. The singer's voice is raspy but perfectly in tune. Noelle and I sit together, fully absorbing this experience. Several times during their set, they invite random bar patrons on stage to join them.

"It must be a tradition," Noelle comments, and I nod my head. She's watching the band intently, almost as if she's imagining them in a different time. I wonder if she's picturing her mother on that very stage, captivating the audience while capturing her father's heart.

Two more drinks are placed in front of us and Noelle's eyes widen. "I don't think I can drink this one," she laughs. "Look at me, my cheeks are red, aren't they?"

I lean closer to her to get a better look and softly touch one of her cheeks. It's slightly warm to the touch, almost as if she has a fever. "You're glowing," I note. "And warm."

"I'm a one martini kind of girl. Anything more and I'll be face first on this table." She pushes the drink away from her and leans back in her chair. "I need some water," she declares, fanning herself.

I signal for the waitress, who quickly returns with two large glasses of ice water. "Thank you!" she shouts as the music gets louder.

Time flies by and soon the house lights come up, the band begins packing up their equipment. Noelle is squinting, trying to adjust to the bright lights. "What time is it?"

I glance down at my watch. "Three-thirty." It doesn't feel as late as it is.

The guitarist from the band approaches our table slowly, and I look up.

"Dude. I can't believe you're here. I hope you enjoyed the set," he says, almost stammering.

I reach out my hand to shake his. "You guys were tight."

Noelle chimes in, "Oh my God. You were seriously amazing. Do you have an album out or anything?"

"Nah. We do this for fun, mostly."

He's young, probably in his early twenties, but his abilities are decades beyond his age. "You have some incredibly raw talent. It could take you places," I state, and his eyes light up.

"Thanks, Heath–uh–Mr. Strickland–"

I laugh and shake my head. "You can call me Heath, dude."

He pulls a yellow Post-It note from his pocket and puts it in front of me. "Can you sign this?" he asks nervously.

I look down and see the set list from tonight scrawled in pencil along with the date at the top.

"Sure," I say. "But I don't have anything to write with."

"Oh shit. Hold on!" He turns and hops back up on the stage, opening his gig bag. He returns with a pencil and hands it to me nervously.

I look down and find a small spot to sign my name. After I do, he takes out his phone. "Will you take a picture with me?" he asks, and I stand up.

"Sure."

He hands Noelle his phone, and we take several pictures together.

"Thank you. That was so cool," he says, backing away. "I won't take any more of your time."

After he leaves, I drape my arm over Noelle's shoulder and guide us to the front door. There's barely anyone left in the place, the bartenders vigorously working to clean up so they can leave.

Our driver is parked out front and when he sees us, he rushes to open the back door for us. "Have a good night?" he asks.

"Amazing," I reply, sliding in after Noelle.

She relaxes against my side, resting her head on my shoulder. "Do you ever get used to it all?" she asks.

"Get used to what?"

"Recognition?"

"I'll never get used to it. It's still so surreal to me that I'm even doing what I'm doing. I don't know how I wound up here."

"How did you?" she asks, curious. "What did you go to school for?"

I tense when she asks me this question. Leaving for college was one of the worst experiences of my life, knowing I was going to Boston alone, without her. I muddled my way through two years before I called it quits. Something I'm not proud of and rarely admit to anyone. For years, I took odd jobs, but mostly staying close to home with an ever watchful eye on Noelle's house. Hoping someday she'd return.

"I declared my major at the end of freshman year. I thought I'd follow in my father's footsteps and practice law. That didn't work out so well for me," I admit, slightly embarrassed.

"Oh," she says. "I'm glad you went though." I can tell she's aware of the awkwardness that hangs in the air between us.

"It didn't feel right going to Boston without you."

She looks up at me with a sad look on her face. "I'm really sorry. I dreamed about what it would have been like to go away with you. I would have been free. And we would have been together."

Her words stab me in the heart, the old pain resurfacing. We missed out on so many years together, and it's hard to digest.

"You were free, in a way," I respond. "You *are* free." I correct myself and tighten my grip on her shoulder, pulling her closer against my side. "Let's not think about what never was."

I feel her nod against me, and her entire body relaxes.

As we drive back to the hotel, I can't help but wonder if things were different.

What if she never disappeared?

What if we actually *were* something?

CHAPTER 23

Noelle
Present

I'M RUNNING THROUGH the streets, chasing something—someone. "Wait!" I call out. "Stop! Please!" The figure turns and disappears around the corner. My feet feel like they're barely moving, yet the buildings seem like they're moving at one-hundred miles an hour in my peripheral vision. I get to the corner and turn, stopping to try to find who I've been chasing. The streets are completely empty, and I begin to cry, my body shaking with sobs, tears forming puddles at my feet.

That's when I hear it. The voice. A beautiful, powerful voice coming from a building at the end of the street. I wipe my face and start running toward it, but it only gets farther away. It's like I'm running on a treadmill, going backward. "No!" I yell and pump my arms harder, trying to propel myself toward the sound of the voice.

I grab onto what looks like a tow rope and suddenly I'm climbing up the side of a building, like Spider-Man, or something like that. I look down and see I'm hundreds of feet in the air, clouds begin to cover the street that I was standing on just a few moments ago. My arms burn as I try to pull myself higher, toward an open window. The voice continues to sing, but the sound is muffled, desperate.

"Hold on!" I yell. "I'm coming!"

Hand-over-hand, I pull myself until my arms feel like jelly. The windowsill is within reach. Once I reach it, I drape my leg over it, propelling myself through the window, falling onto the floor. The room smells musty, dust all over the floor. I look up and see the figure run out of the room. "Wait!" I call out, but watch as it disappears down a long hall.

I hop to my feet and chase again, this time, I'm faster, with almost superhuman speed. The voice is once again getting louder, completely filling my senses. It's beautiful and fueling my chase. I'm almost there. I turn another corner and light suddenly blinds me. Beautiful, vibrant, colorful lights. They're reflecting all around me like a kaleidoscope. That's when I notice thousands, no millions, of light catchers suspended in the air all around me. Beautiful glass reflecting the brightest light I've ever seen.

And her voice. Oh my God, it's stunning. It fills up the room and I can feel the light catchers vibrate around me, carrying her voice to me.

It's so bright I can't see her features, only her silhouette, illuminated by the most brilliant colors I've ever seen.

"Mom?" I ask, waiting for her response.

Her singing gets louder, more urgent. I don't understand the words, it's like she's singing in another language, but somehow I know what she's singing.

"Mom, can you hear me?" I call out. A sense of urgency takes over as I reach out in front of me, trying to touch her, but all I feel is glass. I'm completely surrounded by light catchers.

"Mommy! Please!" I'm crying now, begging for her to acknowledge me. Needing to feel her hand, her touch.

The light begins to fade, the colors turn gray. "No! Don't go! Stay!" Her figure backs away, almost disappearing into the now dark room.

And with her, the light is extinguished. I only hear the clinking sounds of glass all around my ears. I'm crying and flailing my hands around me, trying to find my way out. Trying to find my way toward her.

"Where are you?" I scream. "Please come back!"

"Noelle," I hear in the distance. A familiar voice. "Noelle?"

"Noelle?" A masculine voice pulls me out of my dream. I'm trembling as he pulls me into his arms.

"Are you okay?" he asks in a hushed tone.

I open my eyes and look into Heath's. His brow is furrowed, concern on his face. And he's in my bed with me.

Relief floods me as I realize I was only dreaming. Chasing my mother through the streets, trying to reach her.

I nod against him and inhale sharply. "I had a—nightmare?" I'm not sure what it was.

"I could hear you screaming from my room next door. I thought something happened to you. You scared the shit out of me." He pulls me closer, and I wrap my arms around him, nestling my head into his chest. "I can feel your heart pounding, Noelle. Are you sure you're okay?"

"Yes," I admit. "Better now."

Heath would stay with me almost every night when we were younger, waiting for me to fall asleep before he snuck out through my window and back to his own house. The way I'm nestled against him right now brings me back twelve years. Back to a time when us lying together in bed like this was completely normal. Completely expected. Completely amazing.

"Do you want to talk about it?" he asks.

I close my eyes and see the beautiful figure floating through the air, just out of reach. "It was my mom. She was there, but I couldn't reach her." I say, summing up the bizarre dream.

"I'm sorry," he says, squeezing me tight. "I think we may have over-done it tonight."

We didn't get back to the hotel until almost four in the morning. And now it's five-thirty. The sun is starting to peek through the blinds, and we haven't even had two hours of sleep.

"You mean last night?" I correct him.

"And this morning." He laughs and rests his head against the headboard.

"What time do we have to check out?" I ask, concerned we only have a few more hours here. We both need sleep before we drive another six or seven hours today.

"Not until three. They expect us to check out late."

I relax against him. "Good."

I close my eyes and feel sleep about to take me. "Can you stay with me?" I ask, afraid of his answer. I want to feel his protective arms around me.

"You don't even have to ask. I wasn't planning on getting up," he responds and kisses my forehead. "Get some rest."

I drift off to sleep, comforted to know he's not going anywhere.

"WHAT EXIT ARE WE getting off?" I ask as I glance at the highway sign coming up.

We left St. Louis around four o'clock, and it's almost eleven now. Heath and I have been switching up driving frequently since the sun set a few hours ago. Both of us are feeling the pain of this leg of our trip, and we vowed not to stay out as late as we did again.

"The next one, so stay in this lane."

I turn my blinker on and ease off the highway. He helps me navigate the city streets of Tulsa, Oklahoma. It's late and traffic is pretty light, considering we're in the city now.

Twenty minutes later, we're in our hotel sprawled out next to each other on the large bed in the main bedroom.

"I can't even see straight," I complain. "Is this what jet lag feels like?" I turn on my side and see that he has his arms stretched out above his head. He kicks his shoes off and inhales deeply.

"Jet lag sucks," he states. "It's way worse than this."

"No more Cosmos and late nights," I declare, stretching my hand out to shake his. "Deal?"

"Deal," he says, grasping my hand.

He doesn't let go and pulls my hand down onto his chest, linking his fingers through mine.

"We're sleeping in tomorrow," I state, and he nods.

"We have all the time in the world, right? We can take our time getting to Arizona." A strange look blankets his face, turning into a frown.

"We do have time," I answer. "What's wrong?"

He turns on his side to face me, never letting go of my hand. It's pressed against his chest–against his heart.

"I don't want this to end," he admits, a tinge of regret in his voice. "It's selfish, I know, but I don't think I can say goodbye to you again."

I suck in a breath. He's treading on ground I haven't been ready to talk about since popping back into his life, surprising him.

"Why would we have to say goodbye?" I ask, curious. Is he just going on this trip with me to fulfill some sort of obligation?

"You have a new life now," he states, matter-of-fact.

My heart sinks. Does he not hold onto hope that we'll stay in touch when this trip is over? Do I?

"So do you," I say. "You're a world-traveling, world-famous rock star."

"That doesn't define me," he says. "It's what I do. It's how I pay bills. But it's not everything. I'm so much more than that."

I nod my head. "I know. I'd like to hear how it all came about. Epic Fail."

He pauses and closes his eyes. "If Garrett heard any of this coming out of my mouth, he'd punch me. But I'm a little bit of an outsider amongst best friends."

"Oh?"

"Yeah. They've all been tight since they were in high school. Three of them growing up on the same block. They've all been through some really rough shit."

"How did you become their singer?" I've always been curious as to why he replaced Alex Treadway. When I heard about it, I had to do a double-take. I couldn't believe that Heath, *my Heath*, was the new lead singer for one of my favorite bands.

"Honestly, I did it on a dare," he admits. "I never realized I had a voice, at least one that could put me where I am today. My mom says my voice is a gift, but I had no idea how to even use it. After I auditioned for them, I couldn't believe it when they called me back. And the rest, they say, is history. They've become like brothers to me."

"That's so incredible. It's also surreal." I look into his eyes, and he looks pensive.

"It is surreal. It's also a business. One that I'm not as invested in as the rest of the guys. I didn't grow up with music in my blood like they did. Since they've all known each other for years, they totally gel. They fit perfectly together. I came in on a whim, and I think they initially saw me as a fresh face, someone who would continue to bring the heart and soul into their music that Alex had. His shoes were big to fill, but I was able to do it in my own way."

He pauses and takes a deep breath. "Now they rely on my songs just as they do Alex's. I've been able to fuel their music with my poetry, and it's worked out great. I just don't know how much longer I have it in me."

"Why? Your songs are awesome." I know many of his words are about me. Poetry that I recognize from when we were younger.

"Because my muse came back from the dead," he says, and I suck in my breath.

His eyes lock onto mine, and I'm frozen in his stare. So much of what he's accomplished is because of me. Because I 'died.'

"You can't stop. You're amazing," I say, feeling like a groupie. "And your live performances are–"

"What?" he interrupts me. "You've seen us live?"

I realize I've opened a huge can of worms with my admission. "Yes."

His hand tenses around mine, his fingers not letting go. "When?" he demands.

"In Boston. During your Epic Days tour." I'm sweating now, pulse racing. Why did I tell him this?

"Holy shit." He closes his eyes and drops my hand. I feel the void immediately, almost as if a sheer wall went up between us on the bed.

"I'm sorry, I–"

"I saw you," he says. "I fucking saw you, and I thought my eyes were playing tricks on me."

Dahlia and I were on the floor about twenty rows from the stage. I was in the middle of a sea of people dancing, bodies colliding. I had no idea he could see me.

"You were the only one standing still. Everyone was bouncing around, but not you. You stood there and stared at me–I thought you were a ghost." He rolls over onto his back, covering his forehead with his arm.

"You were singing my song," I state. The poem he wrote for me when I was fourteen. He sang it live that night, and I couldn't move.

"I can't believe you were fucking there."

Is he angry? Confused? I knew I shouldn't have gone to that concert. Dahlia had no idea why I was so out of it. I remember her asking if I was okay. I told her I felt faint and I left the floor, watching the rest of the show from concourse.

"I'm sorry. I didn't mean–"

He turns back to me and places his hand on my cheek. "Don't be sorry. Please. I just wish I knew it was really you and not a figment of my imagination."

His warm hand calms me down, his thumb brushing along my cheekbone. "It's like a light was shining directly on you, showing me that you were alive. And then you disappeared."

"I couldn't handle being that close to you and not touching you," I admit. "I had no idea that you saw me."

He pulls my face toward his and kisses the tip of my nose. "I dreamt about you for weeks after that. Each dream was the same, you were standing in the crowd, almost illuminated. Floating. I woke up every single time feeling your presence, I could swear it was you telling me everything was okay. I thought you were haunting me, in a good way." He smiles, our noses touching. Our breaths mingle, and my heart races.

"It was an incredible performance," I admit, trying to calm myself down. His hand is still on my face, and his lips are so close. *So close.*

"My muse was in the building. I guess that helped with my performance." He smiles, and his eyes leave mine for a brief second as they travel lower to my lips then back up again.

"You had such raw emotion, it was spectacular." I pause. "You can't stop singing–performing. You have a gift."

He nods against me. "Garrett would kill me if I left the band. As much as he hates to admit it, I think he actually likes me." He chuckles, and I'm sure there's a story or two behind his comments. Garrett strikes me as someone who's a little rough around the edges. He's also had his share of spotlight, not all positive. If anyone was considered a womanizer in the band, it would be him. I read somewhere that he settled down and has a wife and son and isn't as controversial as he'd been in the past. I hope that's true.

"Good," I say, relieved that me resurfacing isn't going to split up Epic Fail.

"I'm exhausted," Heath says, his hand sliding off of my cheek and onto my shoulder. "We should sleep."

I nod in agreement, as much as I want him to kiss me and hold me like he used to.

He closes his eyes and pulls me into his chest. We're both fully clothed, lying on top of the blankets, and my heart starts to race again.

He's going to stay with me tonight.

I WAKE UP with a start, staring at the ceiling. Heath is on his side, his leg draped over mine, pinning my lower body to the bed. He's breathing deeply and evenly, his warm breath blanketing my neck. His arm is wrapped around my abdomen, holding me close as if I were a teddy bear.

I can't believe we're here together. So many years have passed, but yet, here we are, almost as if I'd never left.

I place my hand over his arm and feel the heat emanating from his body. It feels so good to have him with me, so comforting.

It's almost dawn, and I'm wide awake. I don't want to wake him; I don't want to move. My father's journal is on the nightstand on my side of the bed, so I reach for it, and open it up to the last page I read. My mother's picture from St. Louis under the Arch is my current bookmark, and her smile warms my heart. To know she was this happy makes me feel hope that I can one day feel the joy that she did. Her eyes are full of promise of her future. Her look is infectious.

I turn the page and squint my eyes to try to read my father's handwriting. It's still pretty dark in the room, but I don't want to turn on the light, afraid Heath will wake up. So I take my phone and turn on the flashlight. Then I prop it on my chest, just under my chin, so it shines on the pages of the journal. His words flow together as I begin to read.

August 24: We arrived in Tulsa early this morning, driving all night from St. Louis. Melanie slept for most of the trip, exhausted from the night before. We decided to stay an extra night in St. Louis so we could go back to the blues bar where she took the stage the night before. Her performance exhilarating once again. The manager asked if she'd be coming back again, hoping she was going to become a new regular. Sadly, she had to tell them 'no,' but I plan on bringing her back here one day, so she can sing her heart out.

After a very long nap, we went to visit the Philbrook Museum. She'd heard about it from her cousin who went to a wedding there a few years ago and had been dying to go. It was stunning. The art itself was breathtaking. All kinds of artwork from around the world, old and new. We spent hours going through the various rooms, taking in the history within the walls. And then we ventured into the gardens and Melanie became a new person. The gardens were absolutely incredible, beautiful and vast. We enjoyed the beautiful serene landscape, even stopping to rest and reflect in the informally designated meditative areas. At one point Mel said, "I could stay here forever and still notice the simple beauty that these gardens give." And in that second, I wanted to stay here forever with her, forgetting about work and the business. Losing ourselves in the timeless splendor that surrounded us in the grounds of that perfect place.

"Where are we going today?" Heath asks, stretching his arm over my belly but quickly tucking it back in place.

"Did I wake you?" I ask, turning off the flashlight on my phone. "Sorry."

"Nope."

"Oh good," I say, relieved.

"So, what's on the agenda? Or do you want to surprise me?"

"The Philbrook Museum. My parents absolutely loved it, especially the gardens."

"Sounds like a plan," he states and kisses my shoulder. His movements are so effortless and comfortable, it's almost as if he's forgotten how much time we've spent apart.

He slides away from me and out of bed. "I'll take a shower first, if that's okay." He rushes to the bathroom as if he has to pee really bad.

I laugh and call out after him. "There's another shower in the other bedroom. I'll go in there."

EPIC LOVE

I slide out of bed and grab my suitcase, rolling it behind me through the suite.

There's a spring in my step as I walk into the bathroom. I'm excited about spending the day at The Philbrook.

It's going to be amazing.

And I feel like I'm getting one step closer to my parents.

CHAPTER 24

Heath

Present

WATCHING NOELLE TWIRL around, a huge smile plastered on her face, takes my breath away. We've been outside exploring the vast gardens here at the Philbrook Museum. Her father was right, it's breathtaking.

I hold my phone up to try to capture the moment forever and hold down the 'burst' function, snapping dozens of pictures.

"What are you doing?" she calls out, laughing.

"Nothing," I smirk, shoving the phone into my pocket.

"I look like a giant dork spinning around out here like I'm in *The Sound of Music*."

She sits on a cement bench, gazing into a small fountain. There's a bird playing in the water, bathing himself, completely unaware of our presence. Or maybe he's having so much fun, he doesn't care that we're here, spying on him.

I sit down next to her and pull her into my side. "It's incredible seeing you like this."

She turns to face me, eyebrow raised. "Like what?"

Alive. Breathing.

"Happy," I state.

"It's been a long time since I've felt this free," she admits, smiling. "Each day we get closer to Arizona, I feel more and more like myself. And less like Sawyer."

"Well, I don't know Sawyer, I only know Noelle. And the Noelle that's emerging is amazing." I place a kiss on her temple, letting my lips linger for a few seconds. She relaxes in my arms.

"I think you'd like Sawyer," she muses.

"It's weird that you're speaking in the third person right now. Heath says 'stop it,'" I joke.

She bumps her shoulder into mine, and we sit quietly for a few moments.

"I feel close to them," she says softly.

"That's a good thing."

"I also feel closer to the man my father used to be. Before my mother died."

I can tell she so desperately wishes she knew the man who penned that journal. The man who was so incredibly in love with her mother, their happiness leading them from state to state.

"They can feel you, and I'm willing to bet they're here with you right now."

Her eyes light up for a second. "Can we stay here until the sun sets and then go eat?"

"Of course," I reply, wanting her to revel in this beautiful place for just a little while longer.

We continue to walk through the grounds, holding hands like a couple in love. She tugs on my arm as several fireflies light up the sky. "Look!" We race to the field where hundreds of fireflies are hovering, displaying their bright lights.

"It's gorgeous!" she exclaims. "Look at them all!"

I capture one in the palm of my hand and place it in front of her.

"I wish we had my firefly house," she says. "Remember that?"

"Of course. How could I possibly forget? That hung outside your bedroom window every night from June through August."

It was a beautiful symbol of love and protection from her father. Although it didn't keep all of the demons away, it gave her hope that those fireflies produced magical fairies that would watch over her.

We capture several more fireflies, cupping them in our hands, rays of light poking through the spaces between our fingers.

"That tickles!" she giggles, opening her hand so her fireflies can fly away into the night.

I do the same and we watch them fly higher, their lights getting dimmer as they get further away.

"As much as this reminds me of my father and what he gave to me when I was little, it reminds me of you more."

"Yeah?" I ask, curious about what she means.

"You gave the magic back to me after things started getting bad with Tonya. I looked forward to seeing it outside my window, filled with fireflies. All because of you."

Tears fill her eyes, and I pull her toward me. "No tears," I demand, kissing them away. My lips brush against her cheeks, and she relaxes in my arms.

"But they're happy tears," she insists, looking up into my eyes.

Suddenly, the sky opens up and rain pours down on us. "Shit!" I yell, trying to cover us with my arms. The main building is far off in the distance, so I search for shelter nearby.

"Over here!" I call as I grab her hand, pulling her underneath a small trellis. The rain is coming down in buckets, both of us completely soaked. The overhang barely covers us as I pull her against my body, our wet clothes stuck together.

"Oh my God!" She laughs. "This is insane! The sky was crystal clear just a few minutes ago."

Both of my arms are wrapped tightly around her waist. She laughs, her happy tears washed away by the rain that pelted us.

"You're so beautiful," I say, and her smile fades, a surprised look on her face.

"What?"

"You're more beautiful than I remember. You're stunning, Noelle."

Our faces are inches apart as we try to stay out of the rain. Her eyes dart around my face, landing on my mouth. "I don't know what to say," she admits, biting her lower lip.

"Don't say anything," I answer her, lowering my lips to hers, softly taking them, making them mine all over again.

She inhales deeply, taking my breath into her mouth as if she's relying on it to survive. Her hands leave my side as she pulls my mouth more forcefully against hers, hungrily kissing me back like something is sparked deep inside of her.

Rain falls all around us, the humid air becoming cooler. Our tongues entwine as our bodies press more firmly, urgently against each other. Our kiss is passionate, probing, like we're learning how to kiss all over again. My hands press into her lower back, holding her in place as I kiss all around her lips, pulling them into mine.

"Heath," she moans softly against my mouth, her fingers caressing the sides of my face. I open my eyes and find her staring at me, her own eyes questioning. "What are we doing?" she asks and pulls away slightly.

"Something we should have done when you showed up on my doorstep," I admit.

She sighs and kisses me softly, resting her lips on mine. "It feels good, whatever it is." She drops down a little so her forehead is resting against my chin, her soaking wet hair touching my lips.

"I've missed you. My life has been such a blur without you in it," I say. "I'm sorry for the circumstances that brought you back to life, but I wouldn't trade it for the world."

I hope that she would have resurfaced regardless of the immediate situation. At least, I tell myself that.

"A piece of me died the day I left. I'm so sorry I did what I did. I'm so sorry I left you wondering and devastated. I should have fought my father. I should have stayed." She kisses me again, more desperate this time, pulling my lips to hers.

I love you, Noelle.

The words echo in my head, unable to leave my lips. How can I tell her this after so many years? So much distance between us?

Instead, I pull her up against me and take control of our kiss. Wanting more. Needing more. If only we were back at our room, I'd show her how much I need her. How much I want her.

My lips travel down to her neck, her pulse beating wildly beneath my tongue as I nip and kiss my way back to her mouth. The rain is starting to let up, but we don't move as we continue to devour each other.

I hear footsteps approach and let go of Noelle.

"The gardens are closed. Kindly make your way to the exit and come back soon," the attendant says, his voice tight.

Noelle blushes and giggles against my chest. "How embarrassing!"

"Thank you, Sir. We'll head out now," I say, tucking Noelle into my side. The remnants of the storm drop a few more raindrops on us as we make it back to my SUV.

"We're going to make a mess of your car," she says, reluctant to get in.

"We're just wet. It's not like we're covered in mud," I assure her. "Get in."

She steps up and slides into the passenger seat. "I don't think I've ever been this soaked in my life."

My heart races as I remember the nightmare I had. I shake my head, trying to get out the image of her as a cold, wet corpse. Seeing her slip away from me, diving down into the depths of the ocean makes the hair stand on my arms.

"You're freezing!" she cries, trying to find something in the back to cover me with.

"I'm okay. Just a couple goose bumps." I crank the heat in the car in an attempt to dry us both.

Seeing her smile begins to shatter the memories of that horrific dream. I don't ever want to imagine her like that again.

I grip the steering wheel and pull out of the parking lot.

"We can't go to dinner like this," she notes. Her tank top is stuck to her still, and her gorgeous hair is wet, heavy over her face.

"You look gorgeous no matter how much rain is dumped on you."

"Gorgeous like a drowned rat!" She laughs, and I take the turn onto the street our hotel is on.

"Why don't we get changed and find that restaurant your parents went to?"

"Sounds like a plan," she says, clasping her hands in her lap.

What I really want to do is stay in our hotel room and make up for all of the years lost, making love to her until tomorrow.

"WELCOME TO CELEBRITY," a much older man says as we enter. He kisses Noelle on both cheeks and grabs her hands, surprising the two of us.

"Thank you!" She laughs as he leads us through the restaurant.

I feel like we've stepped back in time, the place has a 'lounge' feel to it. The walls are painted a deep shade of red, matching the carpeting and the scarlet velvet upholstery on the dining chairs. We're seated in the corner, gold drapes covering the windows.

"This place is so cool," she says, settling into her seat. "My father wasn't kidding when he said the owner was a little 'grabby.'"

I did some reading online before we left the hotel. Apparently, he's been a fixture here for over fifty years and welcomes all of his female clientele in a similar fashion. However common it is here, nothing prepares you for a stranger grabbing and kissing you.

Noelle reads the menu carefully, her finger moving from item to item. "There's so many delicious things on this menu, I want to order one of everything."

"I'm getting the New York strip steak," I declare and close the menu. I'm very easy to please.

"Maybe I'll get fish," she says. "The salmon looks really good."

A waiter arrives and recites six more specials, and Noelle's eyes widen. She orders a glass of wine, and I order an IPA, giving her more time to drive herself crazy over all of the meal choices.

Our drinks arrive, and we order our entrees.

She raises her glass for a familiar tradition on this road trip. "Thank you again for making this trip special. I don't know what I'd do without you. Cheers." She tips it and clinks it with my pint glass, we both take long sips, eyes locked onto each other's.

"You have to stop thanking me," I remind her. "You act like you're forcing me to stay on the road with you. Like it's a burden. Trust me, I want to be here."

She smiles and takes another sip of wine. "I know. But there's that part of me that worries too much. That's all. I'll try to stop thanking you."

I reach across the table to take her hand in mine. "The fact that I can sit here and hold your hand is thanks enough. You have no idea what goes through my mind every time I can touch you–hold you. You're real, and I couldn't be more thankful."

She lowers her glistening eyes to the table, afraid a tear will spill. But she doesn't let go of my hand.

"What else did your father love about this place?" I ask, curious.

"I don't have his journal with me, but if I remember correctly, he said it had an 'old world charm to it' that made my mother giddy. Apparently, she fell in love with this place the moment she walked through the doors, feeling like she went back in time."

"That's exactly how I felt," I admit.

"He also thought the turtle cheesecake was the best dessert he's ever had."

I laugh, "Well, then, we better save room."

The owner comes up to our table and smiles, "I hope you're enjoying yourselves so far." Then he turns to me. "Please consider posing for a picture with me before you leave. We'd love to include you in the many celebrity faces that have come into my restaurant over the years."

I swallow the mouthful of beer I had taken before he arrived. "Of course," I say, nodding. "I'd be honored."

"Fantastic!" he claps. "I won't bother you again, enjoy your meals."

Once he's out of ear shot I mutter, "How on earth did he know who I am?"

Noelle doesn't look surprised at all. "Seriously? You may not act like it, but you do have that 'rock star' swagger."

"Swagger? Really?" She's got to be kidding.

"You exude it. You fill a room with your presence and you don't even realize it."

I shake my head and take another swig of beer. "Now you're talking crap. Stop."

She laughs. "I think it's cool."

We're distracted by another couple across the room. The man is down on one knee, proposing. "Oh my gosh!" Noelle says, covering her mouth with her hands. "How sweet!"

The woman starts crying, her outstretched hand shaking as the man places a ring on her finger. The entire restaurant breaks out in applause, whistling and cheering follows.

"How romantic," Noelle says.

I nod. "That was nice."

Our meals are placed under our noses as we're watching the couple tell their story to a few tables that surround them.

"That was fast," Noelle comments and places her cloth napkin on her lap.

We eat our meals, sharing bites with each other like we've been doing this for years. She savors the steak when I place it in her mouth, little moans escaping her lips. "So good," she says. Everything about her actions tonight are sensual, my libido heightened since our passionate kiss at the gardens earlier.

I need to get her alone. Now.

Our plates are cleared, and she's already ordered the turtle cheesecake. "I'm stuffed, but I have to try it," she states.

I nod in agreement. Anything to make her happy. Anything to let her live the words from her father's journal.

And man was he right. That cheesecake was superb.

Noelle is licking her lips, cleaning the remnants of the crust off of the plate we shared. "I need to walk about ten miles to work off this dinner," she jokes.

I can think of something else that would work this food off even quicker.

"Let's get out of here," I demand, dropping a couple hundred dollar bills on the table.

Her eyes are wide, and a sly grin spreads across her face. "You need to take a picture with the owner first."

She leads me to the front of the restaurant, and the owner steps in front of us. "Thank you for coming to Celebrity, Mr. Strickland. I hope you and your lovely guest had a spectacular meal."

"It was great," I admit, and he leads me over next to the wall. Out of nowhere, a girl appears with a camera. We take several photos and he shakes my hand vigorously and, once again, kisses Noelle's cheeks.

"Thanks again," he smiles.

I place my hand on Noelle's lower back, leading her out of the restaurant. The air is considerably cooler and less humid now that the storms have completely passed.

"It turned into a gorgeous night," she notes as we walk to my SUV.

"It sure did." I open her door for her, but before she can slide in, I turn her around, grabbing her face between my hands. Her eyes widen as I pull her lips to mine, kissing her with purpose. I need her to know what's going to come when we get back to our room.

I release her, but still hold onto her face, caressing her cheeks. Our eyes remained locked, and she's fully aware of my intentions, although words don't pass our lips.

We drive back to the hotel in silence, so much tension hanging in the air. My heart pounds as we pull up to the valet. I can't get her upstairs fast enough.

We walk quickly into the hotel, hand in hand and slip into an empty elevator. As cliché as it is, I don't wait until we reach our floor. I press her into the back wall, slamming my lips into hers, my body grinding against hers. She gasps when I nip at the side of her neck, my teeth and tongue scraping along her skin. I start to hike her skirt up so I can gain better access to her–I need to feel her against me–but we're interrupted by the doors opening.

"Room. Now," she demands.

I grab her around her wrist, pulling her along with me. I feel like a cave man dragging his woman into the cave. I can't promise I won't be attacking her like one.

I fumble for the key card, yet, somehow able to open the door, practically catapulting us into the room. Arms and legs are wrapped around each other, our lips clumsily connecting and then slipping away as we try to navigate the dark room.

My cell phone rings and I fumble it in my hand, trying to toss it across the room, but instead I accidentally answer it. Noelle's lips are on my neck when I say into the phone, "Stuart, not a good time, man." He texted me earlier today, letting me know he was going to call me tonight to talk about a few media things coming up.

"What?" the voice on the other end of the line asks. And it's not Stuart.

I freeze, and Noelle's assault on my neck stops.

Motherfucker.

"Hey, Haley."

Noelle releases me, backing away, eyes wide. I shake my head, trying to get her to calm down. Her expression is scaring me.

"Heath. What the hell is going on?" she shrieks into the phone.

"What do you mean?" I ask, trying to diffuse multiple situations at once.

Noelle goes into the bedroom and closes the door.

"I'm staring at a tabloid that shows you with a dead girl!" she screams. "A fucking DEAD GIRL!"

I can't believe I didn't think of all of the damage control we needed to do. I should have gotten Stuart to be more aggressive. The last person I wanted seeing Noelle before I had a chance to fill her in is Haley.

"You need to calm down. I can explain."

"Explain? How the hell can you possibly explain that Noelle Durand is alive and breathing, and I find out about it from a fucking magazine!"

She could blow this shit up so bad. Noelle's privacy and well-being could be in danger.

"It's a long, complicated story," I state. "I promise you, we'll fill you in when we can. But for now, you need to keep quiet."

"You have got to be kidding me," she says. "Keep quiet? Are you fucking serious?"

"Haley, there are things going on that won't make any sense until she can tell you everything. You're just going to have to trust me on this. Please."

She huffs into the phone. "I don't know, Heath. I'm so fucking hurt right now. Everything that you and I had was obviously a joke to you. I was a side piece while you were hiding Noelle all along. Is that what happened? You're going to pay for stringing me along for so long. The both of you are."

"Haley–"

She hangs up, and my line goes dead.

"Fuck!" I yell into the empty room.

I quickly dial Stuart as the bedroom door opens up, Noelle quietly walking back into the room, her head hanging.

"Heath, my man," he answers, practically singing into the phone. "Glad you got my message earlier today. I wanted to check to see when you're getting home. We have a couple of talk shows lined up for you guys and Howard Stern's people called. He wants you to play in his studio next month."

"Yeah, yeah. All of that sounds great. But we have a big problem," I say, ignoring the appearances he's lined up.

"Is everything okay?" he asks, concerned.

"No. Haley knows about Noelle and she's livid, acting crazy. She saw a picture of us in a tabloid, and she's lost her mind."

"Shit," he mutters.

"Yeah. I need you to call her. Calm her down. Buy her off. Do whatever you have to do, but she can't run her mouth to anyone."

"You think she would?" he asks.

"As sure as I'm standing here." Haley is a woman scorned right now. Add a bit of crazy to the mix and we have a time bomb about to detonate.

"I'll call her right away. Don't worry, she won't talk. I know her type all too well–flash a few zeroes in front of her and she'll forget you and Noelle ever existed."

"I hope you're right."

"I'll text you tomorrow." Stuart hangs up and I'm left staring at Noelle, her head hanging low.

"I don't think I want to know anything," she says, sinking into the couch. She's changed into a tank top and yoga pants, her hair pulled up into a mess on top of her head.

I close my eyes and inhale deeply.

"I thought you said you weren't involved with anyone?" Her eyes glisten, and I can tell she's about to lose it.

"I told you the truth, I'm not."

"Do I even want to know why Haley is calling you in the middle of the night?"

This situation sucks so fucking bad. I don't know what's the right thing to tell her. Do I tell her I've been fucking Haley on and off for almost three years? That Haley fell in love with me and I ditched her just days before Noelle resurfaced?

Fuck.

"I'm not sure any of it's going to make you feel good," I admit.

She starts crying, and I'm helpless.

"I don't know what I expected. I mean, I've been gone for twelve years. In all of that time, of course you've been with other people. Of course you've fallen in love." Tears stream down her face, and I approach the couch, needing to be near her–to comfort her.

"I've never been in love with anyone else," I state firmly. "That is something you have to believe."

She looks up at me, eyes wide.

"Haley and I–we got complicated. And pretty recently. That's why she's upset."

"Complicated? God, I'm going to be sick."

"Please try to understand, my reasons for being with her were purely physical. I thought it was the same for her. But it wasn't. It isn't. The other day, she told me she was in love with me. I didn't handle it well and left her feeling pretty shitty."

I'm saying too much. Telling Noelle things she shouldn't have to hear. Her face sinks further as if I'm ripping all of her dreams away from her.

"How long?" she asks, her voice shaking.

"Too long," I admit. "Almost three years."

"I wish I knew this. I wouldn't have asked you to come with me." Her tone is full of regret.

"I told you I wasn't involved with anyone. That's what you asked me the other night. I didn't lie."

I'm frustrated by this entire situation. Angry she's looking for an explanation of my actions while I thought she was dead.

"This isn't fair, Noelle. I realize you're upset. You're hurt. And your reactions and feelings are very real. I get it. But it's not fair for you to judge me for anything I've done since you 'died.'" I use air quotes to emphasize my point.

"I'm not blaming or judging you!" she yells back. "I just realize I should have made this trip alone. It was obviously wrong for me to include you. To ask you to help me–when you have bigger things to worry about."

"Jesus, Noelle. Haven't you heard anything I've said? I. Want. To. Be. Here!"

I storm over to the couch and pull her to her feet. I've never been forceful with her–ever. I've always been afraid of hurting her or exacerbating the bruises she constantly had all over her body, defense wounds from the abuse she suffered. But I need to get through to her, so I wrap my hands around her upper arms, holding her in place in front of me.

"What are you doing?" she asks, wiggling in my grip.

"Listen to me. Haley is certifiable. I made a huge mistake ever being with her. She's an ugly, vicious, person and I'm afraid of what she's going to do to exact her revenge on me. On us." I breathe deeply, trying to calm myself. I loosen my grips a little bit but don't let go of her.

"I wish to God I never got involved with her. It was selfish of me. It was easy. There were no strings attached. It's been on-and-off for three years–a few hook-ups here and there. The last time I even saw her was almost a year ago. Until I came home from this last tour. She lost it when I didn't share her feelings–and now she's really upset. Really angry."

She closes her eyes for a long time, her body relaxing in my grip. "I'm sorry, Heath. I don't know what to say."

"Say you aren't going to run out that door. Tell me that you want to continue this trip–with me. Say that you still love me."

Her eyes pop open, and she pulls away from me.

"How could you ask me that?" she asks, surprised.

"Easy. You walked back into my life like you walked out of a dream. I've never loved anyone else, Noelle. Ever. Because I never stopped loving you."

Tears spill from her eyes again.

"There isn't even a question," she whispers, covering her mouth.

"What?" My heart races in my chest.

"I never stopped loving you either, Heath. How could I?"

I pull her against me, exhaling with relief.

"But–"

"That's all we need to say right now," I interrupt her. "Let's move forward from here. Clean slate."

She shakes her head against my chest, wrapping her arms tightly around me. "It's not that easy," she admits.

"We need to try," I beg her.

Her cries are muffled against my chest as I whisper into the top of her head.

"Our second chance is a gift."

CHAPTER 25

Noelle
Present

HEATH LEFT THE HOTEL room about an hour ago while I was in the shower. We spent the night wrapped in each other's arms, afraid to let go. He kept telling me how much he loved me, and all I could do was lie there, riddled with guilt.

Yesterday was–intense. So many emotions ripped through me.

Exhilaration.

Bliss.

Happiness.

Lust.

Love.

Hurt.

Fear.

Within the course of a few hours, I was questioning even coming back at all. I should have let my old life be, and traveled on this journey to say goodbye to my parents alone. I should have stayed 'dead.' It wasn't fair for me to involve Heath. He had moved on, made mistakes, but he was living his life. And he was able to move on, something I should have respected. I shouldn't have come back and disrupted things. I feel terrible, guilt overcoming me. He'd be so much better off if I weren't in the picture at all.

When Haley called last night, old jealousy and insecurities resurfaced. When we were younger, she always seemed to be waiting in the wings, almost hoping something would tear Heath and I apart. I realize he isn't committed to her, and actually seems disgusted by her, but I can't help but think she's going to continue to try to insert herself into our lives. I'm afraid she'll try to derail the real reason why I'm back–to lay my father to rest.

I feel sick to my stomach, angry with myself, angry with the situation I was forced into twelve years ago.

I finish getting dressed and shove my clothes into my suitcase. I'm going to get the hell out of here before I make his life any more of a mess than I already have.

I pick up the phone and call the concierge. "Hello, how can I help you?" he asks.

"I need a rental car. Can you help me with that?"

"Of course! Where are you going and for how long do you need it?" I do a quick calculation in my head and realize I'll need the car for about ten days if I'm going to make the trip back to Pennsylvania to pick up my car from Heath's house before heading home to Chappy.

"Ten days. But I'll need to return the car someplace near Philadelphia, Pennsylvania. Is that okay?"

"Yes. Give me about fifteen minutes, and the car will be here. Do you want me to call you when it gets here?"

"No, I'll just come down."

"Sounds good. See you soon."

I finish gathering my things and look around the room.

What am I even doing?

My suitcase is packed, and I place my backpack on top if it as I roll it out the door behind me. Tears threaten to spill as guilt consumes me. I'm running away again and this time I'm the one in control. Heath is never going to forgive me for leaving him again, but I have no choice. He doesn't deserve this heartache and confusion. I'm too much of a mess, and I've caused more problems resurfacing. He has his own life. His own purpose. I'm just a burden, a problem from the past that he feels compelled to fix. To help. And I can't keep putting him in that position.

The elevator doors close, and I begin to descend–away from the only person that still loves me.

THE GPS GUIDES ME onto the highway and has calculated that I should arrive in Albuquerque in about nine or ten hours. That's the longest stretch I've gone so far on this trip, but I'm determined to make it there sometime today, even if it means driving late into the night. My phone starts ringing about ten minutes into my drive, and

I know it's Heath. I send him to voicemail twice, but he keeps calling. Finally, I answer.

"Heath, don't make this any harder than it already is," I beg him as I answer the phone.

"Pull over, Noelle." His voice is calm and even. He doesn't sound angry, but he also doesn't sound emotional.

"What?"

"Pull the fuck over. Now." How does he know where I am?

I look into my rearview mirror and see his charcoal gray SUV right behind me, practically touching my bumper.

"What the hell?" I yell.

There's a rest area just ahead and I veer off onto the ramp and pull into the first open parking spot I see. He parks next to me and jumps out.

I throw open my door, ready to get into it with him. Ready to defend my actions.

He cages me in, his arms on either side of me. "This is not happening," he states. "You're not leaving me again. Not. Happening."

His eyes pierce mine, and I cringe beneath his gaze. "Heath, it's better this way. I–"

"No. It's not better. You leaving is not the answer. Fuck, Noelle." He steps back a little and runs his hand through his hair.

"You don't understand." I shake my head and try to gather my thoughts. "As much as you don't want to hear this, I didn't come back for you. I came back to say goodbye to my father." That didn't come out right. A pained look paints his face, and I reach out for his hand. He yanks it out of my grip.

"This is all so confusing. I should never have involved you, I'm sorry," I say, sitting back in my car, legs hanging out the side.

"Listen to me. You were gone for twelve fucking years. You were dead! Shit happened when you were gone. A lot of shit. Then you come back here, and I realize how much I still love you. For twelve years! I never let you go, despite living my life. Despite making mistakes and causing a shit-storm to bubble up. I own that. Not you."

He's breathing heavily, trying to maintain his composure while I remain speechless.

"You came back to me for a reason. We're on this trip together for a reason. Don't you dare freak out on me and take off, leaving me stranded, wondering if I'm ever going to see you again. That decision is mine now, not yours. Do you get it?"

I've never seen him like this. He's fuming and forceful. A little scary.

But he's right.

"I'm sorry," I apologize again, this time with more truth behind my words.

"Are you?" He folds his arms over his chest. "Are you really?"

I nod my head, and he begins to relax a little.

"I can't lose you again. I just can't." His words are firm. His demeanor is desperate. If I say anything other than what he wants to hear, I'm certain he'll tie me up and throw me in the back of his truck.

"We're in this together, so get in my car."

I look around, "Now?"

"Yes," he demands.

"What am I supposed to do with this car? I rented it." I toss my hands in the air, trying to accentuate my point.

He opens the passenger side of the car and the concierge who handed me the keys just fifteen minutes ago steps out.

"Ma'am," he says, tilting his head. "I'm here to take the car back to the hotel for you. You won't be charged at all. It's our pleasure to help you both out here."

Heath has already opened the trunk to the rental and removed my luggage. My backpack is on the front seat and I grab it, throwing it over my shoulder.

"Thanks. I'm really sorry for your trouble." I step out of the car and place the keys into the concierge's hand. I look back to make sure I have everything and swipe my phone off the console.

Heath holds the passenger door open as I slide into the SUV. The concierge drives the rental car away as I fasten my seat belt.

We pull away in silence as Heath programs Albuquerque into his GPS.

We don't speak for at least twenty minutes. I look out the window, trying to figure out what to say to fix this.

I take a deep breath and finally speak up.

"I thought I was doing what was best," I admit, apologetically.

His tone is much calmer now. "Best for whom?"

"For both of us, I guess." I'm not even believing the words coming out of my own mouth. What's best for me is having him in my life. I've missed him for far too long, deprived from touching him, from him holding me.

"Bullshit. You got spooked and ran. You let Haley get to you. Hell, she fucking riled me up, she's a crazy bitch. But don't you dare lie to me and to yourself that you thought you were making the right decision. We belong together, no matter what. Got it?"

I can't help but smile as his anger resurfaces. I'm not used to seeing this side of him, and strangely, I like it.

"What are you laughing at?" he asks, attempting to scold me even more.

"You're right. All of it is so right," I break down into hysterics, making him wonder if I've completely lost my mind.

"Stop laughing!" he says, but I can tell I'm breaking through his tough exterior.

"I'm sorry. Really, I can't believe I did any of that. And by the way, how the hell did you catch up to me so quickly?"

"I just got off the elevator on our floor when I saw the door close, taking you downstairs. I noticed you had your suitcase, which wasn't a good sign. So I ran down the stairs and made it to the concierge as soon as you pulled away in the rental. It didn't take much to persuade him to get in my car to follow you." He smirks and grips the steering wheel tightly.

"Geez," I say, shaking my head. "A girl can't even stage a good getaway."

We both start laughing at the ridiculousness that's ensued over the past hour. From anger to laughter. Thank God he's lightening up a bit.

And thank God I pulled over.

Everything he said is spot on. I should never have run. Thank God, this time he found me.

A SOFT TICKLE on my arm brings me out of my sleep. "Noelle," the voice is next to my ear, warm breath relaxing me.

"Hmm?" I stretch my legs and realize I'm not wearing pants. I sit up, startled. "Where am I?"

"We're in our room," Heath whispers, and then it all comes back to me.

We drove so long yesterday, taking turns. He took the last leg at around ten o'clock at night, and I promptly fell asleep. He woke me up long enough to get into the hotel, and I immediately passed back out, fully clothed.

"How did I get undressed?" I ask, but I already know the answer.

"I just took off your pants, I didn't remove anything else."

Not that I'm modest, especially around him. He's seen me with nothing on, but that was so long ago.

"Oh," I say, rolling over onto my back. His hand that was once tickling my arm is now resting on my belly.

"I'm sorry, I shouldn't have woken you up."

"What time is it?" I ask. The room is still dark.

"Four."

"Yeah, you shouldn't have woken me up," I groan.

"I haven't been able to sleep. I owe you an apology, and you need to hear it."

I turn my head toward him, "You apologize?" I'm confused. I thought I was the one that was supposed to be apologizing.

He nods his head. "Yes."

I tuck my hands under my cheek and turn onto my side, facing him.

"Okay?"

"So I got crazy earlier. Totally nuts. I shouldn't have driven you off the road like a drag racer. I should have shown you more respect than that. I'm really sorry."

"I get it, I told you that already," I smile. He brushes a strand of hair out of my eyes and drops his hand back down to the bed between us.

"The thought of never seeing you again just couldn't be an option. Not that it forgives the way I spoke to you–the way I yelled at you. It shouldn't have happened. I'm really sorry."

There's so much regret in his face. Too much.

"It's okay," I say, trying to let him off the hook.

"No. It's not. It's never okay to yell and be forceful. I'd never lost control like that, and I can't believe it was with you. But I was desperate. I couldn't let you leave. I would have wrapped my arms around your legs, forcing you to drag me through the parking lot." He smiles weakly.

"Heath, I would have turned around, eventually."

"Really?" he asks.

"I don't know. Probably not, I'm stubborn like that," I joke.

"I never want to feel like that again. I lost you *for real* once. Another time will not happen. Not while I'm still alive and breathing." He looks stern, but tender.

"I believe you," I admit and wrinkle my nose.

He wraps his hand around the back of my head, kissing me softly on the lips. "Now we can sleep," he smiles, pulling me into his chest.

"Good," I state, closing my eyes.

As I drift off, he quietly sings the song he wrote for me so many years ago.

A song about fireflies and the moon.

CHAPTER 26

Heath
Present

NOELLE AND I SLEPT IN today, desperately needing to recover from our long, stressful drive yesterday. I fully admit I was hard on her. *Really* hard on her. I wish I didn't lose my cool the way I did, but thankfully, she knows how bad I feel–and that it will never happen again.

We can breathe a little easier today after Stuart called me this morning. He spoke with Haley, who calmed down considerably. He was able to confirm her suspicions about Noelle. He didn't fill her in completely, but told her that it's dire that she keep Noelle's re-emergence a secret. That Noelle's life depended on it. Haley apparently perked up over being in on a super secret and agreed to back down. She promised not to reveal that she knows the identity of the 'mystery girl' in my life. Of course, Stuart had to make a transfer into her bank account to ensure that she actually keeps her word. Although I know Haley far too well, money is just a play thing for her. And she already has plenty of it. I think this is a temporary reprieve, and Noelle and I are going to have to figure out how we're going to make her return public.

That's when I realize there are a few other people who need to know what's going on.

I pick up my phone and hit send.

"Hello, Dear," my mother answers, her smile coming through the phone.

"Hi, Mom."

"I stopped by your house yesterday and Rosie said you left in a hurry the other day. Is everything okay?" She sounds concerned.

"Everything's fine," I say. "But I have to talk to you about something. Is Dad there?"

"Yes, he is. Should he pick up?" She's getting more worried.

"Yes, if he can."

"Palmer," she calls out, "Can you pick up the extension? It's Heath."

I hear his voice off in the distance and then a click on the other end of the phone.

"Heath!" he says, excited. "How are you?"

"I'm fine. Listen, there's something I need to tell you both."

"What is it?" he asks, concern rising in his voice as well.

"It's about Noelle. She's alive."

My mother gasps, nearly choking while my father remains silent.

"Oh my God! Is this true? Are you serious?" my mother cries into the phone, barely containing her excitement. "How? I don't understand? What's going on?"

"Dad, are you there?" I ask. His silence is palpable.

"Keep going," he urges. "Tell your mother what you know."

He's acting weird.

I tell them everything I can. From Noelle's abuse to Tom Durand's death. I explain why she resurfaced and why she came to me. After hashing out all of the details, my mother asks, "Where are the two of you now?"

"Albuquerque," I state.

"New Mexico?" she asks.

"Yes."

"I don't even know what to say about all of this. I can't believe she's alive. Oh my God, what that poor girl went through at the hands of that awful woman is horrible."

"It's over now, though. She's fine, and we're handling things as they come."

"Well, you certainly seem to be on an adventure," she declares, and I hear her crying softly on the other end of the line.

"Mom, are you okay?" I ask, concerned.

"I'm fine, Dear. I'm just so happy. I can't believe this."

"I know exactly how you feel. I'm still pinching myself to make sure I'm awake."

She sniffles and says, "I need to get a tissue. Tell Noelle we love her and please bring her here when you come home."

"I will."

She hangs up and I ask, "Dad, are you there?"

"Yes, Son. I'm still here."

He was strangely silent throughout my recounting of Noelle's story and what brought her back home.

"Dad?"

"Yes?"

"What do you know about all of this? Did you have anything to do with it?"

He inhales deeply, and I know what's about to come. Anger begins to boil in my blood.

"I didn't know everything, until now. But Tom came to me for help years ago. He showed me evidence that I'd been trying to unearth for a long time. Evidence of Tonya's involvement in the death of her first husband. I helped convict her and put her away for a very long time, with Tom's help. It was then that he told me what they'd done when Noelle disappeared."

"You *knew* she was alive and didn't say anything to me?" I yell into the phone. I've accepted the fact that Noelle had to lie and stay hidden for so long, but why the fuck didn't my own father tell me what was going on?

"Heath, it wasn't that simple. There were so many moving parts. So many things that could surface. Too many innocent people would have been hurt by the actions her father took to fake her death. The only thing I did was help keep it quiet. Help her stay hidden. I also stopped the process of her being declared legally dead."

His admissions rock me to the core. I feel betrayed.

"Please understand that I did this for Tom and for Noelle. Back when they said the home invasion took place, I had my security team pull surveillance footage. When nothing turned up–no masked men breaking down their door–I approached Tom and he looked terrified. He begged me not to look into it any further. That's when I first knew something wasn't right, but I respected his wishes until he came to me, asking me to put his wife behind bars."

I can't listen to this anymore. The fact that my father was part of this conspiracy makes me sick.

"Dad, I don't want to hear anymore."

"Please take some time to digest all of this. Talk to Noelle. You know what we all did to keep her hidden was important. It kept her safe and protected. You would have done the same thing, given the chance."

"But I wasn't given the chance!" I yell. "Jesus, Dad! Why couldn't you trust me with all of this?"

"You were too young, Heath. You would have gone after her, potentially drawing attention to Noelle and away from what we were trying to do to indict Tonya. Listen, I'm not asking for you to forgive me right this second, but I'm begging you to calmly think all of this through. You'll come around."

He's assuming a lot here.

Noelle walks into the room with a confused look on her face. "Everything okay?" she asks, and I nod my head.

"Please tell Noelle we love her, and we're very sorry for her loss. If there's anything she needs done at the house, just let us know. We're right here and will help out any way we can."

"Will do," I state and disconnect.

"Heath?" Her voice hitches and she walks over to me. "I heard you yelling. What happened?"

"Fuck," I mutter. "I just spoke with my parents."

"Oh? I guess you told them I'm alive?"

"I did. My mother cried and is thrilled to hear the news. She wanted me to tell you that she loves you and can't wait to see you when we get home."

She smiles and sinks into the recliner. "I can't wait to see her. She's a wonderful woman, you're so lucky to have her in your life."

I nod and tense up a little. "Apparently, my father knew you were alive. So you can understand why I'm a little angry right now."

"What?" she gasps. "How?"

"Your father asked for help, and my father obliged." I clench my fists, so angry at the time that I could have back with Noelle. I could have gone to find her. Help keep her safe.

"Heath, please don't be angry," she pleads.

"It's kind of hard not to be pissed off, don't you think?"

"Take a step back and try to understand your father's motivation. Clearly, your mother didn't know, did she?"

"Judging her reaction when I told her you were alive? No, she had no idea."

"Your father kept the secret from both of you for a good reason. It's hard for me to say this, but I'm glad he did. Who knows what would have happened if it came out that I was alive back then? Tonya could have imploded and wreaked havoc on everyone. Including you."

She's making a little bit of sense, but I'm still angry.

"Your father did the right thing," she presses. "He loves you, Heath. He did what he needed to do to protect you. You can't blame him for that, and I'm sure he wouldn't change things if presented with the same decision."

"I get it."

She stands up, walks over to me, and wraps her arms around my waist.

"If you can forgive me, you can forgive your father."

She kisses my chin and tucks her head into the crook of my neck.

What's most important is I'm holding the love of my life in my arms right now. She's alive and breathing. I need to draw on this to help me get beyond some of the decisions made without my knowledge.

"What's on the agenda today? Where are we going?" I ask.

She smiles. "Are you ready for this?"

"Give it to me."

"Sandia Peak. We're going on a tram ride." She's bubbling with excitement, despite her lack of sleep. "Maybe we'll do some light hiking when we get there."

"Hiking?" I laugh.

"I said light hiking."

"We'll see about that," I joke. "How far is it?"

"About twenty-five minutes away."

"What are we waiting for?" I ask.

She grabs her backpack, quickly kissing me on my cheek. "Let's do this."

NOELLE INSISTED ON DRIVING to our destination, which I'm thankful for. It gave me time to reflect and calm my nerves a bit after my conversation with my parents and the revelation from my father.

"Can you read my father's entry in his journal about Sandia Peak?" Noelle asks as she merges onto the highway.

"I'd love to," I say, thinking what a great idea this is–getting us back on track on our cross-country trek.

I dig into her backpack and pull out the journal, flipping the pages until I get to the entry she referenced.

"*August 26: Melanie was a sight for sore eyes on that tram earlier today. Her fear of heights emerged completely as we ascended to Sandia Peak. I held onto her tightly, whispering in her ear that she was going to be fine. I tried to get her to focus on the incredible view out the windows, the sun setting behind the ridge. The light danced off of the peak as we traveled along the wire. She told me at least a dozen times that she couldn't do it. She was terrified. But by the time she witnessed that sunset, her breathing became even and she was able to relax a little bit. The sites were impressive. I wish she would have stood up for me so I could get a picture of her with the beautiful landscape as a backdrop.*

Once the ride was over and we made our way back down to the base, and she looked up in awe. Darkness had fallen over the Peak, but she was amazed by her accomplishment, overcoming one of her fears in life. The other is flying in an airplane, and I hope to get her beyond that hump soon, but I'll save that for another trip. I'd like to take her to Paris with me the next time I have to fly overseas for business. She needs to experience that beautiful city, and I need to experience it with her.

Our night ended over a quiet meal in downtown Albuquerque. Her eyes shone bright as she recanted our trip on the tram, she forgot her fears and focused only on the beauty that we experienced, together. Someday, we're going to come back here and do this again. Someday very soon."

There's a single picture taped to the bottom of his entry and I run my fingers over it. "The sunset is stunning. I'm glad we got a later start today," I admit. Noelle seems nervous as we pull into the parking lot at the base. "Are you okay?" I ask her.

"I don't know why it didn't occur to me before how high we have to go," she states nervously. "I'm like my mother, I suppose. Afraid of heights and shit."

I laugh out loud, and she glares at me. "You're going to need to get over that pretty quickly. Like now."

Her face turns pale, the smile completely gone from her face. "I don't think I can do this."

I take her hand in mine. "Trust me, okay? We got this." I place a kiss on her knuckles and I get out of the car, rushing around to the driver's side to help encourage her to come out.

"Are you sure?" she asks, nervously.

"I won't let anything happen to you," I say, pulling her out of the front seat and into my chest. She closes her eyes, inhaling deeply. I place my hands on either side of her face, kissing her tenderly. She begins to relax into me as she wraps her arms around my neck, holding me in place so she can return our kiss, deepening it.

This simple kiss helps the tension from the past few days melt away, almost entirely. "Let's go back to the hotel," she begs against my lips, causing me to smile.

"You can't get out of this that easily, Noelle. As tempting as it is." I kiss the tip of her nose. "Let's go."

Her smile fades, and she grasps my hand tightly. I know she's afraid to fly, but I didn't realize her fear of heights was so intense. We need to overcome this phobia right now.

We get our tickets and enter the tram. She immediately sits on the bench along the far wall and I sit next to her. She grabs my hand so tightly, the tips of my fingers start to tingle. "I don't want to do this," she whispers into my shoulder, her teeth lightly sinking in.

"Are you biting me?" I laugh. She pulls the fabric of my shirt with her teeth and lets go.

"Sorry," she says, squeezing my hand again. "Nervous habit, I guess."

The tram begins to move and she looks like she's going to faint. A voice sounds over the speakers. "Welcome to the Sandia Peak Aerial Tramway. For the next fifteen minutes, sit back and enjoy the landscape as we take you up to the Peak. We should get up there in time for you to witness our spectacular sunset. Enjoy!"

The ride starts off smoothly, and I lean into Noelle. "It's beautiful so far, isn't it?" She's trying not to look down to see us rise above the vast canyons below. Her eyes are fixed on the Peak, our destination. She's completely still and silent for the entire trip, while I twist and turn, snapping shots of the surrounding landscape. Her father's words don't do this place justice at all. I'm witnessing some of the most dramatic and awe-inspiring views I've ever seen. It even rivals the last time I was on tour with Epic Fail when the crew and I took a similar tram-type ride in the Swiss Alps. While that was breathtaking, there's just something so special about experiencing something like this in our own country.

"You doing okay?" I ask, wrapping my arm around her.

"Yup," she mutters, wringing her hands once again. "Doing great." Her voice is tight, and she shifts nervously on the bench.

"We're almost there." I kiss her temple and rest my chin against her head.

The guide announces our impending arrival and Noelle starts relaxing against me. We dock at the station smoothly and Noelle is the first person to stand, practically racing me to the door. Once we're outside, I almost expect her to drop to her knees so she can kiss the ground beneath her feet. She freezes when she sees the sign in front of us, declaring we're at over ten-thousand feet.

"Holy shit."

I don't want to tell her that I've actually been at a higher elevation, she may have a panic attack.

I grab her hand and we walk toward the observation area. Once there, we can see an incredible three-hundred-and-sixty-degree view of the canyons surrounding the Peak.

"Holy shit," she says again, releasing my hand. She turns slowly, her eyes following the various valleys and peaks around us. "It's incredible." Her mouth drops open, and she looks like she's about to cry.

"Are you okay?" I ask, brushing the side of her arm.

"Yeah. I mean–it's like we're steps away from Heaven."

The sun is starting to set, and the sky is vibrant shades of red, orange, and purple.

"It sure seems like Heaven up here."

She walks around, grasping my hand tightly. The various peaks around us are glowing from the sunset, enhancing the incredible red rocks. She reaches into her backpack and pulls out the journal, quickly finding the picture her father taped inside. She holds the book in the air, the setting sun behind it.

"He must have stood right here when he took this picture," she notes. "The sun's practically in the same place as it is now."

Her face completely relaxes, and she closes her eyes, inhaling deeply through her nose. I take out my phone to capture this sight. She looks calm and serene. *At peace.*

She slowly opens her eyes, my phone already shoved back into my pocket. "I wonder if this is how my mom felt once she got to the top?" She stretches her arms above her head as if she's reaching for the clouds above. "It feels incredible up here. It's so quiet and peaceful." She backs up and leans into me and I hold her against me.

We stand like this as the sun sets, completely mesmerized. Neither of us makes an attempt to move as the horn sounds, alerting us that the next tram is departing for the base. "Can we hike down?" Noelle asks, laughing.

"Um–no," I say, pulling her toward the tram. "I think the animals lurking in the terrain along the way are much more dangerous than the tram we're about to get in, don't you think?"

A reluctant smile spreads across her face and she shrugs, "It was worth a try, I guess."

We get on the tram and it's standing room only. Her eyes widen, but she remains somewhat relaxed. "It'll be okay," I whisper into her ear, letting my lips linger. She leans into my side, wrapping her arms tightly around me as we descend, darkness enveloping us. When we reach the bottom, we're the last to exit the tram and she slowly walks through the doors.

"Want to go up again?" I joke, and she pokes me in the side.

"Not exactly," she admits, her tone turning serious. "But I feel like I left something up there."

"What? Did you forget your bag?" I ask.

"Not literally, *figuratively*," she corrects me, and I'm curious what she means.

"Oh?"

"When the sun set and those magnificent colors spread across the horizon, I felt like we weren't alone. I felt my parents." She shakes her head and shrugs her shoulders. "Or whatever, it was probably just the beauty of it all." She walks toward the car, embarrassed.

"I can see what you mean," I say to her, trying to make her feel better about what she sensed. "It's like we were a few steps closer to Heaven, everything up there was so crisp and calm. Like the angels were trying to speak to us."

Her eyes light up, and she throws her arms around my neck. "It was incredible," she says, kissing me tenderly. "I want to go dancing."

I laugh against her lips, "Yeah?"

"Yes!" she exclaims. I think her adrenaline has officially kicked in and she now needs to burn off that nervous energy she had built up.

"What are we waiting for then?"

This time, I drive so she can navigate. I can tell she already has an idea in her head, so I let her tell me which way to go. She flips back and forth between the journal and her GPS. After about twenty minutes, we're on the outskirts of the city.

She directs me as I drive through the city and then directs, "Take the next turn, onto Louisiana." She points toward a bar ahead of us. "There it is."

There's a valet outside as I pull up. He quickly opens the door for Noelle and I jump out, tossing my keys into his hand. "Keep it close," I demand, sliding him a twenty-dollar bill.

"Yes, Sir," he replies, and a hint of recognition twinges in his eyes. "You got it."

I reach Noelle and drape my arm over her shoulder. "Are you ready?" She smiles, and we walk into the bar. The first thing that hits me is the loud music. Frankie Goes to Hollywood's "Relax" is booming through the sound system.

"It's Eighties Night!" she yells over the music. "Isn't this awesome?" I pay our cover charge, and she guides me through the crowd and right onto the dance floor.

She's instantly bouncing up and down, a huge smile across her face. "I love it!" she shouts and twirls around. Her smile widens, and she tries to get me to join her.

I smile and shake my head. "I don't dance, Noelle."

"Nonsense! Everyone dances!"

"Let's get a drink," I say, pulling her toward the bar.

"You're no fun," she pouts.

We make our way to the bar and we slide onto two open stools. Thankfully, it's not too crowded in here. "What do you want?" I ask, pressing my mouth close to her ear so she can hear me.

"Lemon drop!" She's bouncing in her seat as Berlin's "The Metro" begins to play. "This is such a great song!"

I'm not into Eighties music at all, and if I have to sit here much longer and listen to this, my ears are going to bleed. Our drinks are placed in front of us, and she takes a huge sip from the martini. "Only one," I remind her, smirking, remembering what she said the night she had the Cosmo.

She nods and takes an even bigger sip. Her cheeks are already red.

The dance floor in this place seems to go on for miles, hundreds of people jumping up and down to the retro music. Watching the people is interesting to say the least. Many of them have routines for practically every single song that plays. It's funny to witness.

After the song finishes, the DJ's voice booms throughout the bar. "That's it for our Eighties Dance Party! Stick around, we've got some more current stuff for you!" A few patrons start to playfully boo at him, but quickly change their tune when he starts blasting house music through the bar.

Noelle spins back around on her stool and faces me, her lemon drop completely empty. She reaches for her glass of water and practically chugs it. "I think I'm drunk," she blurts out.

"I think you are, too," I laugh.

"Maybe it's the altitude or something."

"Or maybe it's the vodka." I point to her empty martini glass and she smiles, shrugging her shoulders.

A new song starts to play, and Noelle's eyes get wide. "I love this song." She slides off of her stool and jumps onto the dance floor just a few feet away.

EPIC LOVE

Calvin Harris's *"Feel So Close"* begins booming throughout the bar. Noelle's eyes are closed as she starts to sway to the music, her hips moving back and forth.

She looks so fucking hot.

Her eyes remain closed as she tosses her arms into the air and starts jumping in place, in perfect time to the beat of the song. Her hair falls wildly around her face as she moves her head back and forth. She's singing every word of the song, bouncing and gyrating. She's *feeling* every word. And I can't take my eyes off of her. It's as if a light is shining directly above her and she's the only person in this entire bar. She's dancing like nobody's watching, and it's the sexiest thing I've ever seen. For the first time in my life, I want to get out there on the dance floor and feel her move against me. But I don't move, I just watch like a voyeur. Her body continues to move with the music, hips swaying, arms still in the air. She opens her eyes and they look heavy, sultry. She bites her lip before she begins jumping in time with the beat again.

And then the song ends.

She drops her arms to her sides as the next song begins. She pushes her hair away from her face, and she smiles as she walks back to me, almost in a trance.

"That song is awesome," she pants, wiping sweat from her brow.

Yes, it fucking is.

"Let's get out of here," I say, and she immediately nods.

I channel my inner caveman again and pull her out of the bar. The valet recognizes me from earlier and sprints to get my car. He's back with it quickly, and this time I give him a fifty.

"Wow, thanks, man!" he calls out as I drive away.

Noelle is practically vibrating in the passenger seat. "I really felt that song. Like felt it in me. It took over my body and I just want to listen to it over and over again." Her body is swaying in the seat as if the song is reverberating throughout my car.

Fuck. Me.

I pull over and park the car on the side of the street, ripping my seat belt from me and lunge across the console. She sucks in her breath as I crash my lips to hers. My fingers get tangled in her hair as I hold her face in place, diving my tongue between her lips, pulling hers into my mouth. "Heath," she cries out.

"I want you right now." My hand wraps around the back of her head, and she shakes her head.

"Not here. Drive. Now," she says, sliding away from me, trying to adjust herself.

I hesitate for a second then realize she's right. I can't attack her like this on a city street. Her eyes are wide when she demands, "Hurry."

I don't wait any longer before I slam my car into drive and twist and turn through the city streets like a Formula One driver. Noelle is humming *"Feel So Close"* and her hips are moving again and I'm going to lose all control.

As I pull up in front of the hotel, I almost collide with a car exiting. He flips me off, and I don't even care.

As if he senses our urgency, the valet runs to my side, taking my keys from me. "Welcome back, Sir."

Noelle is already out of the car, her backpack slung over her shoulder.

Our elevator ride is quick and this time she's the one fumbling for our room key. She walks into the room ahead of me and begins to remove her clothing as she saunters into the bedroom, her hips still swaying like they were on the dance floor. By the time she's through the door, all of her clothes are gone, the moonlight shining through the window, illuminating her naked body.

She stops at the foot of the bed and I wrap one of my arms around her from behind as I push her hair away from her face, exposing the side of her neck. My lips make contact and she melts into me, pressing herself into my pelvis. I'm already rock hard, and I don't know how much time I have before I need to be inside of her.

She turns around, backing up against the bed. Her eyes are dark and heavy. "I waited so long for this, please don't make me wait any longer." She sits down on the bed and slides up toward the headboard. I strip out of my own clothes as I watch her slowly lie down. I'm on top of her before she takes her next breath, our bodies colliding. Her arms wrap around my shoulders, fingers digging into my back as she presses her pelvis against mine.

Time melts away as my hands become familiar with her body all over again. Our fingertips explore each other's skin, slowly tracing old paths and forging new ones. She arches against me when I glide my hand up her side, slowly grazing the side of her breast. Our eyes have been fixed on each other since I joined her in bed, hers yearning and desperate. Hungry.

I slow down my rhythm above her, my length pressed against her belly and claim her mouth once more. Her lips part slowly, and her tongue darts out welcoming mine. Her hands move to my face, holding me in place so she can take control of our kiss. Soft moans escape her lips as she devours mine.

"Heath," she pants, shimmying up toward the headboard so I'm now perfectly poised at her entrance. I slide my hand down her side and in between us, slowly dipping my index finger into her wetness causing her to whimper, her hips raising higher to meet the palm of my hand. Her lips are back on mine, sucking and biting. "Please," she cries as her eyes roll back, and I remove my finger to grab my length. I position myself so I'm *there*, ready to enter her. Ready to make her mine once again.

"Noelle." I pause, making sure she's ready.

Her eyes pop open and she bites her lip, nodding her head slowly. "Yes."

And that's all I need to push forward. I enter her slowly, our eyes locked once again. This is the moment we become one. I rest my arms on either side of her head so I'm perfectly perched over her, allowing our bodies to touch. Her breasts brush against my chest, and her arms lock around my neck. Sweat glistens on her forehead as I slowly move between her legs, easing in and out of her so we can savor the feeling, savor the tenderness. Her eyes are filled with tears and so are mine. This moment is bridging all of the years we've been apart, our bodies remembering how perfectly we fit together.

Each movement we make is slow and deliberate. I feel *all* of her, soft pulses grab me, pulling me deeper inside. I lower my lips to hers, softly kissing her. Our breathing is in sync, our bodies moving in perfect rhythm with each other.

"I love you so much," I mumble against her lips.

She starts crying softly, tears spilling down her cheeks. "I love you, too, Heath. I thought I'd never see you again." I kiss away her tears, brushing her hair away from her face.

"I'm never letting you go," I state, devouring her mouth once again.

Our tempo picks up as our bodies move more quickly, more urgently together. She arches her back as she thrusts her hips upward. Her mouth drops open as she begins to gasp for air. She convulses around me, her release long and powerful, her cries filling the room. I quickly follow her, allowing her climax to pull mine from me. Our bodies continue to move together until we're both fully satiated. She relaxes against me as I place a soft kiss against her lips, tasting salt from her tears.

"Please don't cry," I beg as I slowly slide out of her, and settle on her side.

"I can't help it," she smiles. "That was emotional. Amazing."

I kiss her again. "Yes, it was."

"I'm sorry about the past few days," she apologizes, and I press my finger against her lips.

"No more apologies."

"But–"

"I'm serious, Noelle. We can't move forward if we're constantly looking back with regret."

She nods.

"This trip has been a journey for both of us, but most importantly, it's our journey back together," I state. "And what we just did proves to me that we should never be apart again."

"Heath." She covers her mouth with her hand as tears fill her eyes again. "I don't deserve this. I don't deserve you."

"Don't ever say that again. Do you understand?" I don't ever want her to feel inadequate or undeserving.

"Do you forgive me?" she asks, nervous.

"There's nothing to forgive. I'm just thankful that you found your way back to me."

She kisses me tenderly and then tucks her head into my neck.

"You're my home," she whispers. "You always will be."

I wrap my body around her as my heart swells in my chest. This feels so good. So perfect.

"Welcome home, Noelle."

CHAPTER 27

Noelle
Present

I WAKE UP TO A FAMILIAR FEELING–Heath's warm body wrapped around mine. We've finally arrived at the South Rim of the Grand Canyon, our final destination. The final resting place for my father. We checked into the lodge late last night and were both asleep before our heads hit the pillow.

The past few days have been beyond crazy but also exhilarating. Heath and I have reconnected in a way I could only dream about for so long. The tension that began in Tulsa has slowly dissolved away as we attempt to move past the hurdles that have jumped in our way. It's still upsetting knowing he and Haley had a relationship of sorts, but I honestly can't blame Heath for any choices he made while I was gone. I just need to come to terms with the things that happened and realize these things were beyond our control. At the end of the day, I can only blame myself to a certain extent. I chose to stay away. I chose to remain dead.

I fully expect the road back to each other will continue to be bumpy. But if I don't give him a chance–give *us* a chance–I'll regret it for the rest of my life. And then there's Heath–he won't let me leave. He's been quite insistent about that.

"Are you nervous?" he mumbles against the back of my neck, placing a soft kiss there.

"You're awake?" I ask, surprised.

"Your heart started racing, it woke me up." His hand is resting under my breast and he moves it up, teasing my nipple gently. I arch into him, a tingling sensation traveling through my belly. He knows exactly where to touch me and he does it expertly, every time.

"I'm a little nervous," I admit.

Today's the day I say goodbye to my father, and I'm not sure I'm ready.

He rolls me onto my back so he's perched over me. "I'm here, Noelle. You're not going to have to do any of this alone."

"I know. But I don't feel ready." My heart is so heavy, I'm not sure I'm going to be able to keep it together.

"I don't think you're supposed to be ready for something like this. We all expect to have to bury our parents someday, but this situation is more unique than most."

He leans down, placing his lips back on my neck. "I love you, Noelle. Please know that you're never going to have to go through anything like this by yourself ever again."

He envelopes me with his body again, reminding me what it feels like to be loved in every way.

WE'RE BOTH OUT OF the shower. We're about to begin my father's final journey.

"Are you ready?" Heath asks, tucking a couple bottles of water into his backpack.

"I think so." Nerves are back, and I suddenly feel nauseous.

I slide my backpack over my shoulders, adjusting the straps so it's resting comfortably. Heath looks at me funny.

"Aren't you forgetting something?" he asks.

"Um–I don't think so?"

He looks uncomfortable, shifting back and forth on his feet.

"What?" I ask him, wondering what's going on.

"Aren't you forgetting–uh–your father?"

I laugh. "What do you mean? I have him," I state and pat my backpack. "He's in here."

His eyes widen, and his jaw drops. "He fits in there?"

"What exactly did you think I was going to carry with me? Yes, of course, his remains fit in here. His ashes filled a large plastic bag that only weighs about four or five pounds."

"Wait. You've been carrying him in your backpack this entire time. Like that?" The expression on his face is one of sheer confusion.

"Of course I have. We took this trip for him. I followed his itinerary. He's been with me this entire time."

He shakes his head in disbelief. "I had no idea. I guess I expected that you'd take an urn or something out of your suitcase." He pauses. "He's in a baggie?"

I laugh. "I guess when you think about it, it is kind of weird. But I wasn't going to lug around some decorative ceramic urn every place we went. *That* would be weird."

"Do you want me to carry it?" he asks. "I mean carry him?"

"No, I've got this. It's okay."

He nods his head and adjusts his own backpack on his shoulders. "I guess it's time to go."

We walk out of our room and through the lodge. He unfolds the trail map that he had tucked in his pocket. "We have to hike just under two miles to reach Grandeur Point, the place that your father mentions in the journal."

When we got here last night, the sun was setting over the canyon and it was spectacular. I've come to terms with the fact that we're thousands of feet above the base of the canyon, but I'm still a little jittery. Heath has promised me that we won't take any trails that I'm not comfortable with. But the point we have to go out on may be a little treacherous, and my nerves are starting to get the better of me. I push my butterflies aside for the moment so we can just get there.

"It's not as hot as I expected," I admit.

"My weather app says it's about eighty-five degrees. A little warm for hiking," Heath notes, and we start walking on the gravel path away from the lodge. We find the trail and I'm thankful it's smooth and easy to navigate. I don't want to have to do any rock climbing or anything that may cause me to dangle or fall to my death into the Grand Canyon.

For the first time all week, I feel the weight of my backpack. I'm cognizant of the precious cargo that I'm transporting to its final resting place, and it suddenly feels like a brick. My father's ashes are pulling me down, almost willing me not to take another step. Maybe he's not ready to say goodbye to me either? We're only about ten minutes into our hike and I already feel like I need to sit down.

"Stop," I call out, bending over to place my hands on my knees. My lungs start to burn, throat closing. "I can't breathe," I gasp, pressure settling in the center of my chest.

Heath rushes to my side, easing me gently onto a large boulder just off the path. He kneels in front of me, holding my head between his hands. I'm looking down at the ground, my feet look blurry.

He rubs the back of my neck, and I suddenly feel cool water drip over my head and neck. "Take a deep breath," Heath directs, continuing to massage me, trying to calm me down.

"What's happening?" I ask, scared as to why I'm unable to move, frozen with fear.

"I think you're having a panic attack," he states calmly. "Keep breathing. Focus on me." He lifts my head so our faces are a few inches apart. He begins taking deep breaths that I mimic. "That's good, keep doing that. You're going to be okay."

I'm able to get my breathing under control after a few minutes and I look at him, embarrassed. "I'm sorry. I don't know why–or how–that happened."

He kisses me, then pulls away. "It's okay. I'm actually surprised something like this didn't happen sooner."

I shake my head. "Thank God you were here." If I actually attempted this trek alone, who knows what would have happened if I had this freak-out while I was by myself on this trail.

"Thank God you let me come," he says. "Can you stand?"

I nod my head, "I think so."

He pulls me to my feet and I take a few more breaths. I'm not dizzy anymore, and my vision is no longer blurry. "I'm good."

He takes my hand and we get back on the trail. "Next stop, Grandeur Point," he states as we forge ahead.

Heath makes a couple of stops to snap some pictures. I've been walking, looking straight ahead, trying not to focus on the steep drops just off to our side. He walks out onto a ledge, and I nearly scream.

"Heath! Be careful!"

He turns back and smiles. "Don't worry."

When he makes his way back to the trail we're on, I smack him on his arm.

"Ouch," he says, playfully rubbing the spot.

"Don't do that. Do you know how high we are? And, for God's sake, why the hell aren't there any guardrails?"

"It's called nature, Noelle," he jokes.

We stop one more time before we reach the point so we can drink some water and Heath can snap a few more pictures.

"It's unbelievable up here," he muses. "I thought Sandia Peak was something special, but this place, seriously incredible."

Sandia Peak was pretty cool, despite the fact that I was terrified on the tram ride. But once I did it, adrenaline coursed through my veins. I'm not getting the same feeling up here. We're on the edge of this incredible landscape, and I'm terrified to inch toward the rim to see what's out there.

"We're here," Heath declares, stopping to take a much narrower trail leading to the point.

I pull my hand from his. "We have to go out there?"

There's a sand covered path that leads out to a point, with large 'steps' down to a flat surface. Nothing on either side of the point but air. It's like a jetty that juts out into the ocean, except without the water and thousands of feet above the ground.

"See, this is the same exact spot that's in your father's picture." He holds up a photo with the point in the background. A small tree that sits on the ledge is the focal point, but that tree has grown so much larger today.

"No fucking way," I state, backing away, shaking my head. "I'm not going out there."

He drops his head, arms at his sides, looking defeated. He mutters to himself and turns back to me.

"Please trust me, Noelle. I won't let anything happen to you, I swear."

I look past him and inch out, little by little.

"We're not on a balance beam," he says, sounding annoyed. "This bluff is at least fifteen feet wide."

I close my eyes and inhale deeply through my nose, practicing 'flower–candle' breathing that my therapist taught me years ago.

Breathe in through your nose—smell the flower.

Breathe out through your mouth—blow out the candle.

"Okay," I mutter. "I'm coming."

He reaches his hand back and grasps mine tightly. We walk slowly out toward the peak, and I try not to look too far to my right or my left.

"We need to climb down one level. I'll go first and you can slide down into my arms."

"How far down is the drop?" I ask, terrified.

"It's only a few feet. We have to get out to where the tree is."

My heart races, and my lip starts to sweat. *Everything* is sweating.

"Trust me," he begs, and I let him lead me out toward the 'step.'

Once we reach it, he jumps down, landing on the flat surface where the tree is. He doesn't have a care in the world, treating this terrain like an obstacle course instead of a death trap. "Will you be careful?!" I scold him.

"Relax," he smirks. "Now, walk to the edge and sit down—it'll be easier for you to slide down into my arms."

Flower–candle.

Flower-candle.

I sit down, dangling my feet over the edge of the rock and he places his hands onto either side of my legs.

"Slide," he directs, his grip tight on me. Once his hands reach my waist, he pulls me the rest of the way down, placing my feet firmly on the ground below me.

The ledge is much wider than I expected, but it's still scary as shit.

"I need water." I state and grab my water bottle. I take a swig and wipe my brow.

I sit on a small boulder underneath the tree. "Can I have his journal?" I ask, reaching my hand up toward Heath.

He hands it to me and I flip to the last few pages. Pages I have yet to read.

"Read it out loud," Heath urges as he sits next to me.

I remove a few pictures that were tucked into a small pocket in the back of the book that I don't ever remember seeing before. I place them face down on my knee and begin reading the passage.

"December 20:"

I stop reading and flip back a few pages. They're all from August when my parents were here together.

"Why did you stop?" he asks.

"Because this entry is dated in December, the year I was born. They were here together in August so many years earlier."

"Keep reading," Heath urges.

I start over.

"December 20: I can't believe I had to visit 'our place' today without you. The memories came flooding back as soon as I got to the ledge where our tree is still standing. It's grown quite a bit, probably five feet or more, but our mark is still on the tree. I had to reach up high, but I traced our initials that we carved together."

"Oh my god," I cover my mouth. "This is after she died. He came by himself." She died on December fifth, earlier in the month.

"You said he wanted his remains to join hers. He must have written this journal entry at that time," Heath suggests, and I'm sure that's exactly what happened.

This is more like a letter to my mother than the journal entries we've been reading all along. I look down and find the place where I left off.

"So many memories of our honeymoon trip have stuck with me throughout the years. But when we descended onto the bluff and sat underneath the tree

to watch the sun set over the canyon, it was one of the most perfect moments in my life. Followed closely by the birth of Noelle. She didn't make a fuss when we traveled here together. In fact, I had her harnessed on my back when I shimmied down the rock to get to the tree. But don't worry, I was careful."

"What?" I cry. "I was here?"

Heath grabs the photos resting on my knee and flips them over. He turns a picture around so I can see it. It's me, strapped to my father's back in some sort of baby–backpack–contraption. I'm asleep, my head resting on his shoulder, my little baby arms outstretched. He's smiling in the picture, the Grand Canyon is in the landscape behind him. He must have asked someone to take this picture of the two of us because this is way before the time of selfie-sticks.

"Holy shit," I say, completely surprised. "He brought me here when he laid my mother to rest."

Giant tears fall down my cheeks, sobs shaking me. Heath slides onto his knees in front of me and pulls me against him, tucking my head into his chest. I don't even know why I'm crying. Am I sad that I never knew my father and I shared this special moment together? Am I sad that my father had to travel across the country with his infant daughter to say goodbye to the love of his life?

"That's incredible," Heath admits. "It's so cool that you've been here before."

I try to compose myself as Heath rubs my arms. "You okay?" he asks, and I nod my head.

"I can't read anymore," I reply, and he takes the journal from my hands. "I'm ready to say goodbye."

We stand up and I open my backpack, removing the clear plastic bag that contains my father's ashes.

"How am I going to do this?" I ask Heath. "I didn't really think through all of the logistics." I look around to try to find a place where I can release his remains into the air.

"I have an idea," Heath states.

He lays down on his chest at the foot of the tree and begins to shimmy toward the edge on his stomach.

"What are you doing?" I yell. "Don't go any farther!"

His arms are hanging over the ledge, thousands of feet of empty space below him.

"Hand me the bag–I mean–your father," he says awkwardly. I'm cradling the bag in my arms, and I don't want to let it go.

"What are you going to do?" I ask.

"I'm going to release his remains here, over the side of this ledge."

This is crazy. He's going to kill himself.

"Are you sure?"

"Noelle, give me the bag, please. I'd prefer not to hang over the ledge like this all day."

I squeeze the bag one more time and remove the pocketknife from the front pocket of my backpack. After I slice through the top of the bag, I get on my knees and gently place it in Heath's hands.

He slides out a little further, his arms now completely dangling over the ledge. He looks back at me and asks, "Is there something you want to say before I do this?"

I nod my head. "Goodbye, Daddy. Please say hi to Mom. I love you."

Heath turns the bag upside down, slowly releasing his ashes into the air. They fall out of the bag without a sound as they descend into the abyss below. I start crying openly, sobbing until I can't breathe. I'm saying goodbye to a man I haven't seen for twelve years. A man who sent me away to save my life, to protect me. His ashes are falling through the air, cascading down and out of sight. I can't bring myself to look over the ledge as I remain planted on the boulder beneath the tree. *Their tree.*

Once the bag is empty, Heath slides his body fully back onto solid ground. He takes a couple of breaths before he eases himself up, joining me once again under the tree.

We sit in silence. The warm air swirls around us, allowing us to reflect, each lost in our own thoughts.

"I'm so sorry, Noelle. I wish I could give them back to you."

"You gave all of this to me. I wouldn't have been able to come out here without you. You helped fulfill his final wishes. Thank you." I say, kissing him gently on the lips.

He pulls away suddenly. "Can I have that knife?" he asks.

"Why?" I ask, reluctantly handing it to him.

"Stay put," he demands, and he jumps to his feet.

We're on a freaking ledge, where could I possibly go?

I turn to see him climbing the tree.

"Heath! What the hell are you doing?"

The pocketknife is between his teeth, his arms and legs wrapped around the tree, as he shimmies up the trunk. He doesn't look at me as he concentrates on getting as high as he can.

I'm going to puke. I look out over the ledge and realize if he falls, he's going to drop thousands of feet to his death. "Heath, get down!" I cry. "Please." But he continues to ignore my pleas.

I crane my neck to see that he's about ten feet up the trunk of the tree. He braces himself as he frees one hand to remove the knife from his mouth and starts hacking away at the bark.

"What are you doing?" I ask him again. "This is no time to be a daredevil!" I shout.

He hacks away for a few more minutes and then calls out, "Catch this." He closes the knife and drops it straight down into my hands. I look up and see him with his cell phone out, taking a picture of whatever he just did.

"Okay, enough, Heath. Stop messing around."

He slides the phone into his pocket and wraps his arm around the tree, working his way back down.

Once his feet are planted firmly on the ground, I punch him in the arm, hard.

"What the hell?" he asks, rubbing it.

"Are you serious? Do you have a death wish?" Angry tears fill my eyes.

He smiles and takes his cell phone from his pocket, swiping the screen so I can see the picture he took. It's four sets of initials.

TD

MD

ND

HS

"Oh my God," I gasp, covering my mouth. "Heath?"

"I wanted to make sure our trip was properly documented, so I carved our initials just below where your father carved his and your mother's."

"I love you so much," I cry, throwing my arms around his neck. "So much." I place my lips onto his, kissing him tenderly. I pull away for a second to scold him again, "You could have died."

His eyes light up. "It would have been worth it." He leans down and claims my mouth.

We sink back down onto the rock and face out toward the canyon. The sun is close to setting and the sky is transforming into a colorful landscape of orange, red, and purple, similar to the one we saw at Sandia Peak. But yet this one just *feels* different.

Heath takes some pictures of the beauty that surrounds us, then turns the camera on us. We take a couple of selfies and then he turns my face so he can kiss me. Once he places his lips on mine, he doesn't move, but puffs out his cheeks, just like our "sticky kiss" from so long ago. I laugh against his mouth but do the same, and I hear the clicking of the phone as he snaps several pictures of us like this. He drops the phone and his lips soften against mine, his hand finding the side of my face, caressing me gently. Our silly kiss turns passionate, our noses brushing against each other. His tongue enters my mouth, probing gently, entwining with mine.

"Wait," he states, suddenly pulling away from me. "There's something I found." He picks up the journal and opens it up. He reaches his finger inside a small pocket that I had no idea was there. When he opens his hand, a ring sits in the center of his palm. It's clearly a woman's ring, diamonds interspersed around the band. He holds it up and reads the inscription inside. *"MD, Forever Yours, TD."*

"It's her wedding ring," I note, wrapping my hand around her diamond that I've been wearing around my neck since I was fourteen.

Heath takes my hand, sliding it over my right ring finger. "It's a perfect fit," He smiles, kissing my knuckles.

"It's beautiful," I state. I can't form any other words or thoughts. Having my mother's wedding ring on my finger seems so surreal.

"We should go," he says reluctantly. "It's about to get really dark out here, and we need to find our way back."

As much as I didn't want to come out onto this ledge, now I don't want to leave. I feel like this place is my home, my parents' home. Our home. But I nod and let him pull me to my feet. We walk hand in hand over to the rock that I'm now going to need to climb up. Heath secures his hands on either side of my waist and lifts me up so I'm once again sitting on the ground above.

"Help pull me up," he says, stretching his hand out. I stand up and grab hold of his hand as he expertly scales the side of the rock and stands next to me. "Wasn't that easy?" he asks.

I playfully lean into him as we begin to walk back to the main trail. I turn to look at the tree and ledge one more time. Maybe someday I'll come back here again, just to say hi. "Goodbye, Mom and Dad."

I blow a kiss into the wind, and a warm breeze swirls around, enveloping us. *Hugging us.*

"I love you," I whisper into the breeze as I run my finger along my mother's wedding band.

Until we can be together again.

CHAPTER 28

Heath
Present

I LOOK AT MY PHONE, willing it to ring.

Ring, dammit.

I miss Noelle so fucking much. She's been back in Chappaquiddick for the past few days, but it seems like a lifetime. She insisted on going *home* so she could talk to her close friend, Dahlia. She didn't want to do it over the phone and felt like it was best to tell her in person. They seem close, and I'm happy she was able to find a true friend in all of this.

We made it back here last week, taking our time coming back from Arizona. We left the lodge the day after she said goodbye to her parents. We drove south, making a pit stop in Sedona before we stopped in Scottsdale. When we stayed there for a few days at The Biltmore, Noelle and I relaxed completely. She went to the spa a few times, but we mostly just stayed in our suite, continuing to find each other again. We made love as often as we could, erasing all of the years that distanced us.

I fell deeper in love with her than I ever thought was imaginable.

We didn't want to leave Scottsdale, knowing there was so much reality we'd have to deal with once we got home. Thankfully, my father was able to keep things quiet. He explained the situation to the new District Attorney, summarizing the events that led to Noelle's disappearance. While most of the details were glossed over, her case was officially 'closed,' because she had been found 'safe and sound.' She also legally changed her name back to Noelle Durand and cried the moment she signed her old-new name on the documents her uncle had drawn up.

There's still some loose ends that need to be tied up, but most of the big stuff is behind us. The one thing that still concerns me is how this news is going to be received by the Constantino family. My father assures me that Tonya's family has distanced themselves as much as they can from her since her conviction several years ago. But that doesn't comfort me at all. I've asked Gus, the former head of my father's security detail, to come up with a plan so we can keep eyes on Noelle as much as possible. Almost like a Secret Service detail, but Noelle would be unaware she's being watched and protected. If she finds out, I'll take the blame, but it will be worth it knowing she's safe at all times.

Noelle was right. I forgave my father pretty quickly for the secrets he kept from me for so many years. It wasn't fair to hold anything against him when I knew that everything he did was for Noelle's safety. I can't argue with that or blame him at all.

I shove my phone into my pocket, and it rings as I'm about to let go. I pull it back out, and my heart sinks when I see it's not Noelle.

"Hey, G," I answer, staring at Garrett's number.

"Are you coming to my place tonight? Stuart's going to be here in about two hours, and he wants all of us here so he can go over the appearances we're making over the next few weeks."

"That's right," I say, forgetting that we have a bunch of stuff lined up to support the Greatest Hits album we've been compiling.

"We're going to be on Howard, man!"

"I know, Stuart told me a couple of weeks ago." Performing on the "Howard Stern Show" is a goal for all of us, and we're thrilled it's finally happening.

"Great, so are you coming?"

"Yeah, I'll be there," I look at the clock, expecting a contractor I hired to do some work to be here in about ten minutes. He finished the work yesterday, and I need to arrange final payment and make sure he's taken care of the punch list I emailed him this morning. "I should be there on time."

"You should bring Noelle," he suggests, and my heart drops.

"She's not in town," I admit. I don't necessarily want to tell him where she's living and how far away she is. I'm not yet used to this long-distance thing we're trying out, and I certainly don't need Garrett to put a negative spin on it.

"Is everything okay?" he asks, sounding concerned.

"It's all good."

"Cool. See you in a few hours." He hangs up just as my doorbell rings.

The contractor is right on time.

"HELLO?" NOELLE answers, groggily.

"I'm sorry, did I wake you up?" I ask.

It's almost midnight, and I just walked in the door from our band meeting with Stuart at Garrett's house. It wrapped up about twenty minutes ago. We all got the run down on what's coming up and what's going to be expected of us during the media blitz that's about to start. Everyone was there, including Tristan, who looked completely exhausted. My heart goes out to the guy, he's been through so much lately. He looked like a disheveled mess and could barely keep his eyes open. Dax kept shooting me concerned looks, like we should do something to help him out, but I honestly can't imagine how we can. The dude needs sleep so he can get back to his normal self before we have to get in front of the cameras in a few weeks.

"I was just dozing off," Noelle says as she yawns.

"I miss you," I state, wishing I could wrap my arms around her.

"I miss you, too."

Neither of us speaks for a few moments, my heart is beating nervously in my chest. "I can't do this," I blurt out.

"What?" Worry fills her voice.

"This distance. It's just not working for me. I need to see you now," I insist.

She sighs. "Heath, I don't live on Mars. We talked about this."

I picture her lying on her bed in nothing but one of my t-shirts, her legs stretched out, eyes yearning for me. "I can't go another day without being with you. *Inside you.*"

She sucks in her breath and says, "Oh?"

"You have no idea," I respond.

"Do you know what song I was listening to tonight?" she asks playfully.

"What song?" I ask, and I know exactly what she's about to say.

"'*Feel So Close,*'" she purrs, and I practically growl. She's awakened the caveman and to my dismay, she's hundreds of miles away.

"I was dancing around my place all by myself," she giggles. "You know how much I *love* that song."

Fuck. Me.

"I'll be there in the morning," I state, making a mental note to text Stuart when I get off the phone so he can book me a flight.

"You will?" she asks, knowing exactly what her teasing would provoke.

"What time is the first ferry from the Vineyard to Chappy?" I ask.

"Early," she states.

"Define early."

"Six-forty-five."

"Ouch," I say.

"It runs all day," she assures me. "But that's the earliest."

Now I need to make sure I can get an early flight from Philly to Boston and then to Martha's Vineyard.

"That song better be blasting throughout your house when I get there," I demand, and she giggles again.

"I love you," she says softly.

"I love you more," I respond. I close my eyes, inhaling deeply.

This time tomorrow, I'll be convincing her to come back here for good.

CHAPTER 29

Noelle
Present

WE JUST FINISHED LUNCH in our favorite cafe and now Dahlia is staring across the table, her face completely blank. She's blinking rapidly, and I snap my fingers, trying to get her attention.

I honestly can't blame her for the reaction she's having. Over the past hour, I told her my story. My *entire* story. In that short time, she experienced a wide range of emotions. Tears flowed, anger bubbled, more tears, and now disbelief.

Her body jolts at the sound of my snap, and she shakes her head quickly. "I don't have any words," she says quietly.

I nod my head and let her digest everything I've told her. It's a lot to absorb and completely overwhelming.

"Take your time," I urge, placing my hand on top of hers. "I'm so sorry I couldn't be honest with you from the beginning."

Her face softens, tears threatening to spill. "Oh my God! Please don't be sorry. That's the last thing you should even worry about. I just–I can't–" she stammers, trying to find something else to say.

"It's been a journey," I state. It's really the best way to explain everything I've been through. A long, winding road filled with many bumps along the way, some bigger and more painful than others, but bumps all the same.

"You can say that again. I'm so sorry for everything you've been through. I would do absolutely anything to take away all of the pain you've endured." Her words are familiar and remind me of the same vow that Heath proclaimed.

She sits back in her chair and scratches her head. "So your dad was in the mob?"

I laugh out loud, realizing she's gotten some of the finer details jumbled.

"No, my dad wasn't in the mob. His wife was. Not my mother, but my stepmother."

She nods her head, "The one that abused you." She's sad again, her voice strained.

"I realize this is a lot to comprehend, but it's all behind me."

"You're alive again, Sawyer–I mean–Noelle. Sorry, it's going to take me a while to get used to this."

I smile and squeeze her hand. "Thank you for listening. My life has been crazy, and even I can't believe everything that's happened to me. It kind of plays back like a soap opera."

"I love you no matter what. And so does my family. We would do anything for you."

"I really appreciate it, Dahlia. You have no idea."

Dahlia's pledge of support makes me realize who my true friends are–in this life and my old one. Haley and I had a long, honest talk after Heath and I returned. I went to her house, and she experienced a similar range of emotions that Dahlia did. But all too quickly, her true, selfish nature resurfaced. My disappearance became all about her and she quickly glossed over the fact that my life was ever in danger. All she cared about was what she didn't know. During our entire conversation, she never once showed concern over my well-being and what I actually went through at the hands of Tonya. While it was eye-opening, I wasn't surprised at all. She'd been like this when we were younger for longer than I cared to admit. She showed sparks of jealousy of my former life, even when she had no idea what was really going on.

I'm glad I could tell her my story, but at the end of the day, I'm happy to close the door on an acquaintance that was only ever one sided and based on her jealousy and narcissism. Someone like her is so good at literally sucking the life out of others, while the world only revolves around her. Haley felt absolutely no emotion when I walked out of her house, and I just felt relief. *Good riddance.*

"Please don't disappear from my life," Dahlia begs, standing up to squeeze me tight. Her tears flow and I know she's absorbed so much tonight. "I couldn't bear losing you."

Familiar words fill my heart. Words that Heath constantly says to me, making me fall more in love with him every single day.

We sit back down as Dahlia composes herself. "Now I need to know, when were you going to tell me about Heath?" Her smile is wide, and her eyes eager.

"I'm not sure. You know, I almost told you when we saw Epic Fail in Boston."

"Holy shit! I would have died!"

I thought about making up a story about meeting him in college and hooking up, just so I could tell her *something*. But I thought better of it and kept Heath as my own secret. Now that the cat's out of the bag, she's dying for more.

"I'm so in love with him, Dahlia, it hurts my heart when I'm not with him." My admission solidifies the fact that I need to make a decision about what to do about staying here in Chappy. This island has become so much a part of me, though, I don't know how I can possibly leave.

"You do what you need to do to keep that heart healthy," she says, her smile getting bigger. "I've never seen you this happy, and I want it to continue, forever."

"I love you," I say to her, and she jumps up to embrace me again.

"You're the best friend I've ever had," she cries. "Even if you move far away, you're never getting rid of me. Ever."

"You make me so happy," I whisper into her hair.

It feels really good to have a true best friend.

Really good.

I PULL INTO MY DRIVEWAY, thinking about how my revelation could have gone with Dahlia, and I'm so thankful that it went the way it did. Disappearing from my *real* life was devastating, but finding her was a blessing. And now that Heath's back in my life, I make a vow to never to lose him again.

As I approach my house, I hear music. Really loud music. Bass reverberating from within and I almost squeal with excitement. I run up the steps and throw open my front door. The deep rhythm from *"Feel So Close"* is causing my house to shake. Heath is sitting in the chair, totally relaxed, legs stretched out in front of him. His eyes lock onto mine as I stop in the foyer. As much as I want to run into his arms, that's not what he wants just yet.

I drop my purse, kick off my flip-flops, and reach behind my head, pulling out the elastic hair tie that's holding my messy bun in place. As soon as I do, my hair falls down around my shoulders. I slip my fingers into the sides of my maxi skirt, sliding it down over my hips and then let it drop to the floor so I'm only wearing my tank top and panties.

The song reaches the crescendo and I throw my hands in the air, bouncing through the foyer and into the living room where Heath is sitting–waiting.

I close my eyes and let my body feel the song. My hips swaying back and forth, my heart beating in time with the deep bass. I get closer and closer to Heath, but he makes no move to get up from the chair. His eyes devour my body, and I've never felt so wanted. So loved.

I squeeze my eyes shut. As I sing the last words of the song, I can only imagine how terrible I sound. Thankfully the music is loud, so hopefully Heath can't hear me. I'm jumping up and down, hands still in the air when, suddenly, his arms wrap tightly around my waist, causing me to stop in place. My heart is still beating in time to the music. I feel his breath near my lips, and I open my eyes. We're nose-to-nose and his stare pierces my soul. So much love and lust mix together as he slides his hand behind my head. He then skims his hands down my back so he can cup my ass, lifting me up, my legs wrapping around his waist. He positions me in the perfect spot. I can feel the hardness in his pants as I press against him, tingles traveling through my core into my belly.

He devours me, our noses banging, our teeth scraping. He's hungry for me, and I'm ready. So ready. He walks through the living room and to the hallway, stopping to press my back against the wall. He drops one of his hands between us, pushes my panties to the side, and slides two fingers into me. Pleasure begins to coarse through my body, and my mouth drops open, head falling backwards into the wall. "God!" I cry out.

He sucks and bites along my neck as his fingers thrust in and out, pushing me to the edge of a quick release. "Do it," he groans into my neck. "Let go."

He speeds up his rhythm, plunging and curving his fingers in the perfect spot, causing me to build and build until I scream. "Heath!" Suddenly, his fingers are gone and he expertly removes himself from his jeans and plunges deep inside, bringing back the intense sensations. His free hand is once again grasping my ass, holding me in place so he can control his thrusts deep inside me. I'm panting and begin to quiver, legs shaking. Our bodies move together as my fingers dig into the back of his neck. He's pushing me over the edge again, filling me completely. He drives one last time, and my body convulses around him, riding our waves of pleasure.

"Fuck," he mutters as he slides out of me. My legs are still shaking as he helps lower me to the floor.

I lean into the wall and look through the door, into my bedroom. "We didn't make it far, huh?" I ask, gesturing toward my comfortable bed.

"I couldn't help myself," he says.

"I really like that song," I smile, as I saunter past him into my bedroom.

"So do I," he says from behind me as he closes the door behind us.

"I'M NOT LEAVING here without you," Heath declares as I walk into my bedroom with our coffee. He's still in my bed where we've been on and off since yesterday afternoon.

"Are you going to squeeze me into your suitcase?" I ask, amused.

He knows how hard it is on me being so far away from him, and I've been considering making a change soon. I don't think I can part with my home here in Chappy, though. This place saved my life in more ways than one. Not only was I able to escape the physical abuse and danger I was in, but I was also able to *heal*. Tonya's abuse shattered my self-esteem and so much more. I was afraid to fight back–to protect myself. I allowed the abuse to continue because I was terrified of what she could do to my father. When I came here, I was only eighteen years old, but I grew up quickly. I was also able to get the help that I so desperately needed.

When I visited my therapist the other day, she and I spoke extensively about me leaving Chappy. She told me I could do anything I put my mind to. She reminded me that I can feel safe anywhere I am as long as I believe in myself.

"No need to squeeze you into anything. We're going to drive off of this island together."

I sink down onto the bed next to him and curl my legs under my body. "I don't have a place to stay in Pennsylvania."

He shakes his head. "There's no question about where you'd stay, Noelle."

"I'm selling my father's house," I state.

He raises his eyebrow with a mix of confusion and sadness in his face. "Really?"

I nod. "Heath, I don't think I could live in that house."

"I understand. But that's not where I was suggesting you live." He places his hand on my knee and circles his thumb on my skin.

I have a feeling I know where he's going with this, and I smile. "I'm sure I can find a new place. Or maybe I can live in the house that my father bought at the beach."

His face drops a little as I tease him with this option.

"That's also *not* what I was thinking."

"No?"

"My place," he grins.

While I already guessed what he was thinking, I'm not sure it's the best idea. We're still reconnecting and learning things about each other that we missed over the years we were separated.

"I'm not sure it's a good idea to rush into something like that just yet."

He shakes his head. "There's nothing you can say that will change my mind about this. You know this, right? We've spent too many years apart for us to waste any more time." He squeezes my knee lightly, and I squirm.

"That tickles!" I exclaim.

"You can decide when you want to come *home*, but the house is already waiting for you."

"What do you mean?" His house is *ready* for me?

"I've made some modifications that I think you'll absolutely love." His smile is huge and now I'm curious.

"What modifications?" His house is gorgeous as it is. It's a custom home in a private neighborhood, not unlike the neighborhood we grew up in. His yard is gorgeous and private. The house is large, but not obnoxious.

"I'll just say this, my mother approves, and you'll see when we go home tomorrow."

"Tomorrow?" I swallow hard. Am I ready to go home with him? Live with him?

"I told you I wasn't leaving here without you, and I meant it."

I lean back against my headboard and look out of the sliding doors. The ocean is breaking against the rocks, and I point to the gorgeous view. "How can you expect me to leave here? I mean, look at my view." This view has calmed my nerves on more than one occasion. It's perfect.

"And we'll see it often," Heath says, raising my curiosity.

"Really?" I ask.

"We could come here anytime we want. You've made a life for yourself here. You've made life-long friends here. I would never ask you to sell this beautiful place–it's so much a part of you. And I want it to become a part of me, too."

He pulls me against him, and I smile. "You're amazing, you know that?" He realizes how much my home here in Chappy means to me. "But, let's not rush things, okay? I promised you that I won't leave, ever again, and I meant it. I just need some time to figure things out, but I will go home with you tomorrow, *temporarily.*"

"Sounds like a plan," he smiles, kissing my neck. "But you should know that I'm really good at getting my way."

"I believe you."

And then he gets his way with me over and over again.

CHAPTER 30

Heath
Present

"NOELLE, WAKE UP," I say, trying to coax her from her sleep. We caught an early ferry from Chappaquiddick this morning and were able to get one from the Vineyard to the mainland shortly after. Noelle passed out cold as soon as we got through Connecticut and has been asleep ever since.

Every time I look over at her sleeping peacefully, I can't believe she's here with me. Coming home with me. The past few weeks have been a whirlwind and full of memories and emotion. But somehow we've managed to close the distance that time stole from us. And now, as we pull into my driveway, we're about to make a new home for the two of us. We've agreed to keep her home in Chappaquiddick and spend as much time there as we can. She's also decided to keep her father's home in Point Pleasant. Her uncle has already put her house next to my parents' on the market and it's not expected to last very long. Although my mom and dad are bummed they're going to have new neighbors soon, they know it's what Noelle wants and they fully support her decision.

"Where are we?" she asks, groggily. A smile spreads across her face when she realizes where we are.

"We're home," I state and throw the car into park. We drove her car here since I didn't have one with me.

"That sounds awesome," she says as she stretches in her seat. "I don't think I can move my legs, they're still asleep!"

"Take your time. The house isn't going anywhere," I joke. Although I'm dying to get her inside.

A few minutes later, she's standing in my driveway on wobbly legs, trying to work out the pins and needles.

"Ready!" she exclaims.

We walk into the house, and it smells incredible. Rosie must have cooked all day today so she could stock the refrigerator for us.

"It smells delicious," Noelle notes as we walk through the foyer.

"Lasagna," I say. "Rosie's specialty."

"I can't wait to try it."

"You won't be disappointed," I promise, turning toward her. I sweep her into my arms and kiss her underneath the large chandelier in my foyer.

"What was that for?" she asks, playfully.

"You have two options."

She raises her eyebrow and rubs her nose against mine. "What are my options?"

"One, we could go upstairs and properly celebrate your homecoming."

"Or?" she teases me, pressing her lips to mine.

"Two, I can show you the surprise."

Her eyes open wide. "Surprise?"

I can tell she's excited to find out what I've been hinting at for the past few days.

"I guess it's number two?" I ask, and she nods wildly.

I kiss her one more time before releasing her. I grab her hand to lead her through the hallway into the newly renovated kitchen. A project that would normally take about six weeks was completed in just over two, construction crews working around the clock until every detail was complete.

As soon as we enter the room, she gasps, "Oh my God, Heath."

Her eyes light up as she spots the new breakfast nook at the far end of my kitchen. I had it designed and built to mirror the one in my parents' house. This one has bigger floor-to-ceiling windows and a higher glass dome for the roof. The way the glass is shaped over the nook gives it an incredible greenhouse look and feel.

She walks closer to the addition and stops next to it. As her eyes travel to the windows and glass ceiling, inaudible squeals escape her lips.

"It's incredible," she says and points in the air toward a shiny object hanging in the window. "Is that–?"

The light catcher that I gave her for her fourteenth birthday is hanging in the center of the window facing the backyard. Tears fill her eyes when I nod my head. "Yes."

"And those?" She points to the six other light catchers adorning the other windows. She's about to cry, but happy tears.

I walk into the nook and point to the first one that's the shape of a lion cub.

"I bought this for you in Columbus at the zoo. I saw it in the window of the gift shop across from the lion exhibit."

She watches it as it spins in the window, reflecting colorful light through the glass.

I turn to the other side of the nook and point up. "This one I found in St. Louis." She smiles as she watches the light catcher in the shape of the famous Arch illuminate.

"This is so wild," she gasps. "I have no idea what else to say."

"Then just listen," I state as I point up to the glass ceiling.

"Okay." She slides onto the bench in the nook.

"This one here is from Tulsa. I was out buying it when you tried to take off." My tone changes slightly, scolding her once again for her bad judgment.

"Is that a rose?" she asks, ignoring my mild jab.

"Yes."

"It's beautiful."

"And this one is from Sandia Peak." It's an incredible light catcher that captures a perfect sunset. The glass inside deep oranges, reds, and purples.

"It looks like the picture we took," she says. "It looks like Heaven."

"When we were in Albuquerque is when I realized you were never going to run away again. You were finally home."

She stands up and throws herself into my arms. "I'm sorry for putting you through so much. I wish I could take it all back."

"I told you never to apologize again, and I meant it. Okay?" I kiss the top of her head and squeeze her tight.

She nods against my chest.

"I have one more to show you," I say and release her so I can turn her around to face the breakfast nook. I wrap my arms around her from behind and point to the light catcher hanging from the light fixture above the table.

"I found that one at the lodge we stayed in while we were at the Grand Canyon," I say. It's a large heart, filled with every color imaginable, colorful light fills the kitchen from this single piece.

"Oh, Heath. This is all so incredible." She walks forward, admiring all of the light catchers filling the windows of the nook. "I can't believe you did this."

She reaches out and touches the heart-shaped light catcher, and together we watch it spin.

"When we were traveling together, I realized so many things," I admit, and her eyes glisten. "I've only ever existed for you."

"You have all of me, Noelle. My heart for yours."

When all is forgotten you find new ways to rescue me.

CHAPTER 31

Noelle
Present

"NOELLE!" HEATH calls from the back door. "Will you hurry up?!"

He sounds eager as I take my time tying my shoelaces. "I don't know what your rush is," I joke, winking at him.

"Seriously?" He looks playfully annoyed as I slide on my baseball hat and grab the Wiffle ball bat.

"I've been practicing my knuckle ball. You won't even be able to touch it," I joke and run by him.

He slaps my ass, and I squeal.

"You'll pay for that later. But first, it's time to put it in the books." He smiles and takes a familiar notebook out of his back pocket. As he fans through the pages, I realize it's the book from our childhood. The one in which he kept track of our scores so diligently.

"Oh my God," I gasp, stopping in place. "I can't believe you kept that."

He tosses it to me so I can look through the years of scores. Years of memories. *So long ago.*

"I could never get rid of something so valuable," he declares, pulling me in for a kiss.

"Ready for a whooping?" I ask and nip his lips lightly with my teeth.

He laughs as he grabs my hand, leading me to the backyard. He's been working on building us a field similar to the one that we made together so many years ago. However, this field looks more 'professional' with a real pitcher's mound and a set of small bleachers

EPIC LOVE

on the side. We don't have any 'fans' watching us right now, but he is planning a tournament sometime this fall, and I'm sure the seats will be put to good use.

This is our first time christening the field so he suggests that I throw out the first pitch for good luck.

We toss the ball back and forth for a little while as we get a feel for it all over again. I'm transported back to my childhood, remembering the first time I played ball with Heath. He was my savior back then, allowing me to escape in our games, even if it was just for a few minutes. He taught me so much about the game as well as myself those first few years.

He taught me that it was okay to trust someone else. And he eventually taught me that it was okay to love.

"Are you ready?" he asks, and I nod.

He drops the ball that we'd been warming up with and pulls a fresh one out of the front pocket of his shorts. He tosses it to me, and I hear a strange rattling noise as it lands in my hand.

"What the–"

I grab the ball and shake it gently, the rattling noise louder now. I look up at him and he's closing the distance between me and home plate, a huge smile on his face.

That's when I hold the ball up in front of my face and peer through the elongated holes on top. I shake the ball again to get a better glimpse and see something large and shiny inside.

"Heath?" I manage to say as he drops to one knee in front of me.

I shake the ball again and fall to my knees, arms shaking and tears about to spill from my eyes.

He grabs my hands, holding them steady as he removes the ball from them. I watch as he twists the top of the ball off and the most exquisite diamond ring sits inside.

"Noelle–"

I cover my mouth with my hands as they continue to shake. I can't believe this is happening. My heart begins to flutter as tears roll down my cheeks.

"When I was ten years old, the most amazing girl wandered onto my Wiffle ball field. She was curious and smart. Fun and kind. Generous and sweet. She was perfect. And she became my best friend."

I'm sobbing now, remembering the first day I met him. The way he looked at me curiously. Trying to figure out where I came from and how I wound up in his yard. I had been watching him from the woods as he warmed up. And watched him some more as he played a game by himself, running around the bases and cheering at his accomplishments.

"This perfect girl believed in fairy tales. She believed in the power of moonlight to make dreams and wishes come true. And she made me believe."

He grasps my hands and pulls them against his chest.

"I believe in moonlight," he says, his eyes searching mine.

"I believe in fireflies." He leans forward and kisses me softly.

"I believe in fairies," he says against my lips.

"I believe in dreams coming true."

"And I believe in us."

I smile as he leans his forehead into mine.

"I've waited a lifetime for you. Marry me, Noelle."

I don't even need to think.

"Yes," I cry against him. "Yes!"

He slides the ring onto my finger and pulls me into an embrace, his lips claiming mine once again.

"I love you," I whisper. This moment couldn't be more perfect. More us. So many thoughts and memories flood through my brain, and I'm so thankful to be here, in the present, with him.

"Now show me your knuckle ball." He smiles.

EPILOGUE

Heath
Sometime in the future...

NOELLE AND I ARE sitting in our backyard, entwined together on the couch in our gazebo. We just said goodbye to my parents who were the last guests to leave the party and now it's time to relax. Time to enjoy this beautiful summer night.

The sun just finished setting behind the trees, the display of rich colors throughout the sky is astounding. Lightning bugs fill the night air, and I'm tempted to run through the grass, capturing as many as I can. Noelle looks up into the ceiling of the gazebo, miniature lights strung above us. "This is beautiful," she says. "It seems like everyday, you're giving us a new gift."

I unveiled the new gazebo this morning as we were getting ready for the party. It's a giant replica of the firefly house Noelle had when she was younger. It's a gift for Noelle and *Luna*.

We watch as our two-year-old daughter bounds through the grass, diving to catch the "Fa-Feyes," as she calls them. She giggles, missing every time, but trying so hard.

"You should help her," Noelle urges. "We have a lot of firefly houses to fill."

Dispersed among the lights strung throughout the gazebo are small firefly houses, hanging from wrought iron hooks. If we fill enough of these tonight, we can turn off the lights and be surrounded by magic.

I get up and jog toward my daughter, lifting her high in the air so she can attempt to catch a firefly. "Da-da. Fa-Feye! Fa-Feye!" She reaches out and swipes, just missing one.

"Let me do it, okay?"

She nods vigorously as I place her tiny feet on the ground. "This is how we do it, Luna. Gentle." I cup my hands around one of the illuminated bugs and we walk slowly over to the gazebo where Noelle is waiting with one of the firefly houses.

Luna and I repeat this for fifteen more minutes, capturing at least fifty fireflies. Noelle has hung the houses around the canopy of the gazebo, Luna watching intently and talking toddler gibberish.

I get down on my knee next to her and say, "Fireflies are magic, Luna."

Her eyes light up and she points up. "Fa-Feye!"

"Tonight, after you go to sleep and when the moon shines on these houses just right, the fireflies turn into fairies."

Luna's eyes widen, and she claps her hands wildly.

"And then the fairies fly all around, looking for a place to live in our yard. They're so tiny, you can't even see them. But they're always here, watching you. Protecting you."

I'm not sure how much she's comprehending, but she throws her arms around my neck so I can pick her up. "Ma-ma." She points to Noelle. I carry her into the gazebo and she slides out of my arms and into Noelle's lap, immediately curling up in her pre-sleep, pre-pass-out position.

"It's past her bedtime," Noelle reminds me as she kisses her forehead. Luna's curls fall around her face as her eyes become heavier and heavier.

"Happy Birthday, little one," Noelle says to our daughter. "Being two is so special. Mama and Daddy love you."

Luna's body goes limp as she falls asleep in her mother's arms.

"I can't believe you did all of this," Noelle whispers as she looks up at the firefly houses. "It's completely magical."

"Anything for my girls," I say, wrapping my arms around my family.

"Today was nice," she muses. "So many people were here. And Luna had a great time."

"It was pretty cool." I nod my head. "But, now I'm glad it's just us. I've been waiting for this moment all day." I kiss her softly on the lips, and she places her head against my chest.

"I wish my parents could have been here," she muses.

I watch dozens of fireflies circling the gazebo, flying random patterns in the air. The moon is perched just over the tree line.

"They're here, Noelle. They're all around us."

"Thank you for giving all of this back to me." She pauses. "Thank you for preserving my childhood and passing it on to our daughter."

"I'll never stop," I respond, pulling them closer to me.

Luna's soft breathing relaxes us. Comforts us.

I softly sing the words I wrote so long ago.

> "Take me back to two weeks ago.
> My blue oil lamp painting
> the fireflies dancing in the ink night sky
> of your backyard in amber rose mosaics.
> *When the moon is asleep I will*
> *find a way to rescue you.*
>
> Take me back to two nights ago.
> Your eyes afire again with the tales
> your father told.
> I know his promises taste like a lie
> or a line or paper stack of let downs.
> *When he has forgotten I will*
> *find a way to rescue you.*
>
> Take me back to two moments ago.
> Setting fairies free to twirl
> under the watchful moon, back with her
> unwavering glow, moving the tides of
> unruly seas and your smile pulled at the
> corners of your mouth like a forgotten
> treasure.
> *When all is forgotten you find*
> *new ways to rescue me."*

Noelle nuzzles closer against me. She has given me so much of herself, every single day. My heart was full before, but now with Luna, it's overflowing.

"Thank you for giving us fireflies and fairies," she says.

"Thank you for giving me so much more," I say.

She looks up at me and raises her eyebrows. "More?"

I run my fingers through our daughter's golden hair.

"You gave me the moon."

THE END

COMING SOON

EPIC

BESTSELLING AUTHOR
TRUDY STILES

HOLIDAY

A STANDALONE NOVEL
EPIC FAIL SERIES

ADDITIONAL CONTENT

Heath and Noelle's cross-country photo album:
http://trudystiles.com/photo-album/

Epic Love Playlist: http://trudystiles.com/playlists/

Epic Love Page: http://trudystiles.com/epic-love/

PLAYLIST

The playlist for Epic Lies can be found here:
http://trudystiles.com/playlists/.

Featured Bands/Artists Include:
Calvin Harris – On REPEAT!
Foo Fighters
The Airborne Toxic Event
A Silent Film
Soul Asylum
The Proclaimers
Phantom Planet
Florence and the Machine
Fleetwood Mac
The Dandy Warhols
Collective Soul
Bloc Party
The Postal Service
Bright Eyes
Brand New

NOTE TO MY READERS

Dear Readers,

Abuse is a horrible thing. Words can't describe the pain and terror an abused person faces every single day of their lives. Physical, verbal, emotional–it doesn't matter, it all tears down an individual equally. The aggressor doesn't care what he or she is inflicting on their victim.

I've witnessed abuse and it's horrifying. Some of the things I've seen have been subtle and other times have been blatant. But it's all the same and it's wrong.

Too many victims don't say a word and unwillingly allow their mistreatment to continue out of fear. Did I want Noelle to speak up and tell the truth. ABSOLUTELY. But it just didn't feel right in the context of her situation. Did it make her weak? No way. She was only doing what came natural. She was trying to protect someone she loved at the expense of her own well-being.

Should Heath have spoken up sooner? Of course. But he also loved Noelle and wanted to do everything she begged of him. I think, in a way, he was in denial of her situation. I don't think he wanted to admit that something so horrific could be occurring under his nose. Unfortunately, he found out too late.

Don't be like the teenage Heath. If you suspect that someone you love is the victim of abuse, say something. Go to someone you trust– a guidance counselor, family member or even law enforcement. There's always someone that can help.

Thank you for, once again, taking a chance on one of my stories. Heath and Noelle's journey is one that will remain with me for a very long time.

xoxo

Trudy

PS: Did you enjoy this book?

Please consider leaving an honest review on the site from which you purchased it.

Want to talk to others about your thoughts?

Join The Forever Family Group on Facebook: https://www.facebook.com/groups/808886315794103/

ACKNOWLEDGEMENTS

Wow. I can't believe I've published my sixth full-legnth novel. It still seems so surreal to me that you, the reader, have stuck with me for almost three years. My publishing journey has been amazing and each time I write acknowledgements, I realize there are more and more people to thank.

My husband and family: Every single day is a fairy tale with you. You make me believe that anything is possible and bring magic into my life. I love you Kevin, Cara, and Danny.

Forever Family: I love my reader group! Thank you all for always supporting me and waiting so patiently for my books. I realize that my life sometimes gets in the way and you have to wait, longer than I'd like, for my stories. Thanks for sticking with me and trusting me to take you on some epic journeys. Also, without you screaming from the rooftops about me and my books, I wouldn't have the expanding readership that I do. Thank you so much.

J.R. Rogue: Your words are magic. They are inspiring. They rip your soul out, piece-by-piece, and if you're lucky, sometimes put you back together. You write from a deep, scarred, place. And that's exactly what I needed for Epic Love. You were able to harness the depth of emotion and fantasy I needed for the poem, Take Me Back. Thank you for giving Heath the song that haunted Noelle. Your words encompassed everything he was about and showcased his need to protect her. Thank you so much for your dark magic.

Chelle Lagoski Northcutt: Thanks, once again, for reading this book through your amazing beta lens. You continue to give me confidence that I'm actually writing something that people want to read. Thank you for your flexibility and for reading this when I dropped it in your lap. Your own life is a bit hectic, and I can't thank you for making the time for me. Love you bunches.

Jade Piccolomini-Grandi: Thank you AGAIN for jumping in when I needed you. You always see things that I'm unable to see up close. Your feedback was tremendous and completely on point. You know how much I love you.

Dina Littner: I'm amazed that you still love me, as much as you hate my aggressive timelines. You constantly provide me with an ever important gut check, helping me keep my characters true to their voices. Thank you so much. Big love to you, my friend.

Erin Noelle: You. Are. Awesome. Thank you for squeezing me into your schedule and editing *Epic Love*. I always find it so unique working with an editor who is also an amazing author. You heard my voice throughout this book and helped me stay true to it. You helped make this story perfect, in every way. Thank you so much. And you have a beautiful name.

Julie Deaton: What more can I say to someone who's been with me since the very beginning? You're amazing and I can't thank you enough for all that you've done for me. There isn't anyone else in this industry that I would trust to put final eyes on my work. Thank you.

Sarah Hanson: Thank you again for the incredible designs you created for this entire series.

Elaine York: Just like the outside cover, the inside of a book needs to look perfect. And for the third time, you've done that for me. You're awesome to work with and so incredibly accommodating. I love these books so much, and what you're able to do on the inside just makes me love them even more.

Bloggers: With every new book that I release, there are more and more of you that jump in to support me. I can't thank you enough, for without you, I would have no readers. Thank you so much for sharing and screaming from the rooftops about me.

FTN: Thank you so much for everything that you do to support me. FTN is a safe place for me and it wouldn't be that without all of you. You all know who you are and you all know how much I love you.

Authors: Thank you to my closest author buddies. The support you have given me over the past few years has been amazing. I love all of you so much!

Readers: As I said in my note to you, thank you for constantly trusting me to take you on a journey that is sometimes bumpy, but will always make your heart smile. I thank you all from the bottom of my heart for sticking with me and diving into each story that I write. Please don't go anywhere–I have more stories to tell.

ABOUT THE AUTHOR

Trudy Stiles is a USA Today Bestselling Author, writer of New Adult Romance, mom to two beautiful children, and married to the love of her life. She's the author of the bestselling **Forever Family** series including **Dear Emily, Dear Tabitha,** and **Dear Juliet. Epic Sins, Epic Lies** and **Epic Love** are the first three books in the **Epic Fail** series and will continue with at least one more standalone novel, **Epic Holiday.** She plans to write many more stories about some of the characters you've already met, and maybe a few new ones. Emily will get her own story, **Sincerely, Emily,** to be released in 2017. Sara will also have her own story, **Forever Sara,** also to be released sometime in 2017.

She's also a contributing author to the USA Today Bestselling anthology, F*cking Awkward, a hilarious group of short stories sure to make you cringe, laugh and everything in between. All proceeds from this project benefited The Bookworm Box and its charities.

Trudy is a music junkie and you'll know that she's writing when you see her plugged into her laptop with her earbuds in. Her playlist is unique and is a must for her writing sprints.

When she's not writing, she's carting her children to their various activities while avoiding any kind of laundry or housework. She also loves to run along the boardwalk of the beautiful New Jersey shore.

She celebrates Wine Wednesday almost every day.

To learn more about Trudy, visit her website here: http://trudystiles.com.

To contact Trudy:
Email:authortrudystiles@gmail.com
Facebook: http://www.facebook.com/authortrudystiles
Instagram: https://instagram.com/trudystiles/
Website: www.trudystiles.com
Goodreads: http://www.goodreads.com/trudy_stiles
Twitter: @trudystiles (http://www.twitter.com/trudystiles)
Amazon: http://www.amazon.com/Trudy-Stiles/e/B00H3O0OJ8

OTHER BOOKS

The Forever Family Series
Dear Emily
Dear Tabitha
Dear Juliet
Sincerely, Emily (coming soon)
Forever Sara (coming soon)

The Epic Fail Series
Epic Sins
Epic Lies
Epic Love
Epic Holiday (coming soon)

Links to all of her books can be found on her website:
http://trudystiles.com/books/